STAR TREK®
NEW FRONTIER

BOOK FIVE

MARTYR

PETER DAVID

New Frontier concept by
John J. Ordover and Peter David

POCKET BOOKS
New York   London   Toronto   Sydney   Tokyo   Singapore

This book is a work of fiction. Names, characters, places and incidents are products of the author's imagination or are used fictitiously. Any resemblance to actual events or locales or persons, living or dead, is entirely coincidental.

An *Original* Publication of POCKET BOOKS

POCKET BOOKS, a division of Simon & Schuster Inc.
1230 Avenue of the Americas, New York, NY 10020

A VIACOM COMPANY

STAR TREK is a Registered Trademark of Paramount Pictures.

This book is published by Pocket Books, a division of Simon & Schuster Inc., under exclusive license from Paramount Pictures.

ISBN: 0-671-02036-6

First Pocket Books printing March 1998

10 9 8 7 6 5 4 3 2 1

Printed in the U.S.A.

3 1502 00432 9064

FIVE HUNDRED
YEARS
EARLIER . . .

ONTEAR COULD TELL which way the wind was blowing.

Even so, it seemed that everything and nothing was clear to him as he looked at the Zondar horizon. The smoke that hovered over the cityscape far in the distance was drifting off to the north. It was not his favorite direction, for the stench from the charnel pit was wafting in as well.

How many of his people had died, he wondered, during the bloody civil war that had enveloped the planet? One million? Two? He'd lost count. For that matter, he'd even lost interest, which was both ironic and unfortunate, considering that the war had been fought in his name.

Ontear felt old . . . older than he had felt in quite some time. He had been sitting at the entrance to his cave, but now he rose to his feet, stretching his cramped legs. He was bald . . . indeed, completely devoid of body hair, as were all his people. His skin was leathery and shiny, with a sheen that made it look as if the Zondarians were perpetually wet or glistening. His eyes were set wide apart, and when he blinked, it was with eyelids that were clear and made a soft clicking sound. His nostrils flared visibly as the charnel stench moved toward him and then past. He wondered how many bodies burning there were people he knew. People he had blessed, or at whose birth he had officiated, or weddings he had performed. For that matter, how many of them had come to him for guidance, had sought out the wisdom of the prophet Ontear? Ontear, the prophet who had seen a great and glorious destiny for Zondar. Ontear, who knew all that was to come. Ontear, who could not help but feel that he was single-handedly responsible for the chaos that had erupted all around him.

He had long felt that he was in direct communion with the gods. But today, of all days, he believed that the gods were going to communicate with him directly, and with a vengeance. Today, Ontear felt, was going to be his judgment day.

He heard scambling below him, heard grunts and arguments and words of indecision. He was being approached by acolytes. They were not exactly being subtle about their advent, and whatever it was that was on their minds, clearly it was accompanied by a certain degree of volume. This was not of tremendous consequence to Ontear, because truthfully there was very little any acolytes could say that would come as a surprise to him. This was an inevitable state of affairs, after all, when one is a prophet.

There were three of them, approaching Ontear with bedraggled and exhausted mien. It was not the easiest of climbs, for Ontear's cave was set upon the upper ridges of a small mountain. There were paths that led to the plateau where Ontear was seated at that moment, but they were not forgiving for the clumsy of foot. There was a thick layer of pebbles along several lengthy patches, and those wishing to come and visit

Ontear oftentimes felt the ground slipping beneath them and they would skid several yards back down the steep path before regaining their footing and slogging forward once more.

Based on the difficulty of approach, no one was quite sure just how Ontear managed to survive there. There was no food to speak of, although water might be available through a mountain stream (not that anyone could really be sure). Perhaps Ontear had hidden resources. Perhaps he had unknown allies. Perhaps, as some speculated, he was actually dead, and merely a very animated and lively corpse.

The trio continued to approach, and Ontear recognized the closest of them as Suti-Lon-sondon, one of his oldest and most dedicated students. He remembered the first time that Suti had come to him, scared and confused, daunted by the task that had been put to him: to approach the prophet and learn at his feet. That had seemed an eternity ago.

It had not been difficult to convince Suti of his veracity as a prophet. Indeed, it was no more difficult than it had been to prove it to anyone else. Unlike other prophets, false prophets, who had contented themselves with speaking in broad and unspecific predictions (the more precious of them choosing to quote their vagueness in rhyme, as if that added some aura of respectability), Ontear had been amazingly specific in his prognostications. He had predicted the great earthquake of Kartoof. He had predicted the rise in power of Quinzar the Wicked and Krusea the Black, and the defeat of Krusea's son, Otton the Unready.

Oh, there were the skeptics who believed that Ontear's predictions were so specific that they became self-fulfilling prophecies. For instance, his prediction that a conqueror named Muton would be born in the eastern territories and dominate half the region had resulted in no fewer than two thousand eastern territory newborns in the last year being given the name "Muton." The confusion this created in schools alone was nothing short of calamitous.

But the debates over Ontear meant nothing to Suti, for he believed in the man and his powers. There was a serenity about Ontear, a confidence that seemed to lift him above all that surrounded him.

Suti was surprised to see Ontear seated in front of his cave. Ontear rarely left the confines of his rocky home. He had a particular spot that he simply sat upon, apparently day and night, for Suti never saw him move from it. Yet here was Ontear, outside, apparently taking a tremendous interest in the skies which were darkening overhead. Suti gestured for the others who had accompanied him to hang back, desiring to address Ontear on his own first. Slowly he drew near to the prophet, and Ontear acknowledged his approach with a slight nod of his head. Suti began to speak, but Ontear put out a raised hand and Suti promptly lapsed into a respectful silence.

"Can you smell it, Suti?" asked Ontear after a short time. "There is a storm coming. A storm of great significance. I have foreseen it."

This, to Suti, did not exactly seem to be the stuff of prophecy. One did not have to be a seer to tell that a storm was on its way. One merely had to look at the growing blackness. Of far greater concern to Suti, however, was the smoke on the horizon. The smoke that was a lingering and mute testimony to the war that had enveloped Zondar. A war that had begun in the western regions but had spread to consume the whole of the planet.

"I do not dispute that, Ontear," Suti said, "but we have other matters to consider at the moment." Suti's skin had the same characteristic sheen that Ontear's possessed, but his eyes were darker and the contrasting youthfulness in his face was quite evident.

"Other matters?" asked Ontear.

Suti drew close and knelt nearby Ontear. "The war, Ontear. The great war."

"Wars are never great, Suti," Ontear said softly, thoughtfully. "There can be great acts of heroism. There can be great causes. But the wars themselves are always terrible, terrible things."

"The Unglza, Ontear. The Unglza refuse to surrender."

"Do they?"

Suti was beginning to feel frustrated. It was as if he was having an impossible time just managing to capture and hold Ontear's attention. "They refuse to surrender," he repeated, trying to give added significance to the statement through weight in his voice.

"Yes, so you have said."

"But you said they would!"

"Yes, so I did."

Suti could hear mutterings from his companions nearby, and he did not like the sound of it. He began to pace furiously, the incoming wind whipping the hem of his acolyte gown. "Ontear . . . this . . . this war is because of you!"

"Is it?" Ontear still seemed to be only partly paying attention to what was being said.

"For years, Ontear . . . for years, the Unglza and the Eenza have desired the extermination of each other. They are two peoples who have racial and border disputes going back centuries! Every time there has been a move toward peace, the talks have broken down and new bouts of attempted genocide on the parts of both peoples broke out once more! But it's never been a full-blown civil war before! Never spilled over into . . . into an unyielding bloodbath! That's what it is, Ontear! A bloodbath!"

"That can be a good thing, Suti. A cleansing thing."

Suti made no attempt to keep the astonishment from his face. "A *good* thing? Ontear, as of six months ago, there had actually been greater advancement in the peace talks between the Unglza and the Eenza than ever before! And then you suddenly came forward with your . . . your . . ." He waved his hands about as if unable to find the words.

"Prediction?" Ontear prompted gently.

"Yes! Your prediction that there would be a great war! Your prediction that the Unglza would surrender, bow in defeat! Your prediction that the Eenza would finally dominate their hated rivals, once and for all! These were statements from your own lips, Ontear! I was there when you made them! We heard them. We *all* heard them."

"I remember, Suti," Ontear said patiently. "I was there. I may be old . . . I may even be approaching the end of my days . . . but my mental faculties remain as sharp as ever."

"But don't you see? When you made your predictions, the talks broke down!"

"I knew they would."

"But to what end?"

"End?" Ontear actually seemed puzzled by the question. "The end is the end, Suti. I am not responsible for—"

And to the shock of Ontear—in fact, to the shock of Suti himself—Suti grabbed Ontear by the front of his robes, and turned and pointed urgently at the haze of smoke hanging on the horizon. "You are responsible for *that!*" he bellowed. "You are responsible for the Eenza breaking off talks, emboldened by your predictions that the Unglza would be crushed! Don't try to deny that you had a hand in that!"

"I deny nothing," Ontear said with apparently infinite calm. "But the actions taken by the Eenza are ultimately governed by their own free will. My predictions are merely that. They are not absolutes, nor are they designed to absolve the participants of their own culpability."

"People are dying, Ontear!"

"People have died for eons before I came along, Suti, and will continue to do so long after I am gone."

There was a crack of thunder from overhead, as if the gods hidden by the rolling clouds agreed with him. Suti did not release his hold on Ontear. "Why haven't they surrendered? The Unglza—why haven't they?"

"They will."

"They haven't! Your predictions have only strengthened their resolve! They have sworn to fight to the last man, woman, and child!"

"Have they indeed?"

"Yes!"

Ontear shrugged. "They are to be commended, then."

Suti was stunned. He felt his fingers go numb, and Ontear gently disengaged Suti's hands from their grip on his robes. "Commended?" asked Suti incredulously.

"Yes. They fly in the face of prophecy. They fight a hopeless battle. It is only the hopeless battles, Suti, that are the truly interesting ones."

"The Eenza are asking me when the Unglza are going to surrender, Ontear! I don't know what to tell them! And I have asked you, and your response has simply been, 'Soon.' In the meantime, hundreds of thousands have died! Perhaps millions! When is 'soon' supposed to be, Ontear?"

And there began to be something in Ontear's eyes . . . something that Suti had never seen before. A sort of burning intensity that caused a chill to spread down Suti's back. "That depends upon your point of reference, Suti. To you, 'soon' means sometime within your immediate lifetime. Days, weeks, months at most. For one like myself, 'soon' relates to the galactic whole. What may seem an infinity of time to you is barely a fraction of heartbeat in the body of the great cosmos. I speak within the frame of reference of our world's vast history, Suti. I speak on behalf of Zondar, and within the time frame of Zondar, the Unglza will surrender soon."

"You're . . ." At first Suti was having trouble framing words, so paralyzed was he by the enormity of what Ontear was saying. The other acolytes, who were outside of hearing range but could see the stunned reaction on Ontear's part, looked at each other with growing apprehension. "You're saying . . . that the Unglza may not surrender in my lifetime? Within the lifetime of *my entire generation?* That their surrender could be *centuries away?!*"

"Of course."

Suti's entire body began to tremble. "You're . . . you're insane!"

Ontear drew himself up, looking annoyed for the first time, and his glistening brow darkened in anger. "Do not take that tone of voice with me."

"Tone of voice? *Tone of voice?* Our people are dying on your behalf! The Eenza fight under the banner of Ontear, in the belief that their triumph is imminent! And you're telling me that you have absolutely no idea when the Unglza will surrender!"

"The Unglza and Eenza need no excuse to battle each other. Theirs is a hatred that transcends generations."

The wind was getting louder, and it was getting harder and harder for Suti to hear. "Ontear, you have to tell them!" he cried out. "You have to tell them that you were wrong! You have to—"

"Wrong?"

"You have to—"

"Wrong?" and his time his voice was audible above the increasing howling of the winds. And with a fury that seemed to mirror the anger of the storm clouds overhead, Ontear shoved Suti with a strength that was far greater than Suti would ever had suspected possible in the old prophet. Suti stumbled backward, losing his balance and hitting the ground with a bone-jarring thud, his elbows absorbing most of the impact and sending a jolt of pain through him. He gaped in utter astonishment at Ontear. High above, the entire sky had become black, and currents of air were beginning to surge. Ontear was buffeted by the gusts, but didn't appear interested in acknowledging it. *"Wrong?"* he shouted over the noise of the wind.

Suti glanced in the direction of his companions, but they were already in full retreat, running before the pounding of the air. It was as if the very elements had risen up against them to defend the wounded honor of Ontear. Never before had Suti felt quite so vulnerable, so exposed. He knew that, at this point, survival was the primary consideration. Not vanity, not wounded pride . . . not even the lives of those already gone, because Suti had come to the realization that if he or Ontear died at this moment, that wouldn't do a damned thing toward bringing back any of those who had already been killed.

"You weren't wrong! I was . . . I was mistaken!" cried out Suti. "We need to seek shelter, Ontear! To get to the cave! To—"

"The cave will not serve as protection! I have foreseen that! I have foreseen all! Do you have any idea what it is like, Suti? Any idea what it is like to *know?* To be *aware?*" He pulled at his face as if he were seeking some way to tear the very skin from his bones. "It never stops, Suti! The knowledge never stops, no matter how much I desire it to! I am accursed, Suti! How can you have sought out my wisdom? I know everything and nothing! Everything and nothing!" He voice went to a higher and higher pitch, bubbling just short of total hysteria. "You want predictions? You want to know what to expect from the future? Look to the stars, Suti! All of you, look to the stars, for from there will come the Messiah! The bird of flame will signal his coming! He will bear a scar, and he will be a great leader! He will come from air and return to air! And he will be slain by the appointed one! Read the writings, Suti! Read of the appointed one and keep that knowledge secret, within the acolytes, for the appointed one must not know the destiny that awaits until the time of slaying! For in that slaying, the Messiah's death will unite our planet! And if he does not die in the appointed way, then the final war will destroy all! All! *All!*"

"What writings?! What do you mean?" Suti called out desperately.

There was a crack of thunder from overhead, a blast so massive that all Suti could think of at that moment was his childhood. He would tremble upon hearing the sounds of storms, and his parents would spin him fanciful yarns of how the gods would be having sport with one another, and that there was nothing to fear. He would take comfort in that, nestle in his mother's arms, no longer afraid.

He longed for those times now, for if there were indeed gods, they were furious about something.

Wind hammered Suti, stinging his eyes even though he tried desperately to shield them. He slammed shut his clear eyelids, and they afforded him some protection even as thousands, millions of infinitely small pebbles ripped up from the pathway, creating dust and dirt. Thunder doubled and redoubled, and lightning blasted from on high. The storm was everywhere, ripping down from the skies, and he felt as if the storm were within him. As if he had become a focal point for it somehow.

Through his eyelids, he saw Ontear.

And he saw something else. Something that filled him with undiluted terror.

Dropping down from on high, like a great black tongue, a blasting cyclone of air was descending and licking up everything with which it came into contact. The base of it was half a mile wide, and the howl of the air was so earsplitting that Suti was screaming at the top of his lungs and still couldn't hear himself. And it was bearing down directly toward them.

Completely panicked, Suti scrambled backward, trying to get out of the way of the oncoming cone of black air. He managed to gain his feet, ran some yards, and then lost his footing once more. He slid on a trail of pebbles, ripping the skin off his forearms, and suddenly he was yanked to a halt. For one horrified moment he thought that the wind had him, but then he felt the sharpness of the ground and twisted his head around to look. His foot was trapped, wedged into a crevice in the mountain path. He yanked in terror, but it seemed as if all the effort he put into it simply caused his foot to become more solidly imprisoned.

The entire sky was illuminated once more, and Suti howled in fear and sent a prayer to whatever gods there might be, hoping and praying that they were listening and were intending to do *something*. The mass of black air bore down on him, he felt the rippling of his clothes, and knew that he was beyond hope, beyond prayer.

And Ontear, with his arms outstretched, appeared to be laughing. Suti couldn't hear him, but his head was tossed back, his shoulders shaking with barely restrained amusement, and it was as if he were welcoming this mass of destruction that had erupted from the heavens like an inverted volcano. And the cyclone, which was driving straight toward Suti, suddenly veered off. Whether it was simply a shift in the air currents or—the more fanciful interpretation suggested—that Ontear was somehow actually summoning it, Suti would not presume to say. Perhaps it was even that this incredible destructive force had just noticed Ontear, and was abruptly realizing the reason for its presence.

Whatever the reason, amidst a blasting of rock, pebbles, and debris, the black air angled right at Ontear. It pulled at his robes as if inspecting him, trying to determine whether he was worthy of its attention. Ontear, for his part, was no longer laughing, nor was he showing any element of fear. Instead, he was serene, at peace with whatever his fate was going to be.

He did not have to wait long to determine what that fate was.

Suti saw air appearing between the bottoms of Ontear's simple footwear and the rocky surface upon which he was standing. The outlandish sight made no sense to him at first, but then he realized what was happening. As incredible as it seemed, Ontear was being lifted into the air.

Ontear kept his body perfectly still and stiff as he began to rise higher and higher. He was so unafraid, so completely at peace. In some ways, it seemed as if he were going home.

Then the wind turned on him. As gently supporting as it had been, suddenly it became savage. Ontear was about ten feet off the ground when he was abruptly snapped from one side of the funnel to the other. For the first time, Suti saw confusion, even fear, in his eyes. As if he had been expecting this, and had prepared himself for it . . . but now, faced with the reality of it, panic was setting in. It was, however, too late for any such last minute considerations or doubt. Ontear was whipped away from Suti's sight, caught up in the whirl of the destructive force, and now he was thrashing wildly, clearly trying to get away from the unstoppable force of nature that had yanked him away.

The dark air hesitated for a moment, as if choosing its course, and Suti's mind was far too paralyzed to pray or hope or conceive of anything except possibly, just possibly, surviving to the next moment. Then the funnel angled completely away from him, plowing toward Ontear's cave. Suti would have thought it impossible, but the mass of air ripped through the cave, blasting through solid rock. Shards and rubble flew everywhere, and Suti pulled himself into a fetal position, arms crisscrossed over his head to afford himself what protection he could. He felt his belly beginning to heave and he couldn't control himself as he vomited up the entire contents of his stomach. Worst of all, he wasn't even aware that he had done it.

Finally, however, he began to hear himself scream. It took a moment for him to realize that he was hearing his own voice, that the air mass was moving away. He continued to scream as if celebrating, with incredulity, his survival. He lifted his head and saw the funnel moving farther and farther away, apparently picking up speed. He could not make out any sign of Ontear, or what might have been left of him. For all he knew, the wind was of such intensity that it had simply ripped him apart.

Then the funnel suddenly began to retract into the sky. Its bottom dissipated, and then, with a final few crackles of thunder, the black column of air vanished as if it had never been there at all.

Suti's breath was ragged in his chest, and he was unable to tear his horrified gaze away from the last place that he had seen the deadly air funnel. He felt as if, were he to look away, the destructive force might return with more power and intensity than before. But after long moments his breathing slowed down and he managed to compose himself to some degree. With the immediate terror of the moment gone, he was able to work with quiet calm on his foot and was surprised to discover that it took only a few seconds' effort to extricate it from its entrapment. He stumbled to standing, wincing as he tried to put weight upon the injured foot. He took a few careful steps to try and shake it out and relieve himself of the pain.

Gradually he made his way over to where Ontear had been standing. He wasn't exactly sure what he was supposed to feel upon standing at the last spot that he had seen his mentor, but the fact—the embarrassing, humiliating fact—was that he was simply glad that it had been Ontear who had been carried off rather than himself.

Then he looked over to the ruined remains of the cave, and remembered that his original instinct had been to seek refuge there. It had been Ontear who had stopped him. Fortunately, as it happened, for if he had tried to secure himself there, he would have been carried off by the winds. Ontear had saved his life. He had known. Somehow he had known.

He walked up to the cave, pushing aside the remaining rubble with the toe of his shoe. So many times had he come there to discover Ontear sitting in the exact same place: quiet, serene, confident. Suti had sought to emulate it, sought to find the inner vision and peace that Ontear felt, even though there were critics who claimed that the serenity was nothing more than the self-confidence born of utter madness.

And then, when Suti stepped upon the spot that Ontear had occupied for so long . . . this time, he *did* feel something. At first he thought it was his imagination, but quickly realized that such was not the case. There was . . . there was something there. The ground felt different: harder, smoother, *warmer*. Was it a simple heating device? Something that Ontear used to help him subsist through the cold of the winter days?

No. No, Suti got a different sense of it altogether. He took a large step backward, and the moment he was away from the immediate area that had once been Ontear's within the cave, the feeling ceased. That was when Suti realized that it was more than simply the sensation of warmth. It was something that somehow had burrowed deep within Suti's soul, something that he felt permeating his very being. It was a sense of . . . of peace. Of knowledge and understanding. There were no particular facts floating through his head, but instead a simple and serene confidence that anything there was to know, he would eventually come to understand. It was addictive, like a drug. Without hesitation Suti stepped back upon the area and he felt it once more, this time stronger than ever. The ground was cluttered beneath his feet, but he kicked away the debris as quickly as he could and then dropped to his knees to inspect the ground. It was the same color as the rest of the area around him, but it was flat and smooth, and under his hands he could feel something that reminded him of a slow, steady pulse.

Then his fingers discovered an indentation, a tracing. He brushed aside the last of the dirt and dust to find a symbol etched in the ground. It was small, no larger than the palm of his hand, and it did not make sense to him at first. It appeared to be carved in the shape of a torch or flame. Why there was a small carving of a flame in the ground, Suti could not even begin to guess, yet something prompted him to extend one long finger and drag it across the intricate line carving.

He found, with interest, that it was one continuous

line, and he traced it until his fingertip had reached the point from which it had begun. The moment it made that contact, it was as if a circuit had been completed. There was a soft rumbling from just beneath him, gears shifting, as if some sort of machinery had been set into motion. This time, however, he felt no immediate fear. No sense of panic as he had before. This time, for no reason that he could readily discern, it all felt . . . *right* somehow.

There was a loud, solid *click* and the flame symbol actually twisted in place, moving about ninety degrees and then slowly sliding upward, revealing a cylinder about the width of Suti's hand and a foot tall. It was made of gleaming silver metal and sparkled in the daylight, the suns rays filtering down in the wake of the storm that had passed only moments ago. With reverence, Suti reached over and removed the cylinder, hefting it experimentally. He turned it over and over, looking for some sort of seam, some hint as to what it might be and what it might contain, if, indeed, it contained anything at all. Experimentally he twisted the top in the opposite direction from the bottom, and suddenly the top unscrewed in his hands. He blinked in surprise as he felt the unexpected give of the device in his hand, but then did not hesitate to unscrew it as quickly as he could. It made a harsh rasping sound, as if feeling the need to put up some sort of token resistance before yielding its secrets, whatever those might be.

He finished unscrewing the lid and then upended the cylinder. Thin sheaves of papers slid out and onto the ground, where they lay for a moment before unrolling by themselves, without Suti touching them at all. He was hesitant to pick them up at first, but finally he did, and scanned them quickly in an effort to discern exactly what it was they contained. There was line after line of writing upon them, and immediately he recognized the penmanship as that of Ontear himself. His eyes grew wide with excitement as he recognized them for what they were: predictions. Page after page of thoughts and concepts by the foremost seer in the history of Zondar. And they were all in his hands.

He knew what he had to do, of course. He had to make these predictions public. He had to bring them to his people, let them know precisely what their future held. Ontear had been closed-minded, self-directed, and selfish, and the result had been an appalling civil war. Suti would not make that mistake.

He replaced the cylinder on the spot from which he had lifted it, and he saw it slide neatly back into place. The gentle vibrations, the feeling of power that he seemed to sense from beneath his feet were gone. It was as if the machinery beneath him, whatever it was, had gone silent. Perhaps he was imagining it, or perhaps it had somehow been keyed directly to Ontear himself. Was it possible that his foresight came not from within, but from without? That somehow this equipment had been responsible? If that was the case, then from where had the equipment come? Who had given it to Ontear, . . . and would they be back?

That, Suti realized, was clearly part of his destiny. He would wait. He would wait right there, for however long it took, to see if the potential providers of the answers would reveal themselves to him. In the meantime, however, he would use the information left behind by Ontear to continue the work and reunite the world. Information that he became more and more excited about as he read the material over.

Tentative voices called his name and he turned to see the other two acolytes who had accompanied him. They were a short distance away, walking carefully toward him, stepping delicately over the shifts in the path. "Are you all right, Suti?" they asked.

This was it. This was the moment to share the knowledge. To let them know all that was to befall the world, to produce the writings of Ontear. Why, with this concrete view of their world's destiny before them, they could mold it and shape it, they could . . .

They could . . .

They could share the power.

Knowledge. Knowledge was power. That truism rang in Suti's head as he read the writings in greater detail. Yes, that was the way of things, wasn't it? Knowledge was power, and there was tremendous power to be had here. Suti's mind raced: There were so many possibilities, so many things he could accomplish with this information . . . except that it would require that he kept it all to himself. Yes, that was the only reasonable possibility. After all, the world was already in disarray, civil war sweeping the different factions. If the information, the predictions, the last words and visions of Ontear were made public, different groups would endeavor to twist them to their own respective convenience. Everyone had their own intentions, after all, their own incentives. Everyone had an agenda, sometimes hidden and other times right out in the open.

There was information, knowledge here that many Zondarians simply couldn't handle. That was another problem. Either they would be driven mad by the knowledge of what was to come, or else would labor to try and invalidate it as had happened with some of Ontear's predictions. There were those who, once the future was revealed to them, felt compelled to do everything they could to change it out of some sort of sheer need for perversity and contrariness. As if once they were told, "This is how it will be," felt the juvenile need to protest, "We'll just see about that!" and labor mightily to change it all. And if that were the case, then one of two things would happen. Either

Ontear's predictions would become invalidated, and the legends of Zondar's foremost seer would be challenged, diminished, and Ontear, who deserved reverence, would be lessened in the eyes of posterity. Or his predictions would remain true in the face of overwhelming odds, and what would be accomplished then? Fear, destruction, railing against the frustrating inevitability of fate. Nothing much else.

No, no indeed, what Zondar needed was one man. One good man, with a solid ethical foundation, who could use these predictions to lead the Zondarians into a new golden age. An age where the Unglza and the Eenza would be able to cooperate with one another and grow into two compassionate, cooperative groups. They were all Zondarians, after all, and it was simply madness that they were at war with one another.

And Suti was that man, of that he was quite sure. Ontear had been given power, but it had corrupted him. It had dragged him down even as he thought he was elevating himself, and he had completely lost touch with what was good for the people. That was something that Suti would never do. Not ever. And if fulfilling the destiny that awaited him meant keeping a few secrets, for the overall greater good, well, he was willing to make that sacrifice.

His back was still to the other acolytes as, without drawing any attention to it, he slid the rolled up papers into the inner folds of his robe. Then he turned to face the acolytes. He felt taller, more confident, as if the writings which he had secreted upon his person gave him an inner knowledge and strength.

"Hello, my friends," he said softly. There was an odd calmness to his voice.

The acolytes looked at each other nervously, and then back to Suti. "Are you . . . all right? Where is Ontear?"

"Ontear . . ." He paused for dramatic effect. "Ontear is with those who have come before . . . and will come after. I am here now. The power is mine now, but I will share it with you. Bring the others. Summon them to me."

"Ontear is . . . gone?"

He felt a brief wave of impatience. "Yes, he is gone. But I am here, and that will suffice. Now bring the others to me that I may address them."

"Suti, they're waiting for us back at the temple. We can all go to—"

"I said to bring them here!"

The acolytes were startled, jumping back in response to the anger and intensity of Suti's voice.

"They will come here," Suti continued with the same degree of intensity. "We will rebuild the cave, rebuild Ontear's place."

"Rebuild a cave? How—"

"We will find a way! We will do so, and we will create a shrine to Ontear, and that is just the beginning of my plans! And you will not question me again!"

They did not question again, but instead bolted down the side of the mountain to obey his orders.

Suti was annoyed, but it was quickly passing. They were going to have to learn, that was all. He was going to have to teach them.

And if they refused to learn, if they irked him or did not sufficiently cooperate, well . . .

Well, he might have to let the war continue a bit longer. Just to show them what they had passed up by proving difficult to deal with. He would hate to have to follow that course, but he had to start thinking beyond immediate gratification. When the whole of the future was at one's fingertips, one had to keep watch on the big picture.

NINETEEN
YEARS
EARLIER . . .

"Get someone else," said M'k'n'zy.

"There *is* no one else," Sh'nab said. "You are the one. It is the appointed time, M'k'n'zy, and your responsibility. I can't believe that you would want to shirk it."

M'k'n'zy strode back and forth apprehensively within the confines of his fairly modest hut. His long black hair was tied back, although a few stray strands dangled around the twenty-year-old's face. The scar that ran the length of his right cheek had flushed bright red, as it tended to do when there was something truly frustrating facing him.

Sh'nab couldn't quite understand what M'k'n'zy's problem was. One of the tribal elders of Calhoun, Sh'nab had seen M'k'n'zy face down entire troops of Danteri oppressors. He had seen him command troops of men, send them into battle, fight for his life. He had witnessed M'k'n'zy dealing with every sort of challenge and problem under the Xenexian sun, and therefore could not wrap himself around M'k'n'zy's current problem. After all . . .

"She's just a woman, M'k'n'zy!" Sh'nab said, for what seemed to him to be the umpteenth time. "This should not be difficult for you. You are acting as if . . . as if . . ." He shook his head in frustration. "I don't know how you're acting. I am frankly not certain what to make of it."

"Why can't D'ndai do it!" M'k'n'zy said, annoyed with the sound of his own voice. He sounded whining, petulant, and even—gods help him—scared.

"Because," Sh'nab said patiently, "D'ndai isn't here. You know that. He's on Danter at the moment, paving the way for the peace negotiations with the Federation overseeing the process. You know this."

It was true, of course. He had been there, after all, when the Federation had first shown up on Xenex in the person of Jean-Luc Picard, the man who had suggested to M'k'n'zy that he himself consider a career in Starfleet. Considering M'k'n'zy's frame of mind at that moment, perhaps the thing to do was to find out when the next shuttle was going to be available and to head straight out as soon as possible. But M'k'n'zy had not made up his mind yet as to whether Starfleet was the direction that he wanted to go with his life. Never before, though, had he regretted hesitating over a decision as much as he regretted it now.

"We can wait until he comes back, then," M'k'n'zy suggested.

Sh'nab shook his head. "The times are very proscribed for these matters, M'k'n'zy. Catrine's husband has been gone a year. She has not remarried; she has had no wish to, and that is her right by tribal law. But she maintains her husband's name, and her husband's fortunes, and she does not wish the family line to end with her. That is also her right."

"But I'm the warlord! I'm not the chief! D'ndai is the chief!"

"You are his brother. These responsibilities run along family lines. You know that—"

"Yes, yes, I know, I know!" M'k'n'zy's purple eyes flickered with frustration. "Sh'nab, will you please stop telling me things I already know and reminding me that I know them? It's most irritating to me!" He paced back and forth. "Can she wait until—"

"We're going in circles, M'k'n'zy! Besides, she—" Sh'nab paused.

"She what?"

Sh'nab muttered something that M'k'n'zy didn't quite hear, and when asked to repeat it, said, "I said she asked for you specifically. If she wanted to be flexible, she could likely wait until D'ndai's return, but it would put her beyond her current fertile cycle and she'd have to wait three months. She said she did not wish to wait, and she made it quite clear that she found you more . . . desirable . . . than D'ndai. I would ask that you do not pass that information on to your older brother. He might be hurt."

"Fine, fine," M'k'n'zy said with an annoyed wave. "Not a word."

"M'k'n'zy," Sh'nab said, not unkindly, "I admit that I am so accustomed to seeing you handle virtually any situation, that I'm not used to seeing you act like . . . well, like a nervous young man. You are, after all, only twenty summers old, even though you have served to liberate your people from an oppression that has gone on for centuries. Catrine is older than you, granted, but she is a comely woman nonetheless. It's not as if the task that awaits you is unpleasant. And it is not as if you have not . . ."

And then his voice trailed off as he saw M'k'n'zy's back stiffen slightly. "M'k'n'zy," he asked, with growing suspicion in his voice, "You *have* been with other women, have you not?"

M'k'n'zy laughed contemptuously. "Of course I have. I have had . . . dalliances, if you will. Experience."

"How much experience?"

"More than enough."

"M'k'n'zy," Sh'nab said, beginning to fully comprehend the situation, "I'm not speaking now of simple pleasure-giving. Of groping beneath sheets, or stolen moments in the darkness of a tent. Have you ever actually . . ." He found the resolve of his question beginning to fail under the intense glare and scrutiny of the look that M'k'n'zy was now giving him. He cleared his throat loudly and said, "Have you ever fully . . . well . . . consummated . . . ?"

There was silence in the hut for a time, and then M'k'n'zy said slowly, "Define 'fully.'"

"Oh gods, you're a virgin," Sh'nab moaned, sinking into a large, ornately carved chair.

"Only partly," M'k'n'zy replied defensively.

"Partly! One cannot partly be a virgin, M'k'n'zy! I don't believe this!" said Sh'nab. "A twenty-year-old warlord virgin?"

"Say it a bit more loudly. I don't think they heard you on Danter," M'k'n'zy told him with undisguised annoyance.

"M'k'n'zy, I don't understand! Every time you'd walk through the village square, women's heads would turn! Do you think a village elder doesn't notice such things? I was knocked aside once by three young girls who were trying to get your attention! How can you still have no carnal knowledge of women? The average Xenexian male is sexually active by the time he has seen thirteen summers."

"It was my choice, Sh'nab."

"I . . . I see."

Sh'nab was silent for so long that M'k'n'zy turned to look at him with concern on his face. "Do you?"

"Of course I do. It saddens me, I admit. But . . . perhaps it's understandable. Perhaps that is why you are so able to lead troops of men into battle. You are more . . . *comfortable* . . . with them."

It took a moment for what Sh'nab was saying to sink in, and when he realized, M'k'n'zy wasn't sure whether to react with outrage or laughter. His voice caught somewhere in between in a sort of strangled choke. *"I do not prefer to have sex with men, Sh'nab!"*

"Oh," Sh'nab said mildly. "I thought that was what you were trying to say."

"If I had been trying to say that, I would have said that! Kindly do not 'help' me with a pronouncement of that magnitude, if it is all the same to you! All right?"

"Well, then I do not understand, M'k'n'zy. If you don't . . . I mean . . . if . . ."

Sh'nab was still seated in the ornately carved chair as M'k'n'zy sank onto the floor opposite him. M'k'n'zy had known Sh'nab for many years, felt a closeness to the elder who had on a number of occasions schooled him in some of the gentler arts of Xenexian life and culture. M'k'n'zy was not comfortable discussing such matters with anyone, really, but if he was going to speak of it, then at least Sh'nab was someone he considered an appropriate sounding board.

"Sh'nab, I did not expect to survive the uprising. Do you understand? I did not think that I would manage to live through the rebellion. I thought the Danteri would catch and kill me, or that I would die in battle. I faced death a thousand times, and to some degree I still cannot believe that I survived it all when so many others who were just as brave, just as resourceful, and just as skilled in battle as I wound up losing their lives. I saw the way women looked at me, Sh'nab. If it wasn't lost on you, it certainly wasn't lost on me. I'd see the lovelight in their eyes, and I . . . I did not desire any woman to form an attachment to me, for fear of not being there for her. I did not want any loved ones because I did not wish to leave a loved one behind. It might have hampered me in what I needed to do, and it would have been unfair to her. So now we are faced with a possible peace, and I find the prospect of . . . of intimacy . . . to be some-what daunting. For that matter, I am suspicious of women."

"Suspicious of them?"

"Well," M'k'n'zy shrugged, "it is unfair, I suppose, to single them out. I am suspicious of everyone. But now I have a reputation as our greatest fighter, our greatest warrior. What if a woman is attracted to my title and reputation, rather than to me, for myself? For that matter, what if she expects me to be as . . . as skilled in the art of lovemaking as I am in the art of war? What if"—and he lowered his head—"what if I cannot perform to her satisfaction? What if I cannot perform at all? Can you imagine that? Can you imagine the things that would be said as word spread? People calling out to me, 'So, M'k'n'zy, having prob-lems getting your sword out of its sheath, eh?' The humiliation of the thought, the . . ." He shuddered, his voice trailing off in contemplation of such embar-rassment.

"M'k'n'zy," Sh'nab said softly, "you are a strate-gist. That has always been your greatest strength. As such, it has been necessary for you to give a great deal of thought to whatever situation you might be faced with. In my opinion, you are treating the prospect of sex with the same gravity that you would plan a military engagement. You are trying to foresee all possibilities, plan for every possible contingency. Inti-macy is not a war, M'k'n'zy."

"I know of some couples who might disagree with you, Sh'nab."

Sh'nab allowed a smile. "All right, I'll grant you that," said the elder. "But you are overthinking things here. Simply allow matters to develop naturally."

"That is not my nature, Sh'nab. I am one who feels the need to steer matters to a conclusion that I find satisfactory."

"Relationships do not work that way, M'k'n'zy. In war, you give instructions to your men and they follow orders. Women do not take to that. Except the most passive of women, and I doubt that you would be satisfied with someone like that."

M'k'n'zy made no immediately reply, and Sh'nab continued gently, "Go to Catrine, M'k'n'zy. She is a good woman. If you do not wish to attend to her wishes, then tell her so. The likelihood is that she will understand. Give her some sort of explanation, though. She is entitled to that much, at least."

"I suppose so," M'k'n'zy sighed. "All right, Sh'nab, all right. I'll go to her and explain the situation. I'm sure I can get her to understand that it would be better for her to wait for D'ndai's return. He has far more experience in these matters. I should know. He certainly boasts of it enough."

It had rained the previous night, and the great square was more like a large pool of mud. M'k'n'zy stepped through it carefully, his feet sticking in place every so often, and he'd have to fight to pull his boots free. He made his way across it, and angled off down the side road toward Catrine's home. The sun was already setting, its rays stretching across the horizon, and M'k'n'zy scanned the skies urgently in the hopes that, at the last moment, D'ndai's ship might suddenly show up overhead. But there seemed to be no sign of it.

Just his luck.

M'k'n'zy knocked gently on the door of Catrine's home, so gently that it seemed as if nothing short of a miracle would enable anyone to hear him. He waited exactly five seconds, got no immediate response, and promptly came to the conclusion that she wasn't home. He turned away, prepared to bolt, when the door creaked open and Catrine stood in the doorway.

She was at least ten summers older than he, with copious blond hair that framed a round and amused face. In contrast to the smile, though, there was sadness in her eyes. Sadness or, at the very least, loneliness. She wore a simple white shift, and there was gentle lighting from within that backlit her, tracing the curves of her muscular body.

"Greetings, M'k'n'zy," she said. He was surprised to notice that her voice had a somewhat enchanting lilt to it. "You have come to honor my request and give me a child?"

"I have come to discuss it," he replied.

"Discussing it is not how it's generally done," was her comment, and then she gestured for him to enter. He did so, looking around at the long tapering candles which decorated the inner hallway. "I appreciate your taking the time to come to me."

"I wasn't otherwise occupied," said M'k'n'zy.

He suddenly realized that she had taken his hand in hers. His palm felt clammy to him, but if she noticed it she said nothing. "Do you have a woman, M'k'n'zy?" she asked.

"You mean at present?"

"Yes."

"No. No, there is no one. I have not had the time. I have been . . . rather busy. Where are we going?"

"My bedroom." She stopped, turned, and smiled at him. "Unless you wish to take me right here on the floor."

"No!" he said quickly, his voice sounding higher and sharper than he would have liked. He composed himself and repeated, "No," in a slightly deeper voice that sounded like forced casualness.

"All right, then."

She brought him into the bedroom, and there were more candles surrounding the bed; so many, in fact, that he felt as if he were about to be tossed onto a slab and offered up as a sacrifice. The bed looked softer than a slab, though. Nonetheless M'k'n'zy looked tense, rigid, nervous. In short, he looked like a man who was about to do many things, other than have sex. The scent of her filled his nostrils, and he felt slightly dizzy. Her eyes picked up the flickering candlelight and seemed to be flickering with a heat all their own.

"Well?" she said.

He shifted his feet uneasily. "Uhm . . . well, uh . . . well, what?"

"What would you like to do? Do you wish to undress me, or shall I do that for you? Do you wish me to—"

"I don't know. Whatever you desire is fine. I am doing this for you, Catrine. It is . . ." He tried to find the words and adopted a scolding tone. "It is an obligation. That is all. Just an obligation. I'll do as you wish, since this is your desire, not mine."

If he could have pulled the words out of the air before they had reached her, he would have. But naturally, that was not an option. He saw the hurt on her face though, her large eyes going round with pain. She did not cry, but she sank slowly onto the bed, her back rigid. "I am sorry," she whispered.

"You have nothing to apologize for."

"No, I . . . I do. For you are young and beautiful, and I am . . ." Her fingers trailed along her throat. "I am . . . old. Old and unattractive."

"What?"

"Obviously that is the case. I—"

He wanted to console her, wanted to speak words of love or sympathy to her, but he didn't have the tools to do so. So all he sounded was brusque as he replied, "Don't be ridiculous. You are . . . you're beautiful. You are. You're beautiful."

"I'm not. I am old."

"You are . . ." He tried to find a way to phrase it that would pierce through her veil of self-pity and, in so doing, his voice automatically adopted a more sympathetic tone. "Every summer that you have lived has graced you with sunlight that you continue to carry with you. You shine with an inner light."

"Oh, please," she said with what sounded like cautious dismissal, as if she wanted to believe his words, but was reluctant to accept them for what they were. "Please, you will say whatever comes to mind so that I will not be sad. I'm flattered by your efforts, but do not patronize me."

"I would not patronize you," said M'k'n'zy firmly. He took her by the shoulders and turned her. "I knew your husband, Catrine. He was a good man. A good fighter. I respected him. If nothing else, I would not insult his memory by treating you in such a manner."

"So," her voice was very quiet and he had to strain to hear. "You . . . do find me attractive?"

"Yes. Very much so."

"And do you"—she looked up at him with hesitation that almost seemed girlish—"do you want me?"

"I—" He suddenly felt as if the temperature in the room had risen. "It is simply that . . . well . . ."

"M'k'n'zy, you act as if you've never been with a woman before. . . ." Her voice trailed off as she saw his reaction.

With an annoyed grunt, he turned away. "What is

it, emblazoned on my face? Has the news been circulated throughout the town? How is—"

And then he heard something that he had not expected: laughter. Gentle, floating laughter, as he turned to see that her body was shaking with mirth. Somehow it was not exactly conducive to salving his wounded ego. "I'm sure it's very funny to you," M'k'n'zy said sourly.

"No! No, I . . . I think it's sweet!" she said.

"Sweet!"

"Yes. You were so busy fighting for the freedom of our world that you never had time for romantic entanglements. Besides, after a day of hacking and slaying, it must be difficult to be in the mood for soft words and softer women."

He was completely astounded to hear her say that. "Yes!" he affirmed, sitting next to her on the bed. "Yes, that's it exactly! How did you know?"

"It's obvious. Obvious to me, at least. Don't worry, M'k'n'zy," she said confidently, patting his hand. "Your secret is safe with me."

"That is . . . that is so kind of you," he said, squeezing her hand in return. "I cannot begin to tell you." Relief flooded through him and he flopped back on the bed. "I thought that you would—no, actually, I had no idea what you would say or do. I wasn't even planning to tell you. I was just . . . I . . . I don't know what . . . I just wanted . . ."

She lay down next to him, propping her head up with one hand. "What did you want?"

"I don't know," he said softly.

"You can leave if you wish. I'll wait for D'ndai to fulfill the requirements of law. I just . . ." She stared down at him.

"You just what?"

"Nothing, M'k'n'zy. It really doesn't matter."

He looked up into her face. She was quite lovely, really. And there was a mixture of sadness and resolution that reminded him, in many ways, of himself. "Catrine," he said slowly, "I do not . . . anticipate remaining on this world. I am seriously considering leaving Xenex. I am thinking of going far, far away. You've had such great loss, such great sadness. You deserve so much more than I can give, I think. You deserve more than simply what the law dictates. You deserve a man to be with you, to wake up next to you, to care for you. If you wait, I'm sure that man will come to you. If we did what you ask now, then—"

"Then I would have your baby. A baby who, I can only hope, will grow up to be as strong, as brave, as determined, and good as his or her father."

"But you should have a mate to—"

"You do not understand, M'k'n'zy. I'm not looking for such a man. My dear, lost husband . . . he was a good man. He was my soul mate. Perhaps someday in the far, far future I may be ready for another, but I do not envision such a time. But I am ready for a child now. A child to love, to raise in the teachings of Xenex."

"Catrine, I—"

She leaned over and her lips brushed tentatively against his. When he did not resist, she kissed him more thoroughly. The kiss was like a fine wine, sweet and bringing warmth to him. His hands, seemingly of their own accord, were running along her body, tracing the curves of her hips. Slowly she undid the front of his shirt and looked at his chest. She saw scars, bruises all over his torso, and she traced the line of one of the scars across his left breast.

"Sword slipped past my guard. Grazed me," he said, and he was surprised how choked his voice sounded.

"So many scars. So much fighting," she sighed as she gazed into his face. "How much death have these eyes seen?"

"Too much," he admitted. "Far too much."

"Tell me, M'k'n'zy of Calhoun, would it not be nice for a man who has seen so much death, slain so many people . . . would it not be proper and just and honorable if, the very first time you made love, it was for the purpose of putting a life back into the world?"

She kissed him on the throat and he sighed, his body trembling. "Yes," he admitted. "Yes, it . . . it would."

He somewhat lost track of what happened after that. He knew that her simple white shift had fallen to the floor, and his own clothes soon joined them there. She was gentle with him, and loving, and any fears he had over being unable to perform were quickly left far, far behind, along with the concerns of the real world.

She moved atop him, her face smiling down at him, and he was lost in the beauty and glory that was Catrine. Even though the goal was a straightforward one, she managed to prolong the moment, the heat building within him but not finding release until she was ready to let it go. And when she finally did, and he exploded into her . . .

He was silent. There was no outcry, no shout of joy. Nothing but complete and utter silence. Even in a moment of total ecstasy, M'k'n'zy could not completely let go. Catrine was struck by it as he sagged beneath her, spent and quiet, so very quiet. She touched the side of his face. "Did you . . . enjoy it, M'k'n'zy?"

He smiled ruefully. His breath was coming in slow, ragged gasps as he said, "You have to . . . remember who you're talking to."

"I don't understand."

And she was astounded to see a single tear roll down his cheek as he said, "I enjoyed it more than anything else . . . that doesn't involve killing an enemy. Do you understand now?"

Slowly she nodded and wiped away the tear. She brought the wet finger to her mouth and tasted it. Then she slid off him and lay next to him, her arm draped across his chest, her head on his shoulder. "Can we stay like this for a time?"

He nodded almost imperceptibly and she drew against him. Even though it was early evening, and the sun had only just drawn below the horizon, Catrine nonetheless fell into a deep and peaceful sleep.

When she awoke six hours later, he was gone. The side of the bed he'd been lying on was cool to the touch. Catrine turned over to face away from "his" side of the bed, as she would continue to do for the rest of her days, and ever so softly cried herself back to sleep.

NOW . . .

I.

In the starkness of her room, Selar twisted and turned on her bed, the single sheet becoming completely ensnarled around her naked body. Sweat was pouring from her, even though the climate control for her quarters did a more than adequate job of duplicating the arid, dry-heat environment of her native Vulcan. Several times during the night she woke up, crying out the name of Voltak, her late husband, and then she would lapse back into her fitful sleep.

An assortment of images tumbled through her mind. She would relive the night of their mating, the horrible circumstance in which a heart attack took Voltak from her while they were in the throes of *Pon Farr*. She would see his face, floating away into the void. And then she would see another face, a curiously angled face with a smile that bordered on a smirk, and two-tone blond hair cut low to the scalp. It was the face of Burgoyne 172, the Hermat chief engineer who had taken a fancy to Selar and made

41

several impassioned overtures before Selar had made it clear that she simply wasn't inclined to sate the demands of *Pon Farr* with the odd Hermat. But Selar had changed her mind, only to spot Burgoyne arm-in-arm with astronavigator Mark McHenry, heading off to what was clearly an assignation. This left Selar high and dry . . . and mightily frustrated.

Burgoyne was smiling at her, hish fangs peeping out from under hish lips. And then Burgoyne reached out with hish long, tapered fingers, and Selar saw herself, her arms reaching out toward Burgoyne. Burgoyne reached for her.

And there was a high-pitched beep.

The sound repeated itself, and it was enough to jostle Selar to wakefulness. Sitting up quickly, she misjudged her position and rolled off the bed, crashing to the floor with a rather loud thud. She lay there, entangled in the bedsheet, musing over the rather odd situation that had brought her to this particular sequence of events. Then, in the darkness, her brain fully cleared and she responded via voice prompt. "Computer, Selar here," she said, her voice so casual that it never would have betrayed the fact that she was lying on the floor, naked and tangled up in a sheet.

"Doctor," came the concerned voice of Doctor Maxwell. "Are you all right?"

"I am in perfect health, Doctor. Why are you inquiring?"

"Because you're over an hour late for your shift, and, well . . . that's unlike you."

That explained why Maxwell had paged her via her comm badge rather than patch directly to her quarters. He'd assumed that she was already out and about, since Selar never slept late. Selar checked the chronometer on the wall. Had she been human, she would have moaned to herself, or jumped up in a panic. "I . . . appreciate the summons, Doctor. I shall be along shortly."

"Take your time, Doctor," Maxwell's reassuring voice came. "Things are somewhat quiet here, for a change of pace."

"Indeed. You are saying, then, that I am not needed."

There was something in her tone of voice that clearly was puzzling to Maxwell, but he endeavored not to let it show. He was only partly successful. "We can always use your guidance, Doctor. You are the CMO, after all."

"The thought is appreciated, Doctor, as is the half-hearted argument regarding my indispensability." She paused, and then her thoughts began to drift, because she was feeling the building of the warmth once more. It seemed to have its origins in her loins and in her heart, and the two radiated outward, the circles of sensation intersecting within her. Something within her snapped her attention back to the fact that she had an open comm link and a puzzled doctor at the other end. "I will be some time more, Doctor, if, as you say, all is calm. I have a meeting I must attend to."

"Not a problem, Doctor. Sickbay out."

Once again she had nothing but the silence of the room. For some reason, she fancied that she could hear distant wind chimes, and sense a warm desert breeze sweeping over her. Something had to be done about the *Pon Farr*. She had a plan; her research had been very beneficial in that matter. Now it was just a matter of summoning up her courage and doing what needed to be done. She had hoped she would be able to wait . . . wait indefinitely if need be. But that didn't seem to be an option. Nor was returning to Vulcan much of a solution either. For one thing, finding a Vulcan male in the right state of *Pon Farr* was possible but difficult in the time she had left. She could hardly just announce her need on the Vulcan planetary internet, and discreet inquiries took time. Besides, a choice of mate on availibility alone would hardly be logical. Selar still retained enough of her logic to know that. She would at least choose a highly qualified father for her child.

No, she knew what she was going to do—what she had to do.

She dressed as quickly as she could, annoyed that her fingers were trembling slightly, thereby making it difficult for her to put her uniform on with efficiency. She glanced once in the mirror and turned away as quickly as she could from what she saw. She stumbled towards the door of her quarters . . .

. . . and it didn't open.

She stepped back, looked at the door as if to wonder whether anything on the vessel was going to go right for her this day, and tapped her comm badge. "Selar to Ops. We seem to have a maintenance problem with the door to my quarters."

"We're aware of that, Doctor," came Lefler's voice. "It's not just you. Engineering has some systems glitches they're trying to lock down. Doors all over the ship are opening by themselves or not opening when they're supposed to."

"Including turbo lifts?" asked Selar.

"No, thank God. Just doors. Burogyne estimates another hour or so before they've got it cleared up . . ."

Selar tensed inwardly at the mention of Burgoyne's name. At that moment, the door to her quarters slid open, even though she was standing two feet away. "The door is open; apparently I have been liberated."

"We'll keep working on it. Ops out."

Selar headed out, relieved to be out of her quarters and away from the face she'd seen in the mirror. A face that she barely recognized as hers. One that seemed to have more ties to Vulcans of the past, with that burning and smoldering savagery, than anything that she vaguely related to her modern-day perception of her race.

A face burned in her mind, one that had not appeared in any of her dreams. And she was going to go to that person and have her situation attended to.

Or else she was going to die.

II.

"The Great Bird of the Galaxy."

Admiral Edward Jellico's face, incredulity written in large letters all over it, glared disbelievingly out from the comm screen at Mackenzie Calhoun and Elizabeth Paula Shelby, who were seated in the conference lounge in apparently relaxed fashion. Jellico's tone of voice came as absolutely no surprise to Shelby; she'd had a sneaking suspicion what he was going to say before he said it. She could see the nice view Jellico had outside his window at Starfleet headquarters: the Golden Gate Bridge, the occasional shuttle floating past. It seemed pleasant enough, and yet she wondered how he managed to tolerate it. If Shelby didn't have stars to look out at, she was certain she would go completely mad.

"The Great Bird of the Galaxy?" he said again.

"Yes, Admiral, that's correct," Calhoun said.

"You're telling me," Jellico leaned forward as if somehow that would bring him closer to the captain of the *Excalibur*, "that the entire planet of Thallon

46

was smashed apart by a giant flaming bird, clawing its way out to freedom, and that it then flew away to who-knows-where?"

"I find it hard to believe myself, but yes, Admiral, that's essentially what I'm saying."

"Captain Calhoun, what do you take me for? Calhoun . . . Shelby," Jellico began again with an air of forced patience, "I know you don't think much of me—"

"That's not true, sir," Shelby assured him.

"Absolutely not," agreed Calhoun. *In point of fact,* Calhoun thought, *we actually don't think of you at all.*

Calhoun reached down subtly to rub his right shin where Shelby had just kicked him under the table. He fired an annoyed look at her, and blocked his mouth from Jellico's view with one hand as he murmured, "Striking a superior officer?"

Shelby reached up to scratch the back of her neck, shielding her face from Jellico's view long enough to mutter back, "If you want to *stay* a superior officer, don't say whatever it is you're thinking." Without waiting for him to respond, she turned to Jellico and said, "Admiral, how you are viewed or not viewed by the command personnel of the *Excalibur* has nothing to do with the matter at hand. The ship's log, the science log, even our visual records, all confirm what it was that we saw."

"Visual records can be arranged, Commander. To imply that seeing is necessarily believing is a charmingly antiquated notion that hasn't had a shred of truth to it in about four centuries now."

"Granted, Admiral, but the fact remains: Somehow this creature burrowed into the heart of the planet Thallon, and provided the energy-rich resources which enabled the Thallonians to become the dominant world that they grew into. It was the creature's imminent . . . *hatching,* if you will . . . that caused the drain of power, the destruction of the world, and the fall of the Thallonian Empire."

"Commander," Jellico said patiently, "empires fall because of any number of things. Economic collapse. Political infighting. Inbreeding causing a downward spiral in the quality of its rulers. Empires do not fall because giant flaming birds smash the home world to bits!"

"Well . . ." Shelby paused, looked to Calhoun, who shrugged. She turned back to Jellico. "Not as a rule . . ."

"Commander—"

"Admiral, be reasonable. Do you really think someone would go to all this effort just for the purpose of perpetrating some sort of massive hoax on you? With all due respect—"

"There's that phrase again," sighed Jellico. "The one that always precedes something said with a total lack of respect."

"With all due respect," Shelby said more forcefully, "doesn't that sound like an odd view of the galaxy? I mean, really now. Ship's log, science log . . . all to pull a joke on us?"

"Or perhaps to cover up some sort of—"

"Of what?" Calhoun now cut in, and the veneer of affable amusement, and even faint condescension, was gone. "May I ask, Admiral, what you are implying?"

"May I ask, Captain, what you are inferring?" countered Jellico.

"I am inferring," replied Calhoun, "that you think there may have been some sort of sloppiness on my part, and that the report we've given you was constructed—in all its outrageousness—to fool us. And that we fell for it. And if that is the case, Admiral," and his voice lowered in a tone that bordered on deadly, "then I am going to have to ask you to apologize."

"Apologize to you, Captain?" asked Jellico with clear skepticism.

"No, Admiral. To be perfectly blunt—"

"As if that were a change of pace."

"I couldn't give a damn what you think of me," continued Calhoun as if Jellico hadn't spoken. "But Elizabeth Shelby is one of the most capable humans I've ever known."

"Captain, this isn't necessary," Shelby tried to say.

But he ignored her and continued. "The notion that she would fail to see through *any* hoax is, frankly, insulting. And if you do not retract that statement, then I shall file a formal complaint with Starfleet Command."

"What 'statement,' Captain?" replied Jellico. "You're asking me to retract an inference that you yourself made. I am simply saying that I find this report of your activities in Sector 221-G, formerly known as Thallonian space, to be somewhat . . . dubious."

"If that is the case, Admiral," Calhoun replied, "if you truly think that running into a figure of mythology or history such as the Great Bird of the Galaxy is too preposterous, then I take it you will not want to hear about it should we happen to encounter . . . oh, I don't know . . . Apollo?"

"Or Zephram Cochrane?" Shelby added. "Or— what was his name—the knife murderer . . . ?"

"Jack the Ripper?" offered Calhoun.

"Yes!" She snapped her fingers as the memory came back. "Jack the Ripper. Thank you. You know, I have to tell you, Admiral, in comparison to those incidents, a giant flaming bird seems a fairly modest claim."

Jellico rubbed the bridge of his nose, suddenly looking rather tired. "Very amusing, Captain, Commander. You refer to Kirk, of course."

"Well, he *was* required reading at the Academy, sir," said Shelby.

"He was required reading because of his tactics and strategy," clarified Jellico. "His more 'outrageous' exploits were hardly required."

"True, sir, but in Kirk's case, sometimes the footnotes were far more interesting reading than the main events."

"That may be the case, Commander, but here's the truth of it: My great-grandfather was in Starfleet Command during Kirk's time. And the fact was, Kirk had some very staunch supporters. That served him well, because he also had any number of people whom he had angered with his constant glory-hounding and utter disregard for regulations. And it was widely believed in Starfleet that, every so often, he would file utterly preposterous reports, just to tweak those individuals whom he knew didn't like his style and his way of doing things. Such as the incident with the giant killer amoeba. And that totally ridiculous alleged occasion in which his first officer's brain was stolen. I mean, come *on*, people. Clearly, these things could not possibly have happened. Every time you heard uncontrolled laughter ringing up and down the hallways at Starfleet Command, you could tell that Kirk had filed another one of his whoppers."

"Did anyone entertain the notion that they might all be true, sir?" asked Calhoun.

"Yes, they did, and every single one of Kirk's crew swore to their dying day that every insane thing Kirk encountered was the absolute truth. To some people, that was sufficient proof of Kirk's veracity. To others, it simply showed the incredible depth of loyalty from his people." For just a moment, Jellico's expression seemed to soften, to become reflective. "Either way, I suppose, that made Kirk a man to be envied."

Calhoun and Shelby glanced at each other in undisguised surprise. Jellico actually sounded almost envious of the legend of Kirk.

Jellico seemed to refocus on Calhoun, and his brow furrowed. "This isn't about Kirk, and it isn't about me. From now on, I expect to receive reports that are not fanciful extrapolations of reality. Is that understood?"

"Fully, Admiral," Calhoun said quietly, but his purple eyes were blazing with undisguised annoyance.

"You have a good deal of latitude, Captain, out there in Thallonian space. You're the only starship out there. You're operating without a net, so don't expect me to be there to catch you when you fall."

"Understood."

Jellico looked from one of them to the other, as if expecting them, even daring them, to say something that might be considered challenging. But they simply sat there, tight-lipped, and Jellico grunted before saying, "Jellico out." His image blinked off the screen.

"That was certainly a little piece of heaven," Shelby sighed, slumping back in her chair. She noticed the way Calhoun was looking at her. "What's the problem?"

"You kicked me," Calhoun said.

"Oh, that."

"Yes, that. That's a hell of a thing to be on the receiving end from the queen of Starfleet regulations. I'd be most interested to see the one where it says that it is acceptable to kick one's commanding officer."

"It's more of an unwritten rule. You were about to say something that would get you is deep, Mac, and in so doing were dragging me along with you. Don't think of it as an assault. Think of it as self-defense."

"I can't say I appreciated it."

"I didn't do it to gain your appreciation. I did it to get your attention."

"Well, next time might I suggest something a little less painful?"

"I would have tried a striptease. That's always worked in the past," she said with no hint of a smile. "But somehow I think the Admiral might have noticed."

"Perhaps. Certainly might have gotten you that promotion you've always wanted."

She blew air impatiently from between her lips as she rose from the table. "Don't bring that up."

"Bring what up?"

"Did you see the promotion list recently? I was scanning it over and did a double take when I saw 'Captain Shelby' commanding the *Sutherland.* For half a second I thought I'd been promoted and someone forgot to tell me, and then I realized it was someone else. It should have been me, Mac. But instead, I'm still . . ."

"Stuck with me?"

She sighed. "You know, Mac . . . the whole world doesn't have to be about you. That's one of the things you always did that drove me crazy. It's my problem, okay? Not yours."

"It doesn't have to be yours either, if you'd only be happy with what you've got."

"With what I've got?" She leaned her back against the wall, her hands draped behind her, and she looked bleakly at Calhoun. "This Captain Not-Me Shelby is in the thick of things. There's a major push going on with about three quarters of the fleet, and he's smack in the middle. And us, we're . . ."

"Exploring," Calhoun noted. "Last I checked, that's what Starfleet is supposed to be all about. *Grozit,* Eppy, you know that as well as anyone. Better than most, in fact."

She glanced at him. *"'Grozit'?* Reverting to Xenexian profanity?"

"Xenexian profanity. Sorry. I'll try to watch myself."

"Not on my account, although your command of terran profanity is fairly comprehensive."

"I have an ear for languages."

She half-sat on the edge of the table. "The problem is, Mac, that first and foremost, I'm a tactician. That's my strength, what I was trained for. Analyzing an enemy's weakness, seeing where they can be out-thought or defeated. That sort of thing is where I really come alive, Mac. But here, I feel like . . ."

"Like you're wasting your time?"

She studied him and, to her surprise, she saw something in his eyes that she had thought he really wasn't capable of: Hurt. He seemed hurt over the very notion that she would want to be elsewhere or that she could think that her time as first officer of the *Excalibur* was not a worthy test of her skill.

"No," she said softly. "No . . . I don't think that at all. Face it, Mac, you'd be lost without me."

"I don't know if I'd be lost," he replied. "But I'd be far less eager to be found."

She was genuinely touched. It was times like this that reminded her exactly how and why she had become involved with Mackenzie Calhoun in the first place. How they had wound up lovers, engaged to be married, until the relationship had broken down under the weight of their conflicting personalities. "That is so sweet," she said.

He shrugged. "I have my moments."

She found that she was looking at him in a way that

she hadn't in quite a long time. When she'd signed aboard the *Excalibur,* it had been for the purpose of more or less riding herd on Calhoun. Of making sure that he toed the line when it came to Starfleet policy. And she had been quite, quite sure that their history together and their past romance would not factor in to their day-to-day interaction.

But now . . .

"Do you really feel that way, Mac?"

He laughed gently, walked over to her, and put his hands on her shoulders. "You want me to be honest, Eppy? When you first came aboard and applied for the job as my first officer, I was relieved to see you. Then, after I agreed to take you on, I decided that I must have been completely crazy to do so. And when we began fighting over protocol and the official Starfleet view of procedures—"

"That's when you were *really* sorry that I was here?" she said teasingly, although she had a feeling, deep down, that she'd actually put her finger on it.

But he shook his head. "No. That's the point at which I became convinced that taking you on was the absolute right thing to do. You make me think, Eppy." He rapped the side of his head with his knuckles. "It's not always easy to crack through this heavy-duty shielding into my head. I don't always agree with what you say, Eppy. But even when we're disagreeing, I'm still thinking about everything you say. You make me think, and that's not always easy to do."

"So you always listen to me, then."

"Always," he smiled.

The door to the conference lounge slid open, and standing there was Doctor Selar. She looked utterly composed, her arms folded across her chest. "Captain, may I speak to you in private for a moment?"

"I'll just excuse myself then." Shelby left, smiling to herself. For reasons Calhoun wasn't certain of.

"This is . . . a delicate matter to discuss, Captain," Selar said slowly."

"I appreciate that," Calhoun said. "And I think you'll find that there is no matter so delicate that I can't be trusted with it."

"Very well, Captain." She paused a moment, as if steeling herself. And then she said, "It is my desire to have sex with you."

"My . . . apologies, Doctor," Calhoun said slowly. "Did you just say you—"

"Desire to have sex with you, yes," she nodded. "There is an explanation, which can be summarized in two words."

"Good taste?" he suggested.

"Pon Farr."

"Ah. Well, that would have been my second guess."

"That is a sort of . . . of Vulcan mating ritual, isn't it?" Calhoun asked slowly. "I mean, I've heard rumors about it, but Vulcans tend to stay fairly closed-lipped about such things."

"It is considered . . . inappropriate . . . to discuss the matter with outworlders," Selar told her. "However, I feel I have no choice in the matter. Besides, it may be that my role as a clinician makes it . . . easier"—she forced the word out—"to discuss matters pertaining to a medical situation. It is not a ritual precisely. It is a . . . a drive. An urge that cannot be denied, no matter how much we may desire to do so." She put a finger to her temple, as if to steady herself, and then said more calmly, "We must mate."

"To conceive a child?" asked Calhoun.

"Yes. You see, it could easily be argued that there is no logical reason to have a child. Ever. They are burdensome, they are limiting, they habitually expel bodily fluids out of a variety of orifices at high velocity, and they are extremely time consuming. So, for a race whose every action is defined by logic, that race would—by definition—face extinction."

"But to allow the demise of your race just to avoid child-rearing is also illogical," pointed out Calhoun.

"In which case, perpetuation of the species becomes a chore. An obligation. To live with such an onerous situation is also not logical. Therefore our very nature, our bodies, have developed in such a way that logic simply does not enter into the conception of children."

"Believe me, it's frequently no different on Earth," Calhoun said ruefully. He paused a moment, pulling himself back to the major topic at hand. "But certainly you can't expect the captain—"

"I can and do," Selar replied evenly. She looked straight into Calhoun's eyes. "You are the most appropriate individual to handle this matter, Captain. At the moment, my options are extremely limited. The *Pon Farr* drive is in remission for the time being, so this need not be attended to immediately. But it will resurge again and again: each time with greater impetus and a greater need to be satisfied. I am requesting that, upon the next resurgence, when the drive is upon me, you satisfy my genetically driven lust. Will you honor my request, M'k'n'zy of Calhoun?"

"I shall *consider* it, Doctor," Calhoun told her. "I'm leaning towards 'yes,' but can I have a little time to think about it?"

Despite her Vulcan training, Selar let out a sigh and sagged slightly in visible relief. "I am . . . pleased . . . to hear that. And yes, of course, take all the time you need. Just . . . not too much."

"A request has been made of M'k'n'zy of Calhoun, the man I was," Calhoun said reasonably. "I can't turn that aside. Doctor, if I do agree to it, kindly let me know when and where you will find my . . . services . . . required. Several hours notice would be appreciated if that's at all possible."

"I will make every effort to accommodate you, Captain. And I would, in turn, appreciate if we could keep this matter between us."

"Sounds like a plan."

She nodded and, as if the matter were completely settled, she turned to leave to find that at some point in her conversation with the captain, the doors to his office had quietly opened by themselves.

At least half a dozen crewmen were walking past at the time. To say nothing of the fact that her voice apparently carried halfway down the corridor.

Selar visibly winced.

III.

Word was beginning to spread.

It was sort of the reverse of a black hole: Instead of everything being sucked away into blackness and disappearing, the information was blasting outward in all directions. And it wasn't as if the stories needed to be built upon; the truth itself was so insane that exaggeration was not required.

Nonetheless, matters did tend to build upon themselves, passing on from one world, one system to the next and becoming bigger and more impressive with each one. The Nelkarites, for example, heard of the two giant flaming birds that had smashed apart Thallon and then fought against the *Excalibur*. The refugees who had settled on Nelkar listened to the stories with unfettered astonishment. By the time word reached the Lemax system, however, and the warring races which inhabited it, the *Excalibur* had apparently morphed into an even greater flaming bird and faced off against the two fiery beasts which had sprung from the smoldering remains of Thallon.

The Boragi, upon hearing the news that two great flaming birds and one large flaming sheep had fought a pitched battled against an armada of morphing ships from the Federation and led by the *Excalibur,* wisely chose—as they oftentimes did—not to believe any information that came their way, and to take no aggressive action unless it could somehow serve them.

On Naldacor, the residents received word of the Thallonian developments, and burrowed deeper into the subsurface hiding places in their world, concerned that somehow the great flaming cat of which they heard so much might somehow come to seek them out.

Comar, on the outer rim, spread word to Xenex, where the triumph of the former M'k'n'zy of Calhoun over the flock of great flaming birds prompted the creation of a planetary holiday.

The news eventually filtered to Starfleet headquarters, where Edward Jellico's head sank into his arms as he became convinced that the entirety of Sector 221-G had organized a massive hoax specifically designed to drive him completely insane.

And everywhere that word was received, there was much cause for speculation and wonderment as to what it all might mean. The name of Mackenzie Calhoun was repeated throughout the former Thallonian Empire with varying degrees of respect, awe, admiration, and even fear. This was, after all, the captain of the brave vessel which had withstood the attack of the giant flaming *whatever.* The valiant warrior who had settled a life-and-death dispute, driven by honor, when a world was literally falling apart around him. Clearly, a new force and power had come to the Thallonian Empire. He captained a mighty starship, with such servants as a being which seemed like a walking mountain, and Vulcans, and a feisty Earth woman (who, truth be known, would probably have blown her brains out if she'd known the word "feisty" was being attached to her). And even the fallen Thallonian noble, Si Cwan, was said to travel with him. The situation seemed ripe with possibilities. . . .

On the surface of it, Tulaan IV did not seem a particularly outstanding or impressive world. There were sections of it that were rather pleasant, with lush vegetation, warm climate, an abundance of water. The weather was fairly moderate, and overall it was attractive.

There was hardly anyone there. Instead there were machines, robots who harvested the food that grew there and shipped it elsewhere. There were a couple of individuals who maintained the robots, but that was the totality of the air-breathing inhabitants.

There was other terrain, however, that was cold and inhospitable. The nights were long, and the wind— nicknamed "monster breath" for the constant and remarkable chill that it always carried—blew steadily. Very little grew there except for a few stubborn patches of vegetation that appeared invulnerable to the hostility of the environment. The temperature never went much above freezing. All in all, considering the alternatives that Tulaan IV offered, this particular area, known as Medita, should have been fairly deserted. Instead, it was where the vast majority of Tulaan's populace resided.

They were not great believers in luxuries or comfort. They felt that it was anathema for their chosen way of life. Theirs, instead, was a life of sacrifice, of thoughtful contemplation, of reading over their holy books. And—most sacred of all—complete domination of any worlds which did not fall into accord with their dogma.

They had a variety of names among many races, usually spoken in fear or hushed whispers. The name that they preferred for themselves was simply . . .

The Redeemers.

They lived in simple homes, and their main gathering place was the Great Hall, the single most impressive structure on Tulaan. That is to say, it was impressive by Tulaan standards. Several stories tall, with spires reaching toward the sky as if trying to caress it, and atop the Hall was a statue carved from a gleaming metal that seemed to absorb even the most meager of illumination as provided by the several Tulaan moons. It was a statue of someone that no living Redeemer had ever seen, but his portraits hung everywhere, and elaborate statues were among the few indulgences that the Redeemers allowed themselves. Probably because they did not consider them "indulgences" so much as objects of worship and respect.

They were representations of the great god, Xant. He Who Had Gone On. He Who Would Return. And the Overlord awaited His return, as had all the Overlords before him, and all those who would likely come after him.

Prime One entered the Overlord's sanctuary and found him much as he always found him: seated in his Great Chair, his fingers steepled, apparently lost in thought. The Overlord's deepest thoughts were generally something that none of the Redeemers, no matter how high up in the Hierarchy, wanted to dwell on for very long.

The Overlord was the tallest of the Redeemers, and half again as wide. His skin was hardened and black, almost obsidian, and his eyes were deeply set and a soft, glowing red. Other races generally tried not to look directly into the face of a Redeemer; it was like experiencing a little foreshadowing of death. His clothing was as black as his skin, with a tunic that hung down to knees and black leggings tucked into his high boots. He wore a large black cape which draped around him, giving him, when he was in a contemplative, forward-leaning mood, a distinct resemblance to a crouching bird of prey.

Prime One said nothing, merely standing there and waiting for the Overlord to acknowledge his presence. This was not necessarily an immediate or swift event; once he had remained exactly where he was for the better part of a day as the Overlord said nothing. Prime One had never been entirely sure whether the Overlord knew he was there and merely elected to let him stand around as some sort of test, or if the Overlord was truly so lost in thought or meditation that he didn't register Prime One's presence. In the end, it didn't really matter: Prime One had waited until the Overlord chose to acknowledge him.

On this occasion, Prime One was fortunate. He waited a mere hour before the Overlord's attention finally focused on him. "Yes?" said the Overlord.

"There is important news, Overlord." Prime One was so excited about it that he actually took a step forward. Any sort of approach to the Overlord was a breach of protocol and potentially punishable, but Prime One had always served the Overlord well and so he was inclined to let it pass for the moment. "I thought you should know as soon as possible."

Prime One remained the Overlord's main point of information. It was a large and annoyingly busy galaxy, and if the Overlord endeavored to keep up with all of the events and happenstances within it, he would never have time for the contemplation that was his first and greatest duty. Indeed, when it came down to it, there was little occurring in Thallonian space that required his firsthand knowledge. He had his meditation, he had the solid hold of the Redeemers upon their own section of space, and that was all that required his immediate attention. Prime One would come to him with news of another Redeemer conversion, or of some particular concern that the Thallonians might have in their ongoing dealings.

A wary truce had existed between the Thallonians and the Redeemers for some time. It was an understanding that went back many, many years, and one which no Overlord had been particularly inclined to disrupt since, truly, there seemed no point in doing so. Why disrupt matters when they were going so smoothly? The Redeemers attempted no conversions of those worlds that were of particular importance to the Thallonians, and the Thallonians in turn made no attempt to press their interests on those worlds which had undergone conversion. Nonetheless, the Overlord had a suspicion that the situation would not last. The Redeemers could afford to be patient, for in the end, Xant would eventually return, and then it didn't matter where the relations with the Thallonians stood. Xant would arrive with His great flaming sword and sweep all away beneath it. In the face of that inevitability . . . what, truly, did the Thallonians matter to the Redeemers?

When the Overlord spoke, it was with a voice that was a deep and forbidding rumble that seemed to originate from somewhere beneath his boots. "What would you have me know, Prime One?"

"The Thallonians . . . are gone, Overlord."

The Overlord's glowing eyes fixed on Prime One with clear curiosity. "Gone, you say?"

"Yes. We had heard rumors, news from other sources, but we waited until we could verify it firsthand before we informed you, Overlord."

"Gone where? Have they abandoned their world?"

"Their world is likewise gone, Overlord."

This fully captured the Overlord's attention. "The world itself? How is that possible? Was it"—for the briefest of moments, there actually seemed to be a moment of concern upon his face—"was it the Black Mass?"

"No." Prime One shook his head quickly to dispel any concerns on that score. "No, not from without, but from within was the planet lost."

Prime One then, very quickly and in as broad strokes as possible, outlined what had happened. As opposed to the exaggerations that were racing through the other populated worlds, the Redeemers' information was fairly accurate. Prime One spoke of the great bird, of the *Excalibur* and Captain Calhoun, of the destruction of the Thallonian homeworld, and of the survival of Si Cwan of the royal house. All of this was absorbed by the Overlord, his face inscrutable except for occasional flickers of greater interest visible in his glowing eyes. When Prime One finished, the Overlord seemed to mull over the significance of it all.

"We live in cold," he said after a time.

Prime One nodded. This much was, of course, evident simply by looking around outside. "And we have lived in cold since the departure of Xant. We are darkness, Xant is light."

"We are darkness, Xant is light," repeated Prime One.

"We are cold, Xant is heat," the Overlord continued, and Prime One—as he had so often in his life as a Redeemer—repeated the prayer. There were ninety-seven of them, each of them describing what Xant was as opposed to what the Redeemers were. It was their most sacred belief that all that they were had to be the opposite of all that Xant was. Only then could Xant truly turn their lives around upon his return. He was their beginning and end, their means to salvation.

There were other religions which endeavored to follow the specific teachings of their gods or messiahs, but to the Redeemers, that seemed preposterous. How could any mortal being hope to have an insight into the workings of as holy a mind as Xant's? When Xant had departed, there seemed only one reasonable course of action all those centuries ago. Rather than try to comprehend and obey His teachings in an imperfect manner, it was decided to operate in as far removed a manner from all that Xant was as they possibly could. Only in this way would Xant then be able to return and show them the right, true, and proper way to live.

And they knew that there would be signs signaling Xant's return. They had no idea what those signs might be, but they would come, of that the Redeemers had no doubt.

"The creature is flame to our cold," the Overlord said thoughtfully. "It is light to our darkness. It is great, and we are small."

"Could it be, Overlord?" Prime One seemed almost afraid to frame the question. "Could it . . . could it possibly be?"

"All things are possible, Prime One. The question is: Are they likely?"

He stroked his chin thoughtfully as Prime One waited for him to voice an opinion. But when none seemed forthcoming, Prime One forgot himself. He blurted out, "Well?" and was immediately mortified, looking for all the world as if he wanted to snatch the word back from the air. Trying to urge the Overlord to speak on a matter! It was presumptuous beyond imagining. The punishment for it would be—

Prime One lost control of his legs as they began to tremble. The Overlord stared at him for such a long time that Prime One felt as if he could actually sense death having entered the room, hovering over him and waiting for the slightest push in its direction.

And then the Overlord . . . smiled.

Oh, it was not much. It was rather small as smiles go, and rather unimpressive. It wasn't as if the Overlord had a good deal of practice at it, so it was understandable. Prime One couldn't quite believe what he was seeing. At first he thought he was imagining it, but it didn't waver and slowly, ever so slowly, the trembling stopped.

"It's a sign," the Overlord said.

Prime One began to ask, *Are you sure?*, but wisely managed to hold his tongue before uttering the words.

"If you wonder why there will be no discipline at this time for your transgression," continued the Overlord, "it is because I would be loath to soil this day with punishment or bloodshed." The Overlord rose from his chair, standing half a head over Prime One, and he clapped a hand on Prime One's shoulder. "Yes, Prime One. A sign, most definitely. We cannot allow our frozen surroundings to chill our imaginations and perceptions as well. Nor should we permit our lengthy wait for some sort of sign to delude us into thinking that there never will *be* a sign. But this cannot be ignored or explained away, Prime One. If these stories are true—and I assume you would not waste my time with them were that not the case—then it presents a clear and concise signal to us, telling us that Xant is preparing to make His return."

Prime One began to tremble once more, but this time it was with excitement rather than fear. "To think, Overlord . . . after all this time, all this waiting . . . Xant is to return, and we are the fortunates who are alive to see it."

"Indeed, Prime One. Come," and he clapped Prime One on the back in a manner that bordered on the jovial. "Come, let us inform the brethren. Let us begin the preparations. Our prayers must not cease, that is to be understood, of course." Prime One nodded in brisk understanding. "Nor must we be lax in continuing to spread the word." The Overlord held up a cautionary finger. "It is, after all, rather tempting to simply sit back and say, 'Ah, well, with Xant on His way back to us, our job is finished. We need not spread His word, for He is come to take up the task Himself. No, Prime One," and Prime One just as quickly shook his head, changing cranial direction so sharply that it caused a slight cramp in his neck muscles. "No, we cannot slacken."

"Not slacken, no, Overlord."

"We cannot let up."

"Never let up, Overlord."

"And after Xant has returned," the Overlord continued, "after the new Golden Age of the Redeemers has been put before us, after we have taken our true and rightful place in the hierarchy of the universe . . ."

"Yes, Overlord, yes!" Prime One was exploding with enthusiasm that was bordering on the orgasmic.

"Then, and only then . . ." The build up was staggering.

"Then what, Overlord?!" Prime One asked in exultation.

"Then . . . you will be disciplined for your transgressions."

It brought Prime One screeching to a halt, both physically as he'd been matching the Overlord's strides, and emotionally as he felt himself brought to the brink of theological ecstasy only to be shoved off into an abyss. "My . . . my transgressions?" It took him a minute to recalibrate himself. "You mean for . . . before? When I . . . ?"

The Overlord nodded. "Of course," he replied matter-of-factly.

"But . . . but you said—"

"I said, 'at this time.' That does not indicate forgiveness, Prime One. Merely leniency. But it will not be for some time yet, so be of cheer! Celebrate!" He nodded approvingly and then, in one of his rare forays from his sanctum (which, in and of itself, was enough to alert the others immediately to the significance of the moment) he strode out with his hands draped behind his back.

And Prime One was left behind, to sink down onto the floor and murmur, "Hurrah," which was about all the enthusiasm for celebration he could muster at that particular moment in time.

IV.

"SI CWAN?"

It was the fourth time that Robin Lefler had said Si Cwan's name without getting any sort of response. She was beginning to get just a little concerned. She sat on the other side of his desk in his quarters and saw him staring off vacantly, as if he'd forgotten that she was there. The quarters remained relatively simple in terms of decoration at this point. By Si Cwan's standards, it was even less than simple. It was rudimentary. Then again, one had to understand that Si Cwan's bed from his time as a Thallonian royal would likely have taken up the entire quarters just by itself. But he'd forced himself to make do, and was actually rather pleased with himself when it came to his ability to adapt. Still, he was much more pleased with himself than anyone else was with him.

She moved her hand flutteringly in front of his face and then said with more force, "Si Cwan!"

It snapped the Thallonian back to attention as he

blinked at her with surprise. "I am sorry . . . what did you say, Robin?" He leaned forward, his fingers interlaced, trying to refocus his attention.

Robin stroked her chin thoughtfully, trying to find a way to phrase it without seeming combative, argumentative, or difficult. "Si Cwan," she said slowly, "I'm supposed to be serving you as your official liaison, correct?"

"Yes, Robin," he replied, looking mildly surprised that she felt a need to state the obvious.

"You've already gone through two other liaisons, in rather short order. There's an old Earth saying about 'three strikes, you're out.' Do you know what that refers to?"

He paused a moment, his red brow furrowing, and then took a stab at it. "Repeated labor disputes can result in the loss of your business?"

She began to laugh it off, but then reconsidered. "Okay, we can go with that," she decided. "And I wouldn't want you to be out of business when it comes to having a liaison. Someone to represent your interests to the captain, and at the same time to serve as an events coordinator for you."

"I should hope not," Si Cwan said reasonably. "We have been barraged with contacts from dozens of worlds, each with their own interests and agendas. There is a goodly deal of administrative work to be done, and I am an ambassador, not an administrator."

She held up a scolding finger. "Technically, you're not an ambassador either. You're forgetting you represent no government. But the captain has made it clear that he has no objection to your using that title, as long as you provide our vessel with guidance and aid in the exploration of Thallonian space."

"Yes, yes, yes." He was making no attempt to hide his mounting irritation.

"The first two people he assigned to this post got

tired of your high-handedness in no time flat and made it clear they did not wish to remain in direct contact with you. The captain was prepared, at that point, to simply close up the position. But I volunteered, Si Cwan," and she leaned forward, tapping herself on the chest. "Me. I actually volunteered. Work an hour a day as your liaison, make myself available to you as emergencies require, and still maintain my bridge duties at Ops. I can do all that because I'm organized, which is the sort of person you need."

"I'm most appreciative, Robin. Can we get on with matters now?"

"Not quite," she said patiently. "What I'm trying to say is that my time is limited. I don't have oodles and oodles to play with in the course of any given day. Which is a roundabout way of saying that I sure don't have time to sit here and watch you nod off and stare into space."

"I was staring into space?" he asked, sounding confused. He started to turn in his chair to glance out the viewing port behind his back.

"No, I meant . . ." and she waved her hands in the direction of the area in front of his desk. He nodded in understanding. "All I'm saying is that something's distracting you, and it's not the most efficient way to manage the time." Then her voice softened. "It's . . . It's Kallinda, isn't it?"

Slowly he nodded, and this time he genuinely did stare off into space, into the great void that glittered at him so frustratingly. "I truly do not know which is worse," he murmured. "To think that she is definitely dead and lost to me, or that she is alive somewhere out there, undergoing who-knows-what form of difficulty."

"Zoran could have been lying," Lefler pointed out.

He nodded. "That is true," he admitted. "Zoran Si Verdin is my oldest, most vicious and unforgiving foe. He would say or do anything to hurt me. It is entirely possible that he created the spectre of my sister's survival in order to gnaw at me. To haunt my days and evenings. And do you know what, Robin?"

"It worked?"

He nodded sullenly. But then he seemed to shake it off with physical effort as he said, "Dwelling on it will serve no purpose, save that which Zoran may have desired to attempt. And it is wasting your time. I have feelers out in a variety of directions, to try and bring me news of Kallinda. Those who are still loyal to me, who are still friends of the old regime, are operating to further my concerns. In the meantime, there is no need to delay you any more than necessary simply because of my inability to focus on important matters."

She put a hand out to lay it on his forearm. She wanted to say something that would comfort him, wanted to establish some sort of "human" connection to the Thallonian. Her hand hovered over his forearm for the merest fraction of an instant, and she allowed it to settle as lightly as possible on the arm. She was surprised by the extreme coolness of his skin. If she were given to flights of fancy, she would have imagined that it was a reflection of the distance he forced himself to keep from the world around him. The distance that was part of the baggage he carried with him, what with being royalty (albeit fallen royalty), an ambassador, and a brother seeking the only member of his family who might still be alive.

He stared at her coolly, appraisingly, and she waited to hear what he would say next. The acknowledgment of her effort, the realization that it was possible to allow others to be close to him. To be his friend, to be . . . whatever.

"I do not like to be touched," he said, not unkindly.

"Ah," was all Robin could think of to say as she quickly withdrew her hand. Suddenly it seemed almost like an alien appendage, just hanging there on the end of her arm. Not quite sure what to do with it, she reached around with amazingly forced casualness and scratched the back of her neck. "That's . . . okay. That's fine, I can understand that."

"I've made you uncomfortable."

"No, not at all. Not at all." She cleared her throat loudly. "It was simply a . . . a human ritual. Don't think about it another minute. So, there's one more planet we've heard from, petitioning for the *Excalibur* to visit."

"That makes, by my count, twenty-nine." Si Cwan let out a soft whistle. "They are very, very curious about us, Robin. They want to know what the Excalibur is up to. They want to meet our captain. And of course . . ." He permitted a small half smile, not bothering to finish the sentence.

"They want to see you," Lefler was kind enough to complete it for him. "Well, naturally. That goes without saying."

"Yes, but thank you for saying it. I will present the captain with a detailed information list on the candidates, with order of suggested priority. He can, of course, deviate from that priority. But to do so would be quite foolish."

"That likewise went without saying."

"So which is the twenty-ninth world?"

She checked her readout. "Zondar."

A jolt of interest seemed to spark in Si Cwan. He had been seated, but now he came from quickly around his desk and leaned over Robin's shoulder to study her data padd. She became, for some reason, rather aware of the nearness of him, and endeavored to keep her mind firmly on her work. "Yes, Zondar. I have to admit, of everyone we've heard from thus far, they certainly seemed to be the most excited about the prospect of meeting with the captain."

"I am amazed," admitted Si Cwan.

"Why? Why should it be so surprising that they would want to see the captain?"

"It's not that. I am amazed that they would want to see anyone." Slowly he circled the interior of his quarters, stopping so often to check, totally unconsciously, for any hint of dirt or dust. "The Zondarians are an extremely acrimonious race. They always have been. They've been in the throes of civil war for well over eight hundred years. They would fight until they were exhausted, then work out some sort of temporary peace, which would hold just long enough for all involved to catch their breaths, and then they'd"—and he made vague stabbing motions—"have at each other again. They're not unique in that they seem rather determined to obliterate themselves from the memory of Thallonian space, but they were certainly the most insistent little bastards that my people ever oversaw."

"Oversaw how?" asked Lefler. She was reluctant to ask for details, for she was always concerned about some aspects of Si Cwan's past that she'd truly prefer not to hear about. But she didn't have much choice in the matter. She had to know as much as possible, and she simply had to acknowledge that, as part of a ruling family, Si Cwan may very well have been party to various acts that outsiders would consider to be barbaric or heartless, but in which Si Cwan had no voice and no choice. "Did you enslave them, or—?"

"Enslave them?" Si Cwan gaped at her in clear surprise. "Lieutenant, honestly. What do you take me for? Slavery!" He *harrumphed* at the very absurdity of the notion. "No, of course not."

"Well, that's a relief to hear."

"No, we threatened to destroy them."

"You—" She blinked in surprise. "You what?"

"It seemed a reasonable threat," Si Cwan said affably. "After all, they were well on their way to doing it themselves. When my ancestors were spreading the influence of the empire and arrived at Zondar, they saw a world at war with itself. One group called the, oh"—and he snapped his fingers for a moment to jog his memory—"The Unglza. Yes, that's it. The Unglza and the Eenza. They have assorted disputes, none of which they seemed interested in settling and, most discouragingly, many that they couldn't even seem to remember the origins of. Now is that the epitome of pointlessness? I ask you.

"In any event, we invited the Unglza and the Eenza to join the Thallonian Empire. They refused. So we took the next step we usually took in such cases, which was to inform them that they officially were members of the Thallonian Empire, subject to our rule, whether they liked it or not. Then we surrounded their world with about a half dozen of our heavy cruisers and informed them that, unless the fighting ceased immediately, we would wipe the planet clean of them. Our logic was that this solution, while violent, would satisfy everyone. Since they were out to destroy each other, this would save them the trouble. And we would be satisfied because we would still have conquered Zondar. Granted, no one would be *alive*. But their decomposing bodies would serve to fertilize the land, and if the Thallonian Empire had to wait an additional century or so in order to take possession, well, we had all the time in the galaxy. But they—as we made clear to them—did not."

He didn't continue immediately, and Robin prompted, "What happened?"

"They didn't believe us."

"What did you do?"

"Well, my great-great-great-great-grandfather gave them one more chance, and then obliterated the eastern seaboard of one of their main continents. Fired down from orbit, of course. Five hundred thousand Zondarians—perhaps more—wiped out, just like that, their shattered bodies sliding into the Great Sea. It's said there were so many bodies in the water, one could have walked from the remains of the eastern territories to the neighboring continent of Kartoof without fear of sinking. An early and rather impressive display of Thallonian might. The Zondarians quickly saw the wisdom in acceding to our gentle guidance, and put themselves under Thallonian rule."

She shifted uncomfortably in her chair. "And do you think what he did was right? Your great-great— your ancestor. Was he right?"

"It does not matter especially what I think. He did what he felt was right at the time. To leave them to their indulgence of slaughtering one another would likewise not have been a particularly positive endeavor, now would it?"

"It's called non-interference. It's the most sacred law of the Federation."

Si Cwan guffawed. "A federation has luxuries that an empire does not." But then he stopped laughing and shrugged. "Then again, my empire has fallen and your Federation yet stands. So who am I to judge, eh? Who am I?" He leaned on the edge of the desk. "The point is, even after that, we've always had to keep a very careful eye on the Zondarians. They would sneak skirmishes as part of their ongoing holy war with each other. They would try to deceive us at every turn. It was like trying to oversee petulant children. But they paid their taxes to us, albeit with complaining, and we had to discipline them only occasionally, so we managed. Not once, though, not ever, did they ever come to us or approach us about anything. They are very, very insular. So for them to be making overtures to the *Excalibur* is a most unusual gesture. The timing could not be better, either, for with the final fall of my family's influence and control over this sector of space, full-blown civil war could easily break out on Zondar at any time, if it hasn't already. The *Excalibur* is in a position to save a lot of lives, if the Zondarians are interested, for whatever reason, in meeting with Calhoun and getting his help or input."

"Well, it's a good thing you feel that way," said Lefler as she glanced farther down the padd. "Because according to their message, they're already in the process of putting together volunteers for a 'pilgrimage' to seek us out. They may be knocking on our back door just about any time."

"If that is the case, then I suggest with all due sincerity that you be certain and let them in. I'll have that formal report together quite quickly. I don't wish to take up any more of your valuable time, Robin."

"Oh, not at all," she said quickly, rising from her seat while making a few last minute notations on her padd. "Not at all. It was . . . it was very educational."

"For both of us," said Si Cwan. "Robin, tell me, why did you *really* take on the assignment of being my liaison?"

She stared at him with a forcefully neutral expression. Stared at the corded muscles on his dusky red forearms, the broadness of his chest, the piercing eyes, the towering presence and charisma that just seemed to radiate from him.

"Aggressively seeking out new duties," she told him, "is a good way to show one's CO that one is a determined, take-charge officer who should be considered for further promotion through the ranks of Starfleet. That's all. Why else?"

He nodded, slowly and thoughtfully. "I had supposed it was something along those lines. Well, thank you for your time, Lieuteuant."

"Not a problem at all," and she exited rather more quickly than she'd intended to.

She headed down the corridor and greeted Commander Shelby. The first officer was heading in the other direction with what appeared to be a great deal on her mind, considering that she didn't even acknowledge Lefler's salutation. Robin Lefler shrugged and continued on her way back to the bridge.

Shelby, meantime, wasn't entirely certain where she was going until her feet, apparently of their own accord, guided her into sickbay. It was only then, as she stood there while various medics walked past her, glancing in her direction before going about their business, that she realized her body had already made the decision on behalf of her mind.

She glanced across the sickbay and saw Dr. Selar in her office, briskly going through assorted reports. She folded her arms since she didn't know what to do with them, and then let them dangle at her sides as she took a deep breath and then strode with authority across sickbay. For some reason that she couldn't quite put her finger on, she felt as if one leg was suddenly a bit shorter than the other. Since no one else seemed to be taking notice, she had to assume that it was her imagination.

She stood in the doorway of Selar's office, and at first Selar seemed to take no notice of her. Finally, however, without glancing up, Selar said, "Yes, Commander?"

"How'd you know it was me?" she asked.

"My hearing is sharper than the human norm, Commander, and you tend to tap your foot if you are impatient."

"I do?" Shelby was intrigued as she sat in a chair opposite Selar.

"Yes. Quite rapidly, I might add. Softly enough so that it does not disturb anyone, but it is detectable to me." She turned away from work and focused her attention on Shelby. "How may I be of service?"

"Selar—do you mind if I call you Selar?"

"If you are asking my preference, I prefer 'Doctor.' "

"Oh. Say, what do you call the person who graduates last in their medical class?"

Selar stared at her for a long moment. "Fascinating," she said at last. "I can easily believe that you and the captain have a history with one another. He reacted in exactly the same manner when I made the same request of him, with precisely the same joke. He was also under the impression that the answer—'Doctor'—was somehow funny. I had once thought that humans were difficult to understand, but I have become willing to widen the parameters to non-Vulcans as a whole."

"It's just that, well, I wanted to discuss something personal, and addressing you with a title seems to keep a distance between us."

"I find that preferable." When she saw Shelby's look, she added, "It is not intended as a personal slight, Commander. I assure you. I prefer distance when it comes to dealing with others. It is one of the qualities that makes me a good doctor: the ability to keep a professional distance between myself and my patients. A doctor must never become emotionally involved with her charges."

"Granted. But a doctor should at least show some empathy, don't you think?"

"Germs do not care about empathy, Commander. Nor do phaser wounds, multiple lacerations, cancer cells, stopped hearts, collapsed lungs, or any of the many calamities that can befall the human body." Selar sat perfectly motionless in her chair. She might have been carved from marble, and Shelby was having a difficult time picturing this woman in the throes of any mating urge. Selar raised one inquisitive eyebrow and asked, "Did you come here to discuss my medical techniques?"

"No," Shelby said evenly. "I came to discuss your request of the captain."

"Yes, that would be the logical reason for your visit. Since discussion of my personal life is doubtlessly moving apace throughout the entire vessel thanks to a faulty door, there is no reason that you and I should not converse about it as well."

"Look, Sel—Doctor . . . I could come to you as a first officer. I'd like to come to you as a friend."

"Friend?" She tilted her head slightly. "I was unaware that you consider us friends."

"I would like to. You must have friends. On Vulcan, at the very least."

"There are . . . others," said Selar after a moment's thought. "Other Vulcans with whom I associate. We have discussions of philosophy, and we devise puzzles of logic in order to hone our skills and direct our thought in proper channels. I do not know, however, that the human word 'friend' would apply. There is a Vulcan term—*Ku'net Kal'fiore*—which roughly translates as, 'One For Whom You Have Use.'"

Shelby tried not to make a face, and was only partly successful. "No offense intended, Doctor, but that doesn't sound very pleasant."

"I said the translation was rough," Selar said defensively. "On Vulcan, that is actually a term of endearment."

"All right, fine. How I want to talk with you is somewhere between a first officer and a friend. Can we agree on that?"

Selar let out a small sigh. "With all respect, Commander, if it will get you out of my office sooner so that I may return to my work, I will agree to virtually anything at this point."

"All right, fine. Here's the thing: You've put the captain in a very awkward position."

"Not yet," replied Selar matter-of-factly. "I do not envision utilizing anything beyond your equivalent of the standard missionary—"

"That's not what I meant," she waved her hands to get Selar to stop. "You asked the captain of this vessel to have sex with you! To sire your child!"

"Yes, I believe the news is just coming through on the Interplanetary Network. Do not worry; if we miss the broadcast, I am quite certain it will be repeated."

Shelby's lips thinned. "I was unaware that Vulcans could be so sarcastic."

"We have many exemplary traits."

"Mm-hmm." Shelby paused, and then pushed forward. "It was . . . inappropriate of you to approach the captain in the fashion that you did."

"Inappropriate for whom?"

"For protocol. A captain should not fraternize with his subordinates."

"That, Commander, is illogical. Since the captain is by definition the most highly ranked individual on a ship, that point of view would require that a captain remain celibate throughout his tour of duty. That does not seem reasonable."

"Perhaps. Nonetheless—"

"Besides, I am not asking for fraternization. Merely to have sex. I doubt there will even be a good deal of conversation."

"Doctor . . ." She tried to find a different way to approach it. "The captain of a ship . . . he's not like everyone else. In a way, he does have to keep himself apart. Because everyone, sooner or later, will come to him for a decision . . . a decision that may very well have consequences for everyone else on the ship. When a captain makes those decisions, he has to be able to make them, free and unencumbered by other, irrelevant concerns. If intimacies of any sort factor into the equation, it can skew the decision into a direction that may be the wrong one."

"I do not quite comprehend, Commander," said Selar. "Are you implying that, in this instance, the captain could develop some sort of attachment to me that would cloud his ability to make appropriate decisions?"

"Doctor," she said and leaned forward, resting her hands on Selar's desk, "trust me on this: I know Mackenzie Calhoun. He's not the type of man who simply has casual sex. If he is intimate with a woman, he immediately considers that they then have an ongoing relationship. He's not a love-'em-and-leave-'em kind of guy. It's not part of who he is, or the way he was raised."

"The way he was raised? Commander, it is precisely because of the way he was raised that I approached the captain in this matter."

Shelby opened her mouth a moment, then closed it. "I'm sorry?"

"Commander, I did not choose the captain simply because of his rank, his rugged good looks, or his 'animal magnetism.' As befits my heritage, I approached this in a logical manner. I researched all the males on this vessel for compatibility and cultural background that would lend itself to attending to my needs. The captain's background on Xenex was the most thorough match."

"I'm not following," said Shelby, her confusion evident on her face. "His background? You mean from Xenex?" In all their time together as a couple, Calhoun had never gone into excessive detail about his life on Xenex. From what she knew of it, it was so filled with memories of war, heartache, and loss, that even to broach the subject was painful to him. So they had not discussed it overmuch. "What about his life on Xenex can possibly apply to your situation. Xenexians don't have *Pon Farr.*"

"Granted, Commander. However, they do have their own traditions and customs. One of them is that if a woman of the tribe has become widowed, and she wishes to conceive, thereby fulfilling what is perceived as the woman's role in the tribal order—and please"—she put up a hand to forestall exactly what she anticipated Shelby saying—"do not spend time telling me that women are capable of fulfilling many more functions besides childbirth. Since you and I have both chosen careers in Starfleet, we can take that to be a given in both our personal philosophies. The point is, if she wishes to conceive, then it is the responsibility of the tribal leader to perform the necessary services. Mackenzie Calhoun was indeed a tribal leader. Therefore I am merely asking him, in a manner of speaking, to fulfill those same obligations."

"But he's not on Xenex!" pointed out Shelby.

"True. And I am not on Vulcan. Our specific geographical location, Commander, is irrelevant. We continue to carry our cultures and backgrounds within us, no matter where we are. Mackenzie Calhoun is, to all intents and purposes, the leader of our little tribe here on the *Excalibur.* I, a widowed female, have asked him to fulfill an obligation that a Xenexian tribal leader routinely fulfills. This is not a question of Starfleet regulations or Federation policy, Commander. It is a question of cultural backgrounds, for both of us. Traditions. As we both know, the honoring of individual cultures and their ways is sacrosanct, even in Starfleet."

Shelby was still working on getting a grip on what Selar had just informed her of. "So . . . so you're saying that Xenexian tribal leaders sometimes act as . . . breeding machines?"

"In a manner of speaking."

"For widows?"

"Not always just widows. If it is a desire of the family and the young woman in question, tribal leaders will have intercourse with young women who have just reached maturity. The purpose there is not conception, but more of a . . . a blessing."

Shelby's voice was barely above a whisper, for which Selar was rather appreciative. "A blessing? The tribal leaders have . . . have sex with adolescent women—"

"It is considered a great honor, and is always consensual."

"Consensual? What girl knows anything about anything when her hormones have just started kicking in, and there's . . . there's"—and she waved a hand in a direction as if she were pointed to an invisible person in the room—"there's M'k'n'zy of Calhoun, big, broad, and studly. Playboy of western Xenex!"

"Such traditions are not completely unknown in Earth culture, Commander, although they are not practiced as much anymore. For instance, the—"

"I don't care, Doctor," said Shelby sharply, and then instantly regretted speaking so harshly to Selar. Even though her face maintained that same inscrutability, it was clear that Selar had an air of polite confusion about her. However, she said nothing as Shelby very, very quickly pulled herself together. Then she slapped her thighs briskly and said, "Well, this certainly has been educational, Doctor."

"Yes, I have learned a great deal, too, Commander," said Selar. And as Shelby walked out of her office, Selar murmured, "I have learned that, when I see you coming toward my office, I should leave immediately."

V.

BURGOYNE 172, CHIEF ENGINEER of the *Starship Excalibur,* seemed utterly engrossed in a message from home that was scrolling across the computer screen, and the other members of the engineering department were tiptoeing around so as not to disrupt Burgoyne's attention. Finally, however, Ensign Ronni Beth had completed an assignment that Burgoyne had assigned her, and felt that delaying the report back to Burgoyne would probably not be a wise thing. So she stepped up behind the Hermat and said tentatively, "Shir?"

Burgoyne turned and looked up at her with those incredibly dark eyes. "That's 'sir.' Sir, or 'chief' since I'm chief of engineering. That would also be acceptable."

"Pardon?" said Beth in surprise. "I thought Hermats preferred 'shir,' feeling that 'sir' was too attached to one particular gender—"

"We did," said Burgoyne, tapping the computer screen. "But some new decisions have come down from the Hermat Language Council."

"The what?"

"The Hermat Language Council," repeated Burgoyne. "It's an organization that meets annually, composed of various scholars and linguists. They review our language: How we use it ourselves, how others use it, our interactions with other races. They adjust the usage, create new words that the language seems to require, or give approval to words that have worked their way into our own language."

"That sounds bizarre," said Beth. "A whole group just to govern your language?"

"If it is so 'bizarre,' why does the French government of Earth have the same thing?"

Beth was caught momentarily off guard, but then she shrugged. "Well, they're French," she said, as if that was all the explanation required.

"Oh," said Burgoyne. "Well, in any event, Starfleet representatives were complaining that we had created our own separate designation. That the fleet had no problem with separate descriptors such as s/he to reflect our bi-gender status, but contended that 'sir' was a form of Starfleet direct address and therefore exempt from Hermat requirements. The winning argument, I must admit, pointed out that it was the equivalent of changing the rank to 'commandher' so that females would have equal time with the word 'man' already included in the title. The Council went back and forth on that one, but finally decided that if we're going to be part of Starfleet, we should accede to their desires in this matter."

Beth leaned forward. "What other decisions have come down?"

"Well, the big one is that they've done away with 'hish,'" said Burgoyne. "It was decided we didn't need both 'hish' and 'hir.' 'Hish' was if you wanted to say, 'S/he bowed hish head.' 'Hir' was for saying, 'S/he didn't know what to do with hir.' But for a long time now, a lot of younger Hermats have been complaining that 'hish' is just too damn difficult to say, and that 'hir' can fulfill both functions. Apparently the Council agreed."

" 'Flutzed?' " Beth's gaze had wandered farther down the screen.

"Yes, 'flutzed.' Slang term, now made official. It means"—hir long, tapered fingers waved in the air for a moment as s/he tried to come up with an appropriate equivalent—"it means, 'messed up.' Not performing as expected due to some sort of error. If you want, we can discuss all the niceties of Hermat language later on. I'll be generating a memo for all personnel discussing all the pertinent changes. Computer off." The screen went obediently blank. "For now, I expect that you have a report for me?"

"Yes, sh—sir. I've been monitoring the readouts of the phase generators as they interface with the coils, and, well, it's still there, Chief."

"The energy wave readout?"

"Yes. I made a recording of it over several one-hour periods. Computer, access file Beth Wave One."

The screen promptly flared back to life. "Accessing," said the computer briskly, and a moment later the distinctive wave pattern appeared on the screen, undulating steadily.

"But it's not affecting engine performance," Burgoyne said thoughtfully, drumming hir fingers on the countertop.

"No, sir. I believe it was the source of some of the systems botch-ups we had earlier, although we have those under control now. In fact, if anything, it's improving energy processing."

"Look at that," Burgoyne said in wonderment. The energy readout seemed to turn steadily in a sort of undulating spiral. "It's almost beautiful to watch."

"It is definitely that, Chief."

"And my own research into this wave," continued Burgoyne, "indicates that we can trace its origin point almost to the minute after we passed through that Great Flaming Bird. Ensign," s/he turned back to Beth and indicated the screen, "do you have any explanation whatsoever as to the current curious status of our energy wave readouts?"

Beth gave it a long moment's thought, and then she said with conviction, "I'd say it's definitely flutzed."

Burgoyne laughed softly, displaying hir sharp canine teeth. "Yes. Yes, I'd have to agree. I want you to find what's causing it, Beth. I want you to make it your top priority. I have my eye on you, Beth. I think you have potential, and it's fulfilling these types of assignments that gets you ahead."

"'These types of assignments.' You mean assignments wherein the chief engineer has absolutely no clue as to what's causing it, and s/he's looking for some lucky sucker to foist the problem on."

"Well done, Beth," said Burgoyne approvingly. "You see, assignment of blame is an even greater skill than assignment of duty."

"Words to live by, sir."

"You'll likely need people working with you. Submit a list of those who you'll want on your team so I can clear them from other duties. Although I suggest you may want to leave Christiano's name off here."

"Christiano," Beth said slowly, feeling her cheeks coloring. "Is there a . . . uhm . . . problem with Ensign Christiano, sir?"

"Not from what I hear," replied Burgoyne teasingly. "My understanding is that you and he have become quite the couple."

"How did you—?"

"Word gets around a starship quickly, Ensign. We're a rather enclosed little community."

Not one to allow teasing to go entirely in one direction, Beth riposted with, "Well, my understanding is that you and Lieutenant McHenry are quite the couple yourself."

"Mark?" Again, Burgoyne laughed, although it was in a slightly different tone. One that seemed to carry a bit of pleasure in it. "Mark is . . . Mark is charming. A very original thinker. Neither of us sees the relationship *going* anywhere, really. We're more friends with fringe benefits, you could say."

"Enjoying each other's company until something better comes along."

"That's it precisely. So," and hir dark eyes twinkled, "any other gossip you've heard about lately?"

It was very odd for Beth, talking to Burgoyne. She never knew quite what to make of hir. There were times when s/he was surly, brusque, bordering on the dictatorial. But there were other times when Burgoyne seemed in the mood to chat and gossip like . . . well, like one of the girls.

"Well, I assume you've heard about the captain," said Beth. "I mean, that's the big one floating around the ship."

"The *captain*." Burgoyne seemed intrigued, leaning forward in hir chair as if afraid that a word might slip through the already minimal distance between them. "No, this I hadn't heard. Smart money is that he and the commander are—"

But Beth quickly shook her head. "No, not the commander. The captain and the doctor."

The smile remained frozen on Burgoyne's face as s/he said slowly, "Which doctor would that be?"

"*The* doctor. Selar."

"Captain Calhoun and Doctor Selar." Burgoyne was having trouble maintaining the smile now. "The . . . the two of them are . . . together now?"

"That's what I hear. Apparently the doctor is having some sort of *Pon Farr* problem. Since she's been talking with the captain, people are speculating that she's looking to him to solve it. That's where my money is, at any rate, although there are some who are speculating that actually it's the doctor and Commander Shelby who—"

"This is none of our business," Burgoyne said sharply, all efforts to maintain hir smile now gone. "You have work to do, Ensign, and so do I. I think we've spent enough time at this foolishness, don't you?"

And Burgoyne turned hir back to her, leaving a puzzled Beth stammering out, "Yes, sir," and walking quickly away.

Shelby entered the bridge and saw Calhoun looking over a report that Lefler had just handed him. He was studying it thoughtfully, and she thought she heard him say something about Si Cwan. She nodded, and then he nodded and said, slightly more loudly, "Sounds like a plan. Mister McHenry."

"Yes, sir," McHenry said briskly from the conn.

"Set us a course at two-two-three mark"—he glanced once more at Lefler's notes—"mark four."

"Aye, sir. Bringing her about."

"Warp factor four, Mister McHenry. Kick it."

"She's kicked, sir."

Shelby went to her chair next to Calhoun's, but she did not sit. Instead she half-crouched, with one bent knee in the cushion of the chair, and turned to face Calhoun. "Mind telling me where we're going, sir?"

"It is Ambassador Si Cwan's recommendation that we meet with envoys from a people called the Zondarians," Calhoun replied. "Apparently they already have people en route. We're going to be rendezvousing with them within thirty-six hours."

"I see." Shelby turned to Lefler. "The purpose of the meeting?"

"We're not sure, Commander," admitted Lefler, "but we are hoping that it is for the purpose of spearheading a peace initiative that will bring an end to a civil war stretching back nearly a millennium." She then proceeded to outline, in quick, broad strokes the details behind the rendezvous.

"Sounds impressive," said Shelby.

"Commander, are you planning to stay with us for a while?" Calhoun commented, noting her rather odd stance. "Feel free to sit down."

"Actually, I'd like to talk to you a few minutes, Captain, if you have the time. In your ready room, perhaps?"

He shrugged. "Of course. Lieutenant Soleta," he called to the science officer, who from her station was busy taking notes from long-range scanners on a collapsing star many parsecs away. She looked up, her eyebrows furrowed. "You have the conn," he said, as he moved toward the ready room at Shelby's side.

Soleta walked around to the command chair and slid into it. From behind her, Security Chief Zak Kebron, the mountainous member of the Brikar, rumbled, "You look entirely too comfortable there."

"I could get to like it," she said, rubbing her hands appreciatively on the armrest.

"I thought I knew you, Mac. I thought I, of all people—"

She was briskly pacing his ready room and he watched her go back and forth as if he were observing a tennis game. "Does anyone really know anyone?" he started to reply.

But she stabbed a finger at him and said angrily, "Don't you dare. I won't see you be flip about this. Not this."

"And I won't see you overreact!"

"Overreact! Mac!" She stopped in her tracks and calmed herself. "Mac, when we first became a couple, I know we agreed that our previous sexual histories weren't really relevant, and we weren't going to inquire."

"Yes, I know."

"But, jeez, Mac!" she said as she leaned against the table to steady herself, shaking her head in astonishment. "You might have mentioned this at least! You were Xenex's official sexual surrogate?!"

"Eppy, why do you care?" he said.

"You're doing it again. Calling me by that annoying nickname in hopes that I'll get distracted. It's not going to work, Mac. Call me 'Eppy' as much as your little heart desires."

"All right, then. Eppy, again . . . why do you care? Our romantic relationship was long ago. Why should you care?"

"Because it colors what went before, that's why! Because it's—oh, I don't know!" she said in frustration, thudding one fist on the table. "I don't know why I care. You're right, I'm being stupid."

"You're being who you are, and saying what you feel. That's never stupid."

She slid into the chair next to him, propping her chin up on her fist. "It's just that"—and her voice was so soft that he had to strain to hear her—"you were . . . you were very special to me back then, Mac. Our relationship was very special. And finding that your life before me included that facet of it, I . . . well . . . it just makes me feel—"

"A little less special?"

"Kind of, I guess. And I'm sorry, I don't care what you say, I am being stupid, because it was a long time ago, and I shouldn't be letting it upset me. I've been through a lot since then, and I shouldn't really." She paused, as if her mind was switching tracks, and then she blurted out, "How many?"

"Pardon?"

"How many women were there? During your 'tenure.'"

"You mean how many women did I service?"

She winced. "That's a bit more blunt than I would have liked. I'd have preferred you put it somewhat more delicately."

"How many women did I fill with the glorious seed of M'k'n'zy?"

"Okay. Let's go back to blunt. How many?"

"Are you sure you want to know?"

"Yes." With a forced demeanor of casualness, she crossed her legs and steepled her fingers. "I admit, I may regret it, but . . ."

"Very well." He proceeded to murmur to himself, counting off on his fingers, muttering a string of names. Shelby felt her heart sinking. He looked at his hands, and then back to her. "I'm out of fingers. I may have to use the computer to calculate it."

"Aw, come on, Mac! Just ballpark it, okay?"

"Okay, okay. Ballpark, rough number, off the top of my head, and don't hold me to this now, but it was somewhere around . . ."

She braced herself.

"One."

She didn't even realize that she'd closed her eyes in a grimace until the moment sustained itself, frozen in time, and she became aware that she couldn't see anything. She opened her eyes and stared at him, to see that he was laughing silently to himself. "*One!*"

"Yes."

"Just one? Just one woman!"

"Just the one. Her name was Catrine, and if you

must know, she was also the first woman that I ever . . . serviced . . . in *any* capacity. Appropriate, I guess. Someone who fought for his planet's freedom from his early teens, naturally my first sexual experience would be in the line of duty."

"But why only the one?"

"You sound disappointed."

"Oh, I'm not!" she said very quickly. "I mean, I guess only in the sense that if I were going to be getting myself so upset about something, it'd have been nice if there were something for me really to get upset about. But one? How can I . . . ? Uhm . . . why just one?"

"I found at that point that I actually had a preference for swordplay."

"Aw, c'mon!"

"Because I wasn't the tribal leader, Eppy! You keep overlooking that. I was the warlord; my brother was the actual leader. How many women he was involved with, I could not begin to tell you, and I seriously doubt that you care."

"Not in the least."

"Good, because if you did, I'd start wondering about you. One time I had to step in while he was off-world and perform that function. I was a nervous wreck, but it all turned out okay."

"And . . . did you have a child? I mean, that's the other thing that kind of threw me, I guess. The thought of dozens of little Mackenzie Calhouns running around."

"Yes. A son."

"What's he like?"

"I wouldn't know. I've never met him."

She was visibly startled. "Never?"

He shook his head. "I had left for the Academy before she gave birth. The one time that I returned, some years later, I learned that she'd moved out of Calhoun. No one knew where. I figured if she'd wanted me to be able to find her, she'd have made it easy for me to do so, so I decided to respect her privacy."

"I'm sorry, Mac. That must be very painful for you. You must miss him."

"Miss him? Eppy, you can't miss someone you never even knew. Don't worry about it. I'm fine. I haven't thought about him in years, actually. Years and years." He paused. "How many?"

She looked at him in confusion. "You're asking me how many years you haven't thought about him?"

"No, I'm asking you how many men you were with before me." He folded his arms expectantly. "It's a fair question, Eppy, considering the grilling you've put me through. How many?"

"One." And she hesitated, and then added, "Half."

"One *half?*" He laughed skeptically. "Bottom half, I assume?"

"It was at a party," she said in annoyance, "and I was, to put it bluntly, tired of being a virgin, and there was this guy who'd been after me for a while, so I let him because I figured 'What the hell,' but he'd only partially, uhm . . ." She hesitated. "Now *I'm* trying to be delicate. He had only partially—"

"Breached your warp core?"

"Yes, thank you. And then suddenly he . . ."

"Fired photon torpedoes?"

"I was going to say 'reached critical mass,' but if you want to mix your metaphors, you're the captain."

"I think you've made the point, Eppy." He smiled. "You know, Eppy, back then, I have to admit that your lack of comfort discussing sex bothered the hell out of me. But now, in a woman your age, I find it somewhat charming."

"Why, thank you. So, have you made a decision regarding Doctor Selar yet?"

"No. But whatever I do decide, understand that I will endeavor to keep the common good of all concerned as my first and foremost consideration. And now, if you'll excuse me . . ." He rose from his chair and exited the ready room.

She stood to follow him, then stopped.

"A woman my age?" she said slowly. "What the hell is *that* supposed to mean?"

VI.

THE APPROACHING SHIP was bristling with armament and ready for war.

It was a sleek, low-slung vessel, small but maneuverable, with foils that clearly indicated it was designed to function equally well in the depths of space or within a planet's atmosphere. McHenry had been tracking it for some time, and when it began to make its approach, he nodded as if confirming his own concerns. "Yeah, it's definite, Captain," he said. "They're definitely set to intercept us."

"How are they running?" he asked.

Kebron checked his sensor array. "Running weapons hot. They are not, however, targeting us."

From the science station, Soleta went over the weapons analysis. "They're packing phase blasters and torpedoes with nuclear warheads. Their weapons could hurt us, sir."

"Any thoughts, Commander?" he addressed Shelby.

She leaned forward, like a bloodhound on the scent.

"They may be suspicious of us. Desirous to ascertain our identity."

"Have you managed to raise them yet, Mister Kebron?"

"Not yet."

The turbolift doors slid open and Si Cwan strode out onto the bridge. "Came as fast as I could, Captain."

Calhoun gestured towards the opposing vessel. "Recognize them, Cwan?"

Without hesitation, Si Cwan said briskly, "Zondarian. Definitely."

"They're not responding to our hails. Any thoughts?"

Si Cwan studied the vessel for a moment. "Turn around."

"You mean the ship?" said Calhoun.

"Well, you could turn around in your chair, but that would hardly alter the situation."

A deep voice rumbled from nearby, "Watch it, Cwan."

"I think I can handle this, Kebron. Thank you," Calhoun said. "Why should we turn around, Ambassador?"

Si Cwan hesitated a moment, as if ready to answer, but then he drew himself up even straighter, towering over Calhoun. "Looming" was perhaps one of Si Cwan's greatest talents. "If one of your officers gave you advice in a pressure situation, you'd take it on faith first and ask questions later."

"Correct," Calhoun said, arms folded. "What's your point?"

"Captain, five hundred thousand kilometers and closing. Still running weapons hot."

"Thank you, Mister McHenry." Calhoun paused, assessing Si Cwan's demeanor, and then he said, "Bring us about, reverse heading."

"Deflectors up, sir?"

"Yes."

Almost as quickly as Calhoun gave an affirmative, Si Cwan said, "No."

Calhoun's violet eyes narrowed. "*Yes,*" he said with emphasis.

Quickly the *Excalibur* turned about, and began to head back the way she came.

"Sir, pursuer is picking up speed! Three hundred thousand kilometers, closing fast, coming in at heading one-two-nine mark nine," McHenry informed him.

"Still no targeting from their weapons array. But they are an intercept course."

"Evasive maneuvers, Mister McHenry!" ordered Calhoun.

"Evasive manuevers. Aye, sir!" replied McHenry, and sent the *Excalibur* howling directly toward the expected point of collision.

There was a unified shout of alarm from virtually everyone on the bridge, Calhoun's voice above all as he shouted, *"McHenry, what are you doing!?"* The alien vessel loomed huge on the screen, looking as if it were about to park itself right on the bridge.

"Evasive maneuver, sir," McHenry said calmly. "Three . . . two . . . one . . ."

The starship passed the point of intersection seconds before the oncoming vessel, and then hurtled away, missing the other ship by barely one hundred meters. Shelby fancied that she could actually hear the roar of the other ship's engines.

". . . Zero," finished McHenry. "Evasive maneuver successful, Captain. Orders?"

"Bring us around behind them. Lock phasers on target, Mister Kebron."

"Gladly, sir."

"Send them a warning that if they do not stand down, we're going to blow them halfway to hell."

"You are going to needless trouble, Captain," Si Cwan said. "They were endeavoring to show 'dominance.' They do not like to have discourse with any race that they feel inferior to. So they make a great show of bluster, like that Earth animal . . . a gorilla . . . pounding on its chest. If you had simply stayed on course, they would have veered off on their own. No evasive maneuvers, as charmingly unorthodox as they were, were necessary."

"If that's the case, Ambassador, I appreciate their desire to deal from perceived strength. But if it's all the same to you, I'd prefer to operate from genuine strength."

"We're getting an incoming hail, Captain."

"About bloody time. Put them on visual, Mister Kebron."

The screen wavered for only a moment, and then two Zondarians appeared on the screen. They were staring, almost in wonderment. "It is you? Mackenzie Calhoun?"

He was struck by the odd sheen of their skin. They looked fairly similar to one another, except that one was taller than the other. "Yes. That's right. Identify yourselves, and explain your attempted attack upon my vessel."

"We would never have injured you, Mackenzie Calhoun," said the shorter one. "We are the Zondarian pilgrimage, come to meet with you."

"You have a very odd way of trying to make a positive first impression," Calhoun informed them. "If you *wanted* to meet with us, why did you take a combative attitude?"

"We would have communicated sooner," said the shorter one, and he glanced in annoyance at the taller one next to him, "but my Eenza associate insisted that he have the honor of having the first communication with you, since it was one of the Eenza who foretold your coming. But it was my belief that I had equal right to the first communication, considering all the hardships my people, the Unglza, have suffered at Eenza hands."

"As if the Unglza hands are clean," snorted the taller one.

"I told you Mackenzie Calhoun would not be familiar with your convoluted methods of greeting newcomers by way of challenge," the shorter one said testily. "Attack, dive. Which idiot member of your clan dreamt up such—"

"Gentlemen," Calhoun said firmly, "there are certainly more constructive ways to spend time than arguing over who said what. I'm willing to chalk this unfortunate incident off to miscommunication and"—he glanced at Si Cwan—"rather odd greeting rituals. The point is, we're talking now. You desired to speak with us. Here we are."

"Yes. Yes, of course. I am Killick," said the shorter one, "and my associate is—"

"I can introduce myself. I am Ramed," said the taller. Calhoun noticed that there was another difference between the two of them. Ramed's eyes were darker, more serious. He had the air of being perpetually disturbed about something. His gaze flickered to Calhoun's right, and he nodded slightly in acknowledgment. "Lord Si Cwan."

"Ramed. We meet again under unusual circumstances," Si Cwan replied.

"Odd how things develop, isn't it?"

"Odd indeed. To see an Unglza and an Eenza side-by-side."

"We have been brought together by common cause," Killick spoke up. "We humbly petition that you meet with us as soon as possible. We wish to share the joy of this moment with you, so that you all may understand."

"Do they have matter transport capability?" Calhoun said softly to Si Cwan.

Si Cwan shook his head. "Not to your degree of sophistication. They can transport from one construction transmat point to the next, but they do not possess the Federation's capture-and-receive technology."

"Very well." He turned back to the Zondarians. "We will bring you aboard our vessel and we can discuss the matter more thoroughly."

"How will you do that?" inquired Killick.

"It's not very involved. Bridge to transporter room," Calhoun called. "Lock onto the transmission origin and beam the senders aboard. I'll be right down to greet them."

"Affirmative, Captain."

A moment later, Killick and Ramed vanished from the screen in a startled dissolve of sparkles. Calhoun nodded approvingly, and then said, "Shelby, Soleta, Si Cwan, Kebron—with me. Mister McHenry, you have the conn. And no evasive maneuvers while we're gone."

"Aye, sir."

"Come, people: Let's see what our new friends have to say."

"You are the Savior."

They were in the conference lounge: Calhoun, Soleta, Shelby, Si Cwan, and the Zondarians seated around the table. Kebron had taken up position directly behind the Zondarians, just standing there with his massive arms folded across his chest, his hard-to-see eyes glittering from deep within his face like diamonds with attitude. Clearly he was waiting for evidence of even the slightest false move on the part of the newcomers, and if they provided him with that opening, he would strike quickly and with finality.

Calhoun was staring at the Zondarians in disbelief. "I'm sorry, Killick, I didn't quite catch that, or even understand it. I am the what?"

"The Savior," repeated Killick, sounding extremely reasonable. "Our Savior. You are He. You are come. Just as was prophesied five hundred years ago." He looked to Ramed for verification, and Ramed nodded agreeably. "You see?" he said as if that constituted the final, rock-solid proof. "If there is something that even Unglza and Eenza can agree upon, then it must be so."

"Far be it from me to dispute the indisputable," said Calhoun, "but may I ask how just how, precisely, you came to this conclusion? That I am your Savior?"

"Yes," Ramed nodded emphatically. "There can be no mistake."

"May I ask how you can be so sure?" Shelby inquired.

"It is in the lore of our greatest prophet, Ontear, and his greatest acolyte, Suti," Ramed told them, and now it was Killick who was obediently bobbing his head in affirmation. "Ontear predicted your coming."

"Was the captain mentioned by name?" asked Soleta.

"Well . . . no," admitted Ramed.

"Well, then," Soleta continued, "unless this prophet said something to the effect that you should be on the lookout for a starship captain with a scar who will show up shortly after a giant flaming bird puts in an appearance, I'm afraid I don't quite see the logic in believing that Captain Calhoun is your anointed one."

Killick and Ramed looked at one another, and then Killick sighed. "You're the Eenza; it's your right. Go ahead and say it."

Ramed slowly stood, and he seemed so consumed with excitement that he could barely keep his legs still. His fingers rested on the edge of the table as if he needed it for support. "'Look to the stars,' he intoned, 'for from there will come the Messiah! The bird of flame will signal His coming! He will bear a scar, and He will be a great leader! And He will unite our planet!"

"That was written by the great Ontear, on his last day upon our world, five hundred years ago," Killick informed them.

As one, the others turned and stared at Soleta. She shifted uncomfortably in her chair. "A lucky guess," she said in an offhand manner.

"It really says all that?" Calhoun asked in disbelief.

"They would not lie about the predictions of Ontear, Captain," Si Cwan said. "It is a subject they take most, most seriously. To even joke about such matters is the equivalent of consigning your soul to . . . well, whatever passes for oblivion in Zondarian theology."

"Is that specific enough for you, Captain?" asked Killick.

"I have to admit, it's a fairly impressive set of coincidences," Shelby agreed. "Perhaps too many to be considered 'mere' coincidence, although I still don't rule out a more scientific explanation."

"Such as?" inquired Ramed politely.

"Lieutenant?" Shelby turned and looked hopefully at Soleta.

Soleta shrugged. "Nothing comes to mind," she said.

"Thanks for the help, Lieutenant."

"Not a problem, Commander."

Calhoun leaned forward, and there seemed to be mild amusement in his eyes. "All right. Just for the sake of argument, let's say I am your Savior."

"Which we are not saying, most emphatically,"

Shelby quickly put in. She looked to Calhoun for confirmation of that, and was a bit disconcerted when she didn't see it.

"As I said," he repeated calmly, "just for sake of argument. If that were the case, what would you expect of me?"

Killick glanced at Ramed, who nodded silently, and then turned back and said, "It is our hope that you would come to Zondar. Your return has long been associated with peace among our people. Were you to come to our world, as a vehicle for peace, we know that they would listen. Both the Eenza and the Unglza are building up arms in preparation for a resurgence of the violence that has dominated our relationship for centuries. But leaders of both groups have agreed to set aside differences for the purpose of sitting at a negotiation table with the Savior Himself. Who, after all, could possibly turn down such an honor?"

"Who indeed?" Si Cwan affirmed. "Captain, in my opinion, it would be foolish of you to deny your obvious heritage. The beliefs of these good people should be—must be—honored."

"You are our Savior," Ramed said with quiet conviction. "Save us, anointed one. Save us . . . from ourselves."

The Zondarians had returned to their ship, impressed by the power of the *Excalibur*'s transporter, and Kebron—the possible threat to security now gone—had returned to his post on the bridge. Calhoun was now meeting in privacy with the remaining officers. "It could, of course, be a hoax," Soleta pointed out. "The prophecies written only recently by those within an inner circle and then 'discovered' in order to fulfill recent events."

But Si Cwan was emphatically shaking his head. "No," he said flatly. "I spoke separately with them.

These writings go back half a millennium, as they said. There's no chance of forgery."

"You can't intend to go along with it, Captain," Shelby said.

Calhoun was scratching his chin thoughtfully. "Why not?"

"Why not?" She couldn't quite believe she had to spell it out. "Captain, you cannot go to these people and present yourself as their . . . their messiah!"

"Why?"

"Because it's a clear violation of the Prime Directive! You're interfering with the development of their society!"

"With all respect, Commander, I disagree," Si Cwan replied from across the table. "The captain has not inserted himself into their society. Their society has reached out to encompass him."

"Some men seek out greatness," Calhoun said sagely, "and others have greatness thrust upon them."

Shelby kept her voice level, endeavoring to explain that which, to her, seemed crystal clear. "Captain, you do not seem to be regarding this situation with the gravity that it quite clearly demands. To set yourself up as some sort of ruler for these people, even if they demand it—even if the title seems yours by some sort of prophetic right—it's against everything that the spirit of the Prime Directive stands for."

"I'm not an idiot, Commander," Calhoun said, a bit more sharply than he might have intended to.

"I never meant to say, or imply, that you were, sir," Shelby replied stiffly.

"I know what you're concerned about. I know the regs. What I also know is that these people stand on the brink of almost certainly heading back into a civil war, now that the Thallonian Empire's influence has ceased."

"There is no 'almost' about it, Captain," Si Cwan affirmed. "The grudges are long-standing, the hatred beyond any rational discussion. They are not able to look beyond their squabbles and stereotypes of one another. But the one thing upon which they do agree, which cuts across all of their hatred, all of their hostility, is that their Savior will reunite them. Indeed, perhaps it's their conviction in that regard that has given them license to attack one another all these centuries. They believed that they were destined to do so. But now their Savior is here."

"He's not here!" said Shelby firmly.

"What would you have me do, Commander?" asked Calhoun reasonably. "Go to the Zondarians and say, 'Sorry, you've got the wrong guy. You're on your own.' And leave? Turn my back while men, women, and children are slaughtered?"

"No, of course not."

"You wouldn't want to take the Thallonian route, I presume. Go in and threaten them with force of arms? Cow them into submission?"

"That is also, obviously, not an acceptable alternative." She sighed. "Captain, I want peace for these people, the same as anyone else. And aiding in peace negotiations is well within the mandate of our mission."

"If that's the case, then I think I have a simple solution," Calhoun said. "In fact, from the look in your eyes, I suspect you have it, too."

"To neither confirm nor deny?" suggested Shelby.

"Precisely."

"I'm not quite following, Commander, Captain," admitted Si Cwan.

"I will not go to the Zondarians and put myself forward as being the fulfillment of their prophecies," Calhoun said. "By the same token, if they ask me, I will not deny it either. I will simply nod, smile, and say something vague such as, 'Who am I to argue with prophecies?' I'm not going in there for the purpose of self-aggrandizement. I'm going in to try and convince a race that seems hellbound on destruction that there are better courses for them to follow. If they want to think of me as some sort of 'Savior,' let them. Let them think I'm God from on high. Let them think I'm J'e'n't, the Three-Headed Xenexian God of Lightning, for all I care. As long as it gets them seated across from each other at a negotiation table, talking with one another, then my job is done."

"The end justifies the means," commented Soleta.

"Of course it does. Always," Calhoun readily agreed.

"Captain," Shelby said cautiously, "I know that your motives are pure and well intentioned. And I agree that this seems to be the most expeditious manner in which to proceed. But expediency doesn't always equal wise. We have to tread very, very carefully. We're walking a fine line here between right and wrong, both from a Starfleet standpoint, and the standpoint of morality."

"I know that I can count on you, Elizabeth, to keep me on that straight and narrow line and warn me lest I fall off."

She smiled wanly. "I'll certainly do my best, Captain."

The door to the conference lounge slid open, and Doctor Selar entered. "Captain, you wished to see me?" she asked.

"Uhm . . . yes. I believe we're done here, then?" There were nods of affirmation from all around. "Commander, kindly inform the Zondarians that we will indeed proceed directly to their homeworld, there to meet with their senior advisors to try and map out some sort of permanent peace between the Eenza and the Unglza. Have Mister McHenry bring us there at warp two. That'll give them some time to build up anticipation over our arrival. Lieutenant Soleta, work with Ambassador Si Cwan, if you will, and dig up any other information you can on this reputed Savior of theirs. Anything I can use to my advantage to pull this off will be of great help. All right, people," and he clapped his hands briskly. "This all sounds like a plan."

Everyone filed out, Shelby the last, and she hesitated just a moment as she passed Selar. A significant look passed between them, one that was not lost on Soleta, who was very aware of the mating urges that Selar was dealing with. She'd heard the rumors flying around the ship regarding the captain and Selar, and had known what aspects to dismiss—also which aspects to take seriously.

There was something else going on, however; some sort of odd dynamic between Selar and Shelby that Soleta could not quite understand. Feeling a need to come somehow to the aid of her fellow Vulcan, Soleta—who was already out in the hallway—said questioningly, "Commander?"

"Yes. Coming," said Shelby, shaken from the spell that had momentarily distracted her. She walked out behind Soleta as the door slid shut behind her, leaving Selar and Calhoun alone in the conference lounge.

Selar waited expectantly.

"I've given the matter a good deal of thought," Calhoun said.

"You mean the matter of having sex with me."

He wanted to say, *No, the matter of whether or not there is a God,* but he wisely decided that that would not be the best course. "That's correct. I've consulted Starfleet regs on the matter, and they seem rather vague on how to proceed in this instance."

"Since this is a condition that we generally like to keep to ourselves, even though others may tend to broadcast word of it"—and she glanced with a clearly annoyed manner in the direction of the departed Shelby—"it does not surprise me that it would not thoroughly be covered in literature."

"Be that as it may, it seems to me that the wisest course might be to say no, simply to avoid the possible entanglements such an encounter might engender. Besides, there may be other possibilities. Have you considered the option, Doctor, of simply returning to Vulcan? Of finding a mate there? I could arrange for transport."

"I am very aware of that, Captain," replied Selar evenly. She looked down at the toes of her boots, and for the first time she actually looked vulnerable to Calhoun. Even a little scared, although he was quite sure that she would never admit to it. "Captain, I find the entire concept of *Pon Farr* to be most onerous. My duties as chief medical officer of the *Excalibur,* on the other hand, give me great satisfaction. It does not seem proper or just to me that I must dispense with the latter in order to accommodate the former. Furthermore, I—"

She hesitated. He thought of prompting her, but he knew that she would tell him in her own time.

"I . . . have no one on Vulcan, sir. No one I would be . . . comfortable with."

"Comfortable? Doctor, the bottom line is you hardly know me, and vice versa."

She returned his gaze, and it seemed to him as if she were dissecting him with her eyes. "You are a good man, Captain. A proud man. Clever, inventive. I have not known many men whom I would classify as heroic, but you would certainly fall into that category. I would be," she began, and it seemed to him—although he might have been imagining it—that she had to make the slightest effort to keep her chin from trembling. "I would be most proud if you were to sire my child."

Calhoun smiled, actually feeling embarrassed, although he'd believed that couldn't possibly be the case. He felt his head nodding even before he said anything. "All right, Doctor. If that's what you want, I'll accommodate you."

"Thank you, Captain," she said with clear relief.

They were standing about a foot away from each other, and the moment seemed to call for some sort of physical contact. They each moved their hands in a vague manner, and Calhoun even thought to hug her except he felt that it would be wrong somehow. They settled for a brisk handshake.

"So, judging by the fact that you're not knocking me onto the conference lounge table, I can take that to mean that you're still in 'remission,' as it were," he said.

She nodded. 'Yes, that is correct. However, the mating urge will resurface, probably within the next week. I will inform you when I will need you. I will endeavor to time it at a point where your duties and requirements are minimal."

"I appreciate your consideration for my schedule."

"It's more than that, sir. You see, as I go more deeply into *Pon Farr*, I will . . . link with you, psychically. You will become as driven by the impulse to mate as I am. You will be consumed by, and be able to think of nothing else but, sex."

"Sounds like fairly typical male behavior," Calhoun observed. Then he grinned at the seriousness on her face. "It was a joke, Doctor."

"Ah. I see. Humor is a difficult concept."

They stood there for a moment, uncertain what else to say.

"Captain."

"Yes, Doctor?"

"If you would like, you may call me Selar."

He nodded appreciatively. "And you may call me Mac, if you wish."

She seemed to roll the name around in her mouth for a moment, and then she said, "If you will not be insulted, I think I would prefer 'Captain.'"

"As you wish, Selar."

"Thank you, Captain."

VII.

THE HIGH PRIEST OF ALPHA CARINAE did not like what he was hearing.

The Alphans were relatively recent converts to Xantism. They were a somewhat barbaric race, really. Large, muscled, fairly savage of mien, yet living with a rather healthy fear of the Redeemers, which was naturally how the High Priest preferred matters.

Different High Priests handled their positions of power in different manners. High Priests on some other worlds, for instance, chose to keep themselves in seclusion, learning of the world through various "eyes" and "ears" among the populace who were loyal to the way of Xant. But the High Priest of Alpha Carinae was far too outgoing an individual to stay hidden away somewhere. He insisted upon moving among the populace, to hear their words with his own ears. To know what they were thinking, to look into their eyes and see whether their love and belief in Xant was sincere.

The High Priest was becoming concerned.

It seemed to him that the Alphans were not looking at him in the same, comforting manner of fear that usually possessed them. Usually, if there was a crowd of Alphans, they would part to make way for him. Recently, however, they'd been slower to do so. Not only that, but when they did get out of his way, they made a major show of doing so as if to draw attention to themselves, as if to make mockery of the High Priest.

And as he walked away, if he strained his ears he could hear muttering. Hear the name of the Redeemers mentioned with what sounded like contempt, and other names murmured as well. Names he had heard bandied about with greater and greater frequency these days. Names such as "Calhoun" and *"Excalibur."* The names, in and of themselves, did not mean a great deal to him. But it was enough to cause a stirring of concern in the pit of his stomach.

He did not yet consider himself to be in any sort of danger. The person of a High Priest of the Redeemers was sacrosanct, and he was certain that none of the Alphans would be foolish enough to transgress in that respect. They knew the consequences. At least, he thought they knew the consequences.

However, he needed to find out more for himself. So, during one of his daily perambulations, he chose at random a cluster of Alphans standing at a street-corner, talking and arguing with what seemed to be tremendous enthusiasm. Something had them rather worked up, and the High Priest reasoned that only two things could get a group of young males quite that excited: sex, or a stimulating religious discussion.

Slowly the High Priest moved toward them. One of the young males had his back to him and so didn't see him approaching. The others' discussion and chatter quickly trailed off as they spotted him coming, and the one whose back was to the High Priest slowly trailed off, looking and sounding rather puzzled until he turned around and saw the High Priest standing directly behind him.

"Saulcram, isn't it?" asked the High Priest. He tapped the young man's chest with his staff.

Saulcram nodded fretfully. The others began to back up as if conspiring to make a getaway, but the High Priest froze them with a glance. He slowly turned his attention back to the first young man. "I would be interested to know that which you are discussing, Saulcram."

"It's nothing, my lord," Saulcram said nervously.

"If it is nothing, then it is of such little consequence that you should not hesitate to tell me what it is. Correct?" He made it sound so pleasant, so simple. He prodded Saulcram under the chin less than gently with his staff. "Now you will tell me, yes?"

Saulcram looked to his friends, and then back to the High Priest. "We're just . . . just discussing, well . . . what everyone is discussing."

"Odd," said the High Priest. "I don't recall discussing it. Why don't you share that which apparently should already be common knowledge, hmm?"

"Well, it's . . . it's about . . . you know . . . the Second Coming."

"The Second Coming." The High Priest nodded approvingly. "You refer, of course, to the Second Coming of Xant."

"Yes. Yes, that's it exactly. Can I go now?"

The end of the staff had a curve to it. The High Priest twisted it slightly so that the curve snagged Saulcram's upper forearm, keeping him serenely in place. "Well, I find this a bit odd, Saulcram," the High Priest told him. "If that was indeed all you were talking about—the Second Coming of Xant—then why did you hesitate to tell me? Why were you so nervous? Why are you so nervous still?"

"I . . . I swear, I don't—"

The High Priest suddenly gripped his staff with both hands and twisted quickly. The abrupt sharp turn of the hooked end bent down and back against the arm, and there was a very audible snap. Saulcram went down, clutching at his broken arm, and there were tears already starting to well up in his eyes.

The others surrounding the High Priest took an angry step forward, and once again the High Priest glared around at them in that forceful way he had. It was a look that was usually capable of thoroughly intimidating the Alphans. This time, the High Priest made a mental note that the Alphans did not appear intimidated at all. Hesitant, yes. Unsure of whether to make a move or not. But it seemed no longer that they would hesitate to attack. Rather, it appeared that they were simply waiting for the right time, although no one seemed to know precisely when that was going to be.

Other passersby were stopping to observe the altercation. A crowd was beginning to grow, and it was not something the High Priest could particularly say he liked. He raised his voice and called out, "The person of a High Priest is sacrosanct! Do not forget that! Let none of you forget that! For to injure or kill a High Priest is to spell swift and immediate doom for your entire world! Know that!"

And from somewhere in the crowd, he heard a voice call out. And the voice said, *"Excalibur* is coming!"

"Excalibur," he murmured in confusion and annoyance.

"Excalibur, the force of freedom, chosen of the flame bird!" someone shouted.

A third person called out, "The liberator is coming! They will destroy you, and the Redeemers, and even your precious Xant will not be able to stand before them!"

Still another person shouted out, "Calhoun! Calhoun!"

The crowd began to take up the chant, repeating it over and over: "Calhoun! Calhoun! *Calhoun!*"

The High Priest had no idea what was going on, but he knew he did not like it. Not in the least.

He stepped back away from Saulcram and his friends. Caught up in the defiance of the crowd, even Saulcram and those with him were calling out *"Calhoun! Calhoun!"*

The High Priest, maintaining as much of his dignity as possible under the circumstances, made his way back to the Alpha Carinae Central Hall of Worship. Even though things seemed calmer once he put some distance between himself and the impromptu rally, he couldn't help but feel that all eyes were upon him. He kept feeling that someone would launch himself from the shadows of a nearby building. Anything from a harsh word to a projectile might have come flying his way at any moment. As it happened, however, his return to his base occurred without incident. And so it was that—with his skin intact, albeit it with nerves somewhat strung out—the High Priest was putting through a transmission to Tulaan IV as fast as possible.

Moments later he was speaking directly with Prime One, the Overlord's good right arm. At first he had been concerned that Prime One might be upset in response to what should have been a minor problem, but instead Prime One seemed amused by it all. "I know whereof the Alphans speak, Brother," Prime One said calmly. "We know well of this 'flame bird' that was mentioned. You will be most pleased to know that the Overlord had officially declared it to be a sign."

"A sign," the High Priest repeated uncomprehendingly.

"A sign that Xant will be returning," Prime One said with a touch of impatience. He outlined the specifics of the flame bird's appearance in as broad strokes as he could, and then concluded, "This is not a time of concern, Brother. This is a time of rejoicing!"

"Rejoicing is a luxury in which you can indulge yourself, Prime One," replied the High Priest. "But the people of Alpha Carinae do not seem to necessarily share your conviction that this is a precursor to the return of Xant. They seem perfectly inclined to attribute some other cause to it."

"Other?" The thought literally had not even occurred to the Prime One. "What other could there possibly be?"

"This *'Excalibur'* they mentioned. And another name . . . Calhoun."

"Yes, we are aware of both of these," said Prime One. *"Excalibur* is a Federation vessel, Calhoun its captain. They were merely on the site when the bird signaled the return of Xant. They have nothing to do with the creature's existence, nor with the return of Xant."

"That may very well be," the High Priest informed him, "but the Alphans seem to feel otherwise. They believe in some sort of link. That, rather than signaling a return by Xant, the circumstances surrounding the creature's appearance is an endorsement of, or a precursor to, the one they call Calhoun. They seem to regard him as some sort of . . . of liberator."

"Liberator?" Prime One was thunderstruck. "Liberation from the word of Xant? From the spirit of

Xant? Who in their right mind would desire to be liberated from that?"

"The Alphans apparently, sir. They have no comprehension or appreciation of all that we try to do for them."

"I will inform the Overlord of this situation," Prime One said after a moment's thought. "He will want to know of the wrongheadedness in many which surrounds this clear signal of Xant's return. He may very well want to address Alpha Carinae . . . and perhaps even other worlds which may be laboring under similar delusions. Thank you for informing me of the situation there, Brother."

"It was my honor as always, Prime One."

"May Xant light your way."

"Yours as well, Prime One."

Prime One's image blinked off the screen, leaving the High Priest to gaze out the windows at the populace below him. It was a populace amongst whom he had never hesitated to walk, but now something told him that he would be most well advised to stay exactly where he was. That perhaps now was not the time to spread the good word and tidings of Xant among the Alphans.

Because somehow, he had the feeling—a feeling that, as it turned out, was a correct one—that the last thing the Alphans were interested in doing at that particular moment in time was listening.

VIII.

SELAR WAS SEATED BY HERSELF in the team room, which was how she was customarily seated. She was carefully nursing a glass of Synthehol when she looked up to see Burgoyne 172 staring down at her.

"Somehow, Lieutenant Commander," Selar said slowly, "I suspected that we would be chatting in the near future."

"Really," Burgoyne said. "So you're saying there's something you want to talk to me about?"

"Not in particular, no," replied Selar. "However, it was my suspicion that you would desire to talk to me."

"Well, now aren't we full of ourselves," said Burgoyne, and Selar could see from the slightest waver in Burgoyne's bearings that s/he had already had a bit to drink. Selar was well aware (since Burgoyne had boasted of it on more than one occasion) that s/he had a fairly impressive collection of scotch back in hir quarters, a drink s/he had apparently developed a taste for while imbibing with a former engineer from another ship.

"Would you care to sit down, Lieutenant Commander," said Selar, "before you fall down?"

"Why don't you ask me to sit?" Burgoyne demanded.

For the briefest of moments, Selar doubted her sanity. Was it possible, she wondered, that the semi-delusional state resulting from heightened *Pon Farr* was enough to cause her to lose track completely of time or a discussion? Hadn't she just asked—

She shrugged mentally. It hardly seemed worth a dispute. "Why do you not sit down?" she inquired.

"Thank you," said Burgoyne, dropping down into a chair next to Selar. Burgoyne was leaning so far over toward Selar's side that she had to slide over a bit so as not to wind up with Burgoyne in her lap. That was a situation that certainly would not have been off-putting to Burgoyne, but was not something that Selar desired to explore at this particular moment in time.

"How may I be of service, Chief Engineer?"

"For starters, you can call me Burgoyne. Or Burgy. Most fother olks do."

It took the Vulcan a mere moment to realize that Burgoyne had meant to say "other folks," and somehow the letters seemed to have gotten away from hir, to say nothing of each other. Although the familiarity was uncomfortable to her, she opted to accede to hir requests rather than risk a protracted conversation. "Very well, Burgoyne. How can I help you?"

"Well, I thought that I could have helped you," said Burgoyne. S/he didn't seem particularly happy at the moment. "But I must have looked pretty foolish, huh? There I was, letting you know I was interested. Talking about how good we could be together. And it turns out you already have something going on. With the captain, no less."

"My involvement with the captain—whatever that may or may not be—is no concern of yours, Burgoyne. If you must know, I . . ."

Burgoyne looked up at her, hir eyes looking slightly bloodshot. "Yes?"

It was at that moment that Selar almost blurted all of it out. Not just the needs of *Pon Farr,* but the fact that she did indeed find Burgoyne attractive. Despite hir over-the-top approach, despite all of hir aggressive and devil-may-care theatrics—or perhaps *because* of them—Selar had slowly come to consider Burgoyne very desirable. So much so that she had been ready to give herself over to Burgoyne during one of the more aggressive flare-ups of her condition. But she had seen Burgoyne with Mark McHenry at the time. There had been something about the cavalier, casual way in which Burgoyne had managed to toss aside Selar and move on to someone else—of another gender, yet!—that had prompted Selar to back off from the Hermat. Had prompted her to look elsewhere for a suitable mate, one who might be just a bit more stable.

"If you must know," repeated Selar, "I find the captain . . . most attractive."

"Good for you!" said Burgoyne. S/he slapped hir hands together in loud applause, drawing looks of casual confusion from other officers sitting nearby. Selar quickly reached over, put her hands on top of Burgoyne's, and pushed them down to the table top.

Burgoyne's tapered fingers wrapped around Selar's for just a moment, holding them, and Selar felt a jolt of electricity between the two of them. It was insane. What the devil was it about the Hermat that caused hir to have this sort of effect upon Selar? Selar didn't know, and it was perhaps that very ignorance that she found the most off-putting. The captain she found suitable for a variety of intellectual reasons. That was something she could grasp. Burgoyne as a choice was totally and utterly illogical, and there was absolutely no reason in the galaxy for Selar to pursue such a relationship. None.

"I mean it," and Burgoyne sounded less blustering, more sincere. "Truly, I mean it. I want you to be happy, Selar. And if the captain is what you want, and if he's what will make you happy, then I would be the last person to stand in your way. I mean that. I value relationships too thoroughly to get between the two of you."

"I . . . appreciate that, Burgoyne. I do."

"Well, good." Burgoyne had still not released Selar's hand. And then s/he looked up at Selar with a look of mischief on hir face. "Threesome?"

"I . . . beg your pardon?" asked Selar.

"Well, I was simply curious, that's all," Burgoyne told her. "Have you ever tried a threesome?"

"I am not certain what it is you are referring to."

"I mean three people. Having sex. At the same time."

Selar stared at hir. "With whom?"

"With each other!" laughed Burgoyne. "I mean, I don't know the captain apparently as well as you do. But if that's something the two of you would be interested in exploring . . ."

"Three . . . together . . . simultaneously . . ."

"Yes, that's the general—"

"Burgoyne, that is not sex. That is a committee."

"Well, only if you start taking votes and things . . ."

"Burgoyne," and Selar began to rise from her chair, "I do not know how things are done on your world—"

"I have a book. With illustrations and footnotes."

"Keep it. We are . . . we are too different, that is all. I do not know why I even considered—"

"Considered?" The moment she'd mentioned the

word, Selar wished that she could have the sentence to say over again. But that wasn't possible, for Burgoyne had quickly picked up on the slip. "Considered what? Me? You and I? Us?"

"No," Selar said flatly. "I was going to say, I do not know why I even considered the possibility of talking to you simply as one individual to another. You are—"

"Dashing? Charming? Wonderfully open?"

"I believe 'insane' is the word I was searching for."

"I'll take that as a compliment. Insane, as in crazy about you."

"Burgoyne, you are intoxicated. It is prompting you to say things that you would not ordinarily say, which is, in and of itself, surprising to me, for you have rarely shown any restraint before in saying whatever comes to mind. But I believe you have set a new standard for yourself with this conversation."

"But I'm happy for you! Can't you see that? I'm just pleased you're not lonely!"

"Lonely?" She gazed at hir with what seemed a distracted air. "Do not dismiss the concept of loneliness, Burgoyne. There is much to be said for it. There is much comfort that one can take in it. Once one adjusts to loneliness, one can never be hurt again. Yes, indeed . . . loneliness is underrated."

"I can think of no worse, or depressing state, than loneliness," Burgoyne replied. "It can be all-consuming. It can and will destroy you. I can think of no sadder state."

"And that," Selar said softly, "is why you will do whatever you can to avoid it. Cast about for bed-mates, flirt shamelessly, do whatever it takes to make certain that you are not alone. I pity you, Burgoyne."

Burgoyne's face clouded. "Save your pity for some-one who needs it. I'm happy. Happy. You understand? Happier than you will ever be."

"As opposed to loneliness, happiness is overrated."

Selar left her drink behind as she headed out of the team room, Burgoyne calling after her, "It's been great talking to you, too!"

S/he plopped down into the chair Selar had just occupied, still feeling her warmth from the seat cushion. Burgoyne shook hir head. "Women," s/he sighed.

McHenry had entered the team room, and now he spotted Burgoyne by hirself. He strolled over to hir, reversed the chair and straddled it. "You look lonely, Burgy."

"You look off-duty, Mark."

"I am."

"You doing anything?"

"Well," McHenry told hir, "I'm reading a quantum physics review article."

"What?" Burgoyne looked at McHenry's empty hands, then over hir own shoulder to see if there was something visible behind hir. "What are you talking about?"

"I have a photographic memory," McHenry told hir. "Some new articles came through the ether this morning, but I didn't have time to sit down and read them. So I kind of glanced at them and just made mental snapshots. Now I'm pulling them out and reading them while we talk. Although if you find that distracting, I can stop."

"No, it's quite all right. About how much of your brain functions does that occupy?"

"Maybe thirty percent."

"I see," Burgoyne said thoughtfully. "And tell me, Mark," and hir small tongue strayed across hir distended canines, "how much of your brain function does sex require?"

"Fifty, maybe fifty-five percent."

"So what do you do with the remaining fifteen percent?"

"Overflow space," McHenry told hir. "In case some of the rest of it gets used up unexpectedly quickly."

"Well, I have an idea," Burgoyne told him. "Why don't we go back to my place and see if we can fill up the unoccupied space, okay?"

"Sounds like a good deal to me," McHenry grinned.

And later, when they were together, their clothes strewn about the floor, McHenry moving atop hir with easy grace, Burgoyne's fingers traced the curve of McHenry's upper ear, and s/he inadvertently whispered the name "Selar."

Fortunately, McHenry was engrossed in a particularly riveting footnote in the article and so didn't hear.

And in the meantime, several decks away, Selar tossed in her sleep and dreamt of a tongue gently caressing canine teeth . . .

Calhoun was sound asleep when he heard the buzzing of his room bell. From long habit, he snapped to full wakefulness. Calhoun had never been one for waking up slowly. Why give an opponent an opportunity to stick a sword between your ribs while you're busy rubbing the sleep from your eyes?

"Who is it?" he called, no trace of grogginess in his voice. He had already stepped from his bed and pulled on his robe.

"Shelby," came the reply.

"Shelby," he muttered. "How did I know. Lights. Come in."

The room lights flared on as the door slid open, and Shelby entered. She looked as if she hadn't been to bed yet, and had a great deal on her mind.

"Let me guess," he said, his hands shoved deep into his pockets. "You've suddenly realized that faster-than-light travel is an impossibility, and we should head home immediately before someone realizes and we all get in trouble."

"I can't agree with the decisions you've made lately," she said, the words coming out all in a rush.

"None of them? I mean, I was thinking about changing the part in my hair. Perhaps now I'd better reconsider it."

"I think this Messiah business is fraught with danger."

"Fraught? Eppy, it's"—he glanced at a chronometer—"it's oh-one-thirty hours. It's the wrong time of night to use words like 'fraught.'"

"I don't want you to be flip with me."

"Neither do I. I'd rather be flipping with my pillow, but you seem to have precluded that." He dropped down onto the bed. "Eppy, I thought we had this settled . . ."

"I've been thinking about it—"

"Obviously."

"And I think we have to set them straight, right at the beginning. Tell them no, tell them this Savior business is pure fiction on their part."

"How do we know that?" Calhoun replied.

"How do we *know?* Mac, you're not their Savior!"

"No man knows his destiny, Eppy. Perhaps I am. Perhaps their predictions got it right. If that's the case, then I'd be violating the Prime Directive by refusing to fulfill that destiny, since I'm already a part of their culture rather than something on the outside interfering with it. In any event, we'll see when we get there. Now if there's nothing else, don't let the door hit you on the way out." He pulled the blanket over himself, even though he had his robe on, and tried to find escape in the pillow.

"There's also the matter of Doctor Selar."

"Grozit. Here we go." He sat back up, stared at her for a moment, and then stood with his hands placed

firmly on his hips. "You know what your problem is? You're jealous."

"Jealous! Oh, get over yourself, Mac."

"I'm over me, but you sure as hell aren't. Why should you care whether I become Selar's lover or not?"

"Because there's questions of protocol! And because she's not thinking clearly!"

"She seemed quite lucid when she came in and asked me."

"She said herself that the *Pon Farr* can affect the way she thinks, affect her perceptions. I think that's the case here."

"Why? Because no woman in her right mind would consider me a suitable father?"

"And what about that?" she challenged him. "What's going to happen when she has the child, huh? Is she going to remain aboard the *Excalibur?* We're not set up for families the way other vessels are."

"I suppose we'll face that situation when we come to it," replied Calhoun. "There are always possibilities."

"And are you going to participate in the raising of the child? Or are you going to walk away from this one, too."

Calhoun's brow darkened. "That was uncalled for."

"Well maybe something is called for, just to get you to think about some of the things you're doing! To think about the damage you might inflict on Selar, or on the people of Zondar!"

"I'm providing a woman with relief for a medical condition, and I'm giving a race of people a shot at freedom. That sounds pretty laudable to me."

"Oh, Mackenzie Calhoun, the selfless martyr," retorted Shelby. "Admit it. This all appeals to your ego. The educated woman who picks you as the main stud on the ship, the race of people who think you're the second coming of God. It inflates your ego."

"No," said Calhoun, raising his voice slightly. "The only thing I'm getting any ego gratification from is the knowledge that you are so totally jealous of Selar and me that you're willing to come in here and make a complete jackass of yourself rather than stand by and watch me become involved with another woman."

"You have no idea what you're talking about." She threw her hands up. "I tried. God knows, I tried. I tried to make you see the error of your ways. I tried to make you realize the danger in what you're doing. If you don't want to listen to me, fine. If you want to risk exacerbating situations under the delusion that you're making them better, that is likewise fine. I don't care. I don't care anymore. I really, really—"

"Don't care. Yes, I get the picture." He tried to put his hands on her shoulders but she pushed them away. "Eppy, I know that look in your eyes. The sleep-deprived look. Once you leave here, you're going to go back to your quarters, and you're going to fall asleep, and when you wake up in the morning you're going to hit yourself in the side of the head and say, Oh God, what an idiot I made of myself last night."

"You just dream on, Calhoun."

"The moment you leave, that is precisely what I intend to do."

With an annoyed huff, Shelby turned and stomped out of the room, leaving an amused Calhoun behind shaking his head and wondering just what exactly he'd gotten himself into by taking command of this vessel.

"I've seen more stable nuthouses," he said as he flopped back into bed. "I bet Picard never had these problems."

IX.

THE HOME OF RAMED, as was typical for a Zondarian home, was heavily fortified. One never knew when there might be stray missiles flying, or when pieces of hurtling shrapnel would suddenly present a danger to life and limb. Nor was anyone there desirous of any intruders. The wandering packs of Unglza raiders were well known to all of the Eenza, and anyone who had the wherewithal to protect his family did not scrimp in the least little bit.

Most of the furniture was heavily curved, symbolizing the Zondarian belief that all was eternal. That what began had no end, and vice versa. Furthermore, most of it was bolted to the floor, so that vibrations from nearby explosions would not send them tumbling all over the place.

It was early in the morning, and Ramed's wife, Talila, had already prepared breakfast for herself and their young son, Rab. For the first time in a long time, she had moved about the house without the perpetual cringing in her shoulders, an involuntary spasm that haunted her most of her waking hours as she prepared herself for the sound of another shell dropping or another bomb exploding in the middle to near distance. There was a cease-fire throughout Zondar, and thus far it seemed to have taken hold. It was as if the entire planet was awaiting the coming of the Savior.

Talila felt so close to the actual event, particularly because it was her husband who was part of the inner circle. He who had studied the sacred writings of Ontear and Suti, probably with greater detail and scrutiny than virtually anyone else on the planet. When he had told her of the possible coming of the Savior, she had been unable to find words. Instead she had simply begun to cry, tears of joy pouring down her face so effusively that she couldn't begin to control them. Nor was she interested in trying.

Since Ramed had joined with Killick of the Unglza (whom she did not particularly trust, but Ramed seemed tolerant enough of him) to go to the Savior and convince Him to come to Zondar and fulfill His destiny, Talila had not known what to do with herself. Little Rab had asked every day since his father's departure when he would be coming back, and she had never known what to tell him. "A few days," Ramed had told her, but who truly knew what that constituted?

Talila had just cleared the breakfast dishes away, and was now preparing to teach Rab his morning lessons. Like most children in their particular sphere, Rab was home taught. It was not an unreasonable course of action. Both Talila and Ramed were, naturally, highly educated. And it saved Rab from having to make that potentially treacherous journey to school every morning. Instead she kept him safe and sound in their home, teaching him the wisdom of the Zondarians while protecting him from the foolishness of those very same peoples.

She heard Rab cry out, and immediately a chill cut through her. A woman in her situation automatically assumed the worst when hearing her child sound a cry of alarm, and she immediately went to the main foyer . . .

There to find Rab wrapped around the leg of his father.

Talila went to him quickly and embraced him with all the fierceness that her small frame commanded. "It seems as if you have been away for ages!" she said.

"I feel the same," he said, stroking the back of his wife's gleaming head. "It is good to see you, wife. Were there any . . . problems in my absence?"

The pause before the word was painfully significant. It was his understated way of inquiring as to whether there had been any threats to the safety of his wife or son.

"None, Ramed," she was happy to reply. "The cease-fire remains in force. It is as if our whole world is . . . is holding its breath. Tell me," and her eyes widened, "tell me what . . . He was like."

"He?" For a moment, Ramed didn't understand what she meant, and then, of course, he did. "The Savior."

"You saw Him, father?" asked Rab.

"Yes," and he embraced both wife and son. "Yes. I did."

"Did He have a . . . glow about Him?" Talila asked. "Did power crackle from His eyes? Did He perform any miracles for you?"

"He was . . . different than I expected."

"Different? How so?"

"He had power about Him. It was a quiet power, however. Almost an . . . an aura. A sense of command, of inner strength."

"As if He wanted to keep His true power hidden?"

"That could be," he agreed. "Yes, that would definitely be one way to look at it." He strode thoughtfully around his living room. "As if mere mortals such as ourselves should not—would not even want to—look at Him in display of His full glory. It might be too much for us."

"Did He know that He was destined to be our Savior?" she asked.

"No. No, it was completely a surprise to Him." He shrugged. "All of us have our places in the grand scheme, my wife. Sometimes we are aware of them, and sometimes we are not. Nonetheless we fulfill our purpose."

"I suppose you are correct. It's so amazing," she breathed. "To think that this would happen within our lifetime. Is He with you? Has He returned with you?"

"He is on His way," Ramed assured her. "We raced ahead to make preparations."

Talila turned to Rab and knelt down to face him. "I want you to begin keeping a journal, my dear. You are young yet, and the events might not be as clear to your recollection when you're older. So you should be able to look back at your words of this age as a sort of tunnel back through time."

"Yes, mother," Rab said agreeably. "Will you help me start it?"

"Of course. Let me just spend some time with your father first—"

"But I want to start it now," Rab protested. It was not an atypical reaction for a child. An idea that had not even occurred to him mere moments before had suddenly become the single most important thing in his world.

Ramed put a gentle hand on his wife's shoulder. "It's all right, wife," he said gently. "Be happy that the boy has embraced the notion. I need a short time to myself to collect my thoughts anyway. I shall be in my study for a bit."

"As you wish, husband." She brought his knuckles to her lips and smiled at him affectionately. She touched his face and whispered, "I have never been more proud of you."

He smiled in response as she went off with Rab to help him set up his journal. But then the smile faded as he retreated into his study.

He knew that Talila would not have entered it in his absence. She respected his privacy; indeed, she might even have been a little afraid of the room. Talila was a sweet woman, a good wife, a superb mother. But she was not the scholar or philosopher that Ramed was. When Ramed and the others in his clan would gather to discuss various fine points of Eenza law, or go over the predictions of Ontear and Suti to see how they applied to the modern world, she was a bit intimidated by it all. She would stand on the outskirts of the group, dart in and out of the room and pick up snatches of conversation, but she did not pretend to understand any of it. Nor did she have need to, really. She was married to a great man. In truth, that alone was really enough for her.

But because of the slight intimidation factor, she kept her distance from such places as Ramed's study. For any number of reasons, he found that preferable, although it was not as if he had ever given her explicit instructions not to enter. It was simply an unspoken understanding between them.

He stood in the middle of his study, drinking in the presence of the words. The shelves were lined with scrolls of knowledge dating back to ancient times, carefully preserved. There had been a movement to transfer that information to more modern, computer-oriented means of information storage, but the Eenza inner circle had fought that notion. There was something pure and sacrosanct about the preservation through writing, through that physical connection to those scribes who had taken the time to write down the words of wisdom those many centuries ago. It was more of a living history in this manner.

His eyes skimmed the repository of Eenza written tradition, each carefully preserved in their cylinders, but he did not focus on any one of them in particular. Instead he went to one cylinder in particular set in the lower right-hand section of the shelving. Unlike the others, however, it did not slide loose from its place in the rack. Instead he pulled on it and it pivoted on a hidden hinge. A moment later, a small section of the nearby wall swung open. Ramed reached into the hole in the wall and pulled out a scroll, older than any of the others on the wall. He unrolled it carefully on his reading table, clipping the upper and lower ends down so that he could read it flat and uninterrupted.

It was not as if he didn't have it memorized already. He had read it so many times that every word, every syllable was seared into his consciousness. Yet for some reason he derived some degree of affirmation, perhaps, by seeing the original writing once more. Words written by the divine Suti himself, as told to him in turn by the sacred Ontear at the time when the mysterious Great Wind had come down and whisked Ontear away to whatever his reward would be.

Words that had only partly found their way into the sacred texts of Zondar.

Ramed had never been entirely certain just how the original, unexpurgated text had wound up in the hands of his family. It had been given him by his father, who had in turn been given it by his, and so on. It was not as if Ramed was a direct descendant of Suti himself; to the best of anyone's knowledge, Suti had never married, never produced any offspring. The words of Ontear and the spiritual well-being of the Zondarians was the sum and substance of his entire life. He had never seemed to need anything more than that.

Perhaps he had passed the complete text to a trusted disciple, and he had held onto it until his passing was near, and in turn had given it to a trusted individual. It was nothing short of miraculous, really, that the scroll had found its way through the centuries to Ramed without word of its full contents filtering outside of the sphere of its caretakers.

There was something else that was in the same secret compartment as the scroll had been. It was a cylinder, about a foot long and made from wood. One side was closed off, the other end open. On the handle, a small emblem that looked like a flame was carved on it. He ran a finger over it lightly, as he had so many times before.

He extended the cylinder straight out in front of himself and pushed in firmly on the flame. And with a quiet *shak* noise, a sharpened rod snapped out of the end of the handle. It was telescoped in three places and extended to about a yard in length. As always, it felt incredibly light. Ramed swung it about him experimentally, satisfied at the whistling sound it made as it passed through the air. Then he lunged forward once or twice, and wondered what it would be like to drive it through the chest of a living, breathing being. Would it be possible? When the time came, would he have the intestinal fortitude to do what had to be done?

He thought of what he had just said to his wife. "All of us have our places in the grand scheme, my wife. Sometimes we are aware of them, and sometimes we are not. Nonetheless we fulfill our purpose."

He had his purpose. He had his own role that had been handed down to him. How would he be viewed, he wondered? As one of the great heroes of Zondar? As one of the most memorable traitors? Would he be a martyr to a great ideal that he, and only he, knew to be the truth? What would they say to his wife? What sort of torment would his son be subject to?

Perhaps the course upon which he was embarking was the wrong one.

He began to tremble. Whether it was in fear, in excitement, or in religious zeal over the rightness of his actions, he couldn't begin to say. All he knew was that he was trembling so violently, he couldn't even hold on to his weapon. It clattered to the floor, although the noise was minimal since the staff was so lightweight.

He dropped to his knees, waiting until the spasms passed. And all during that time, he prayed. Prayed to the shades of Ontear and Suti. Prayed for guidance.

"Please," he whispered to them. "Please . . . help me do the right thing."

He paused a long moment, then picked up the spear. He envisioned the Savior standing against the opposite wall. Standing there strong, confident. Ramed then drew his arm back, as he had so many times before, and hurled the spear. It flew lightly through the air and thudded into the far wall, the shaft quivering, the point squarely in the heart of the Savior.

"May the fates help me," he whispered. "And may the Savior, even in His death throes, have mercy on my soul."

X.

BURGOYNE SAT IN HIR OFFICE in engineering and studied the reports compiled by Ensign Beth, looking over them again and again until it felt as if the numbers were blurring in front of hir. S/he became aware that Beth was hovering nearby, probably looking rather concerned. S/he couldn't blame her, because the information that s/he'd been handed was less than useful. "So let me see if I understand this," Burgoyne said slowly. "We not only do not know what is causing this energy wave, but now it's causing a *drain* on the engines."

"Not exactly a drain, Chief," Beth said. "Look, follow the power curves. The energy reserves begin to build up exponentially. They reach a maximum point of somewhere around eighteen percent above the norm, and then they drain off, reaching standard levels. As if someone were topping off a glass of water and then sipping off the top so that it doesn't overflow. Bringing it down to a more reasonable level."

"But what's causing the overage?" asked Burgoyne

in frustration. "And when it's being drained off, where is it going? You don't think . . ."

"Think what?" asked Beth.

Burgoyne sat back, studying the readouts with just a touch of visible apprehension. "What if we've some . . . thing . . . living in there? Something sentient."

"A sentient energy creature?"

"We ran from one not too long ago," Burgoyne pointed out. Beth was forced to agree with that reminder. "If this is somehow connected with that . . ."

"Is there any way that we can determine it?"

"I'm not quite sure," said Burgoyne. "At the very least, we keep observing it. Also, we'll probably want to bring Soleta in on this. She's the science officer, after all."

"How about medical?" asked Beth. "If there's a living creature rooting around in our energy transfer ducts somehow, then maybe Doctor Selar can—"

"Let's leave Doctor Selar out of it for the time being," Burgoyne said after a moment's thought.

"Are you sure? Perhaps if we—"

Burgoyne turned, and hir canines were extended as s/he said, "Are you questioning my orders, Ensign?" Hir voice was very sharp, hir eyes narrowed and genuine anger was flashing within them.

"No! No, sir!" said Beth quickly.

There was such clear alarm in her voice that Burgoyne immediately felt chagrin. "Sorry, Ensign," Burgoyne said, the ire passing as quickly as it had made its presence known. "It's not your fault."

"I was hoping it wasn't." Beth paused a moment, and then said, "Chief . . . I hope I'm not overstepping myself here, but is everything okay between you and the CMO?"

"Okay?"

"It's just that any time she's mentioned for some reason, you seem to tense up. Personality conflict?"

Burgoyne considered several possible answers, but finally said, "You could say it's something like that."

"I know how it is," Beth said by way of commiseration. "Sometimes you just meet someone, and for absolutely no reason you can think of, you just connect on a negative level. You take an instant dislike to them. It's as if you have a bad history that goes back before the two of you even met."

"That is an . . . interesting way to look at it."

"Sometimes two people just click—like Christiano and I did," admitted Beth with a grin. "And other times, well, two people can't even work together without getting on each other's nerves."

"You're very likely correct, Ensign. It would probably serve us best if we didn't discuss it anymore." S/he went back to the energy wave readouts. "Look at this. This is interesting."

"What do you see, Chief?"

"During those periods when the energy drain slows down, it occurs when the *Excalibur* speeds up. The faster we go, the slower the energy drain. And when we go in excess of warp five, there's never any drain at all. Those are the points at which the energy wave indicates growth."

"That's right," Beth said slowly.

"Of course that's right," Burgoyne said archly. "I said it. Therefore, by definition, it's right." S/he drummed hir fingers in annoyance. "I should be able to figure this out more expeditiously," s/he said. "I've just got to get my mind clear."

"What's on your mind, Chief?" asked Beth.

And for just a moment, Burgoyne allowed hir thoughts to stray to a face that had a perpetual stoic pout, framed by the loveliest pointed ears.

"Just someone I can't work with," Burgoyne said with a trace of sadness.

On the bridge of the *Excalibur,* Calhoun leaned forward in the command chair and said, "ETA at Zondar?"

"Three hours, eleven minutes, sir," McHenry said crisply. As always, he didn't even bother to check his instruments. The first several times, it had been a bit disconcerting to Calhoun, and extremely so to Shelby, but by this point they were accustomed to it.

"Keep her steady on course, Mister McHenry," Calhoun told him.

"Steady on, sir."

Lefler glanced at the captain, who seemed to become involved in conversation with his first officer. Then, very casually, she sidled over from her post at Ops and murmured, "Haven't seen you around much after hours."

"Hmm?" He looked up at her, apparently surprised that she had come over. "What?"

"I said you're something of a stranger off-duty these days. Don't see you in the team room, or any of the usual haunts. What have you been up to?"

"Oh, that," said McHenry. "I've been busy."

"Busy . . . how?"

He shrugged as if it was no big deal. "I've been spending a lot of time with Burgy."

"'Burgy,' is it? Very friendly nickname to be using."

"Is it?" McHenry seemed unimpressed. "I didn't think so especially."

"So what do you guys do? Talk?"

"No, we have sex," McHenry said matter-of-factly.

Now, Lefler didn't fancy herself as a prude, but nonetheless she was still caught a little flat-footed by the frankness of his response. "Oh," was all she could think of to say.

"That's what you wanted to know, isn't it?" He seemed rather amused by her expression. He leaned toward her and said, "Robin, I may seem distracted all the time. I may seem in my own little world. But I'm not stupid. I know what you want to know. What's it like? What's s/he like? Right?"

Lefler squirmed slightly, suddenly feeling that she should be elsewhere. Anywhere else, in fact, which was odd considering she usually was the most frank and open of people. She made vague gestures in the direction of Ops and said, "I, uh . . . I should really get back to—"

But he put a firm hand on her wrist, and she was surprised at the forcefulness of it. The cheery manner never left his face, but there was strength in his grip that seemed at odds with the lackadaisical demeanor. "S/he's amazing, Robin," McHenry told her. "Very free, very open with hir body. Very eager to please, and also eager to be pleasured. The fact that s/he is both male and female probably adds to hir expertise, because s/he knows what men like and what women like. S/he sees life, love, and sex from all angles."

"That's . . . uhm . . ." Lefler found herself completely tongue-tied. She'd always considered herself something of a free spirit, a "party girl" who was open to all manner of experimentation. "And, you're, uh . . . you're not distracted by the, uhm . . ."

"The what?"

"The, uh . . . hir . . . *male* aspect? That doesn't, you know . . . give you navigational difficulties?"

"Not especially. It's nice to have someone who knows what a man wants."

"Oh? And what does a man want?" Lefler said challengingly.

McHenry looked her straight in the eyes. "If I tell you," he said, "will you be sure to jot that down so it can be in the next newsletter."

They laughed together at that point, and then Lefler said, "Lefler's Law number fifty-two: Never underestimate a man's ability to make you laugh."

"Laughing at a man is okay," McHenry said. Then, as an afterthought, he said, "Unless, of course, you're pointing while you're doing it. Laughing and pointing . . . bad combination."

Lefler laughed more loudly at that. She took care, however, not to point.

And then she said, very softly, "Do you love hir?"

"Love?" For the first time, McHenry looked uncomfortable. "We . . . haven't discussed that."

"Why not? Don't you think that's important?"

"To some people, yes. Not to me. I'm not interested in falling in love. I'm not sure how Burgy feels about it; I haven't asked hir."

"Why aren't you interested in falling in love, Mark?"

He stared at her. "Tried it once. It didn't take."

"Didn't take? Why not? I mean, if you don't want to tell me . . ."

McHenry seemed to stare off into space for a time. This was not atypical for him, but there was a different feel to it this time. "Mark?" she prodded gently. "Why didn't it take?"

He returned his gaze to her and smiled a sad little smile.

"She tried to kill me," he said.

Lefler's jaw dropped, and she tried to find a way to frame a follow-up question. But then from behind her she heard Shelby's voice. "Lieutenant, is there a problem? Something I should know about?"

Lefler stood up, smoothing the front of her uniform. "No, sir," she said briskly, all business. "Just consulting with Mister McHenry on some cross-checks."

Shelby nodded, apparently satisfied, but there was clear curiosity in her eyes. Lefler quickly crossed back to her station and sat. Several times for the rest of the shift, she glanced in McHenry's direction. Not once, in all that time, did he meet her gaze again.

Doctor Selar had taken a brief break, returning to her quarters to get some rest. She lay on her bed, able to feel the slow percolating of her hormones within her. She knew that the *Pon Farr* would be back in full phase before very long. However, she didn't wish to deal with it immediately. She knew that the ship was on a mission, heading for the world called Zondar. She knew that the captain was some sort of focal point for these people, and he had to keep his mind clear and focused. It would have been irresponsible for her, she felt, to pull Calhoun into the world of the Vulcan mating ritual at this particular moment in time. She had warned him of how all-consuming the interest in sex became once the Vulcan and her selected mate were in the throes of *Pon Farr,* but the fact that he had joked about it led her to believe that he did not fully grasp the reality of the situation. Since she herself knew what was to be expected, therefore, she felt the onus was upon her to try and act in as responsible and intelligent a manner as possible.

She decided to meditate a bit, to give her mind and body some time to calm down. However, a chime sounded at the door in the midst of her musings, disrupting her, throwing her off-balance. She had been reclining, but now she pulled herself to sitting, her legs securely folded. "Come," she said.

The door slid open, and to her surprise she saw Burgoyne 172 standing there.

"Doctor," s/he said, nodding hir head slightly in acknowledgment. "They said you were here in your quarters. It's nice to see that they spoke truly."

"Yes. I came here for the purpose of being alone."

"Ah. I see," said Burgoyne, stepping in so that the door slid shut behind hir.

"I do not think you truly do see," Selar pointed out, "considering the fact that you have entered my quarters, thereby precluding my being alone." She hesitated. "If there is a matter that you wish to discuss, Lieutenant Commander, then kindly do so and be done with it."

"I was just interested in . . ." S/he cleared hir throat. "I just wanted to congratulate you."

"I see. And why would that be?"

"Because of you and the captain," Burgoyne said. S/he felt a little odd that s/he had to explain it to Selar. Didn't she know the details of her own affairs? "It is my understanding that you and he are . . . involved."

"Very delicately put," Selar said with an ever-so-slight hint of surprise. "That is unusual, to say the least. You are not generally known for your delicacy. Rather, bluntness seems to be your stock in trade."

"You seem to be someone who prefers delicacy. I just . . ." S/he seemed to have trouble phrasing what was on hir mind.

"You just what?" prodded Selar, curious in spite of herself to see where the conversation was going.

"I just wish you had been honest with me."

"Honest?" Selar was far too controlled or thorough-going a Vulcan to allow outright astonishment to creep onto her face. Nonetheless, her surprise was evident if one knew where to look. "I have not lied to you, Lieutenant Commander."

"You asked me to leave you alone, without telling me why," Burgoyne said with ill-concealed annoyance. "Had you simply informed me of your involvement with Captain Calhoun, I could have avoided potentially making a fool of myself. Instead I pursued you, spoke to you of gentle relations, told you that I felt we were destined to be together . . . and all that time, you had an understanding with the captain."

Selar could have corrected hir, of course. Her relationship with the captain was, after all, a fairly recent development. It had purely been Burgoyne's misinterpretation, a mistaken assumption that Selar and the captain were involved with one another at the time that Burgoyne was making advances upon Selar.

Selar's discouragement of Burgoyne had had nothing whatsoever to do with the captain. She had simply found the Hermat so brazen, so aggressive, so over-the-top, that her gut reaction had been to keep Burgoyne at more than arm's length. And when Selar's position had softened, she had seen Burgoyne arm-in-arm with McHenry. At that point, Selar saw little reason to try and pursue Burgoyne in return. She did have her pride, after all. Something about her didn't want to give Burgoyne the opportunity to stand there with hir smirk and say, "Ah, now you want me." Nor did she want to feel like an also-ran to McHenry.

But Selar, who just wanted Burgoyne out of her quarters already, saw no reason not to take advantage of Burgoyne's perception. She had no desire to lie outright. It cut against her Vulcan grain. But she saw no harm in selective revelation of the truth.

"We have an understanding, yes."

"And may I ask what that understanding is?"

She cocked an eyebrow. "You may ask. But no answer will be forthcoming, since I owe you no explanations and since it is none of your business."

"Had a feeling you'd say that," s/he said ruefully. "I suppose, on some level, I agree. But you and I, Selar, we operate on a different level."

"Lieutenant Commander, *you* operate on a different level," Selar replied tartly. "I operate on the level of one who wishes to keep her private affairs private, despite all the best efforts of this ship's personnel to make it the business of the entire crew complement. I would ask you to respect that privacy."

"I do," sighed Burgoyne. "Believe it or not, I do." Burgoyne strode across the room to her and hunkered down opposite her. S/he smiled, displaying hir canines. "Selar, believe it or not, I wish you all happiness."

"Do you," Selar said, her voice inflectionless.

"Yes, I do. I want the best for you, and if you feel the captain represents the best . . . well, truthfully, I'd be hard-pressed to disagree. He is quite a man. And you are quite a woman."

"And you, Burgoyne," Selar said with attempted diplomacy, "are quite a . . ." Then she hesitated and finished with a mental shrug, "A person."

"I appreciate that. And I want you to know something: I still feel a connection to you, even though you obviously do not share it."

I do. But you are completely wrong for me, went through Selar's mind unbidden. Her face, however, remained inscrutable. "I do not . . ." She found it hard to say. She licked her lips, which were suddenly extremely dry, and continued, "I do not wish to cause you any pain."

Burgoyne waved off the notion. "Don't worry about that. I'm fairly resilient; takes a lot more than that to hurt me. But I want you to understand something." S/he took one of Selar's hands in both of hir own. Hir long fingers intertwined with Selar's. "I will always feel the attachment to you, whether you want it or not. Whether you like it or not. I will never do anything to cause you harm, and you will always be under my protection."

"I appreciate the sentiment that you—*ow!*" Selar was startled as she felt an abrupt prick of pain in the top of her hand. She pulled the hand away from Burgoyne's grip to find a small bit of green blood welling up on the top. There was a minute scratch there, and Selar looked up at Burgoyne. Despite her Vulcan training, surprise registered on her face as she saw a trickle of green blood on Burgoyne's fingernails. Selar had never really noticed before, but Burgoyne's nails were rather long, almost conical.

Burgoyne brought hir right hand up to hir face and daintily licked the blood off with hir tongue.

"What are you *doing?*" demanded Selar, rather put off by the entire business.

"Consecrating my promise to you," replied Burgoyne. The green liquid was already gone from hir right fingers. There was a small spot of the Vulcan's blood on Burgoyne's left hand as well; Burgoyne brought that up to hir nose and passed it under, hir nostrils flaring slightly, and then s/he licked that clean as well. "I hope I didn't startle you."

"To be blunt, you did. And I would prefer that you do not puncture, wound, or lacerate any other parts of my body unless you have been granted specific permission for that activity." She shook her head. "It is my desire to, at the very least, be able to tolerate you, Burgoyne. You are not making that simple, and such stunts as these do not endear you to me."

"They may someday," said Burgoyne, and then, with a lazy wink, s/he walked out of Selar's quarters, leaving the doctor shaking her head.

XI.

THE EXCITEMENT HAD SPREAD throughout Zondar as the *Excalibur* drew closer. Statues were being erected to Him. However, since descriptions of Him varied tremendously, one statue would look very different from another. That really didn't matter, though. It was, truly, the thought that counted.

Festivals were held. Parades were staged. There was a general air of euphoria upon the entire world. And, most importantly of all, the Eenza and the Unglza did not launch into immediate battles whenever any members of the two groups happened to run into each other. The cease-fire was in force, of course, but that was only part of it. The cease-fire, after all, was imposed from above by the respective ruling bodies of the Eenza and the Unglza. The true desire to get on with one another, however, had to come from the people themselves. And that seemed to be exactly what was happening. The people seemed to be viewing each other with a new eye, as if trying to contemplate what it would be like to be able to live side-by-side with their "enemies." And the speculation itself did not seem so intimidating once they were faced with the prospect. They began to envision a new age for Zondar, one in which they did not perpetually have to watch their backs against attacks from rival groups. An age where the Eenza and the Unglza would actually be able to work together, perhaps to develop something greater than either of them could accomplish on their own.

These possibilities were being discussed in all sectors of Zondar, including in the home of Ramed. There, Talila bustled about with tremendous excitement as Ramed watched her go about her business with a paternal sort of smile. "You are a one-woman hive of activity, Talila," he said, amusement in his voice.

She was unable to avoid saying what she had sworn she wouldn't say. "Am I going to meet Him, husband?"

"Him? You mean the Savior?"

"Is there any other 'Him' worth discussing these days on Zondar?" she asked reasonably, and he had to admit that she had a valid point. "At the convocation. Am I going to meet Him?"

He paused a moment before answering, as if preparing to discuss something that he knew was going to be very unpleasant. "You will not be attending the convocation, my wife."

She gaped at him, not quite willing to believe what she had just heard. "I am not going to come with you? But . . . but I have already prepared—and Rab! I told Rab that he would be coming as well! Husband! You are one of the foremost speakers of the Eenza! It cannot be that you—"

"This is my decision, Talila," he said flatly. "I must be focused on the matter at hand. I cannot be distracted by—"

"Distracted!" She made no attempt to keep the bitterness from her voice. "After all these years together, after all my time as your helpmate, aiding you wherever and whenever I could . . . is that all I am to you in the final analysis? A distraction?"

"That is not how I meant to . . ." He sighed and put his hands on her shoulders, but she pulled away from him. He stood behind her, looking saddened. "My wife, there are things I must accomplish at the convocation. Difficult, involved matters. I must be able to devote myself solely to the work that must be done for the purpose of saving Zondar. I cannot act in the capacity as husband, as father. I simply cannot. Talila," he said, not without compassion, "you have trusted me all these years. Trust me in this. If you never trust me in any other matter again, trust me on this. I know what I am doing."

Slowly, with clear frustration, she nodded. Obedience to her husband was ingrained as to be second nature, so she found that he couldn't quite help herself. But she was not happy about it. "I feel," she said softly, "as if you are being selfish, Ramed. Or perhaps you are simply embarrassed to have me as a mate."

"Embarrassed!" he said in surprise.

"I am not as wise as you. Not as learned. Perhaps you are ashamed to have me meet the Savior of Zondar. You feel that I am not good enough, or will reflect poorly on you."

Again he took her by the shoulders to turn her around, and this time she did not resist. "Your assumption could not be farther from the truth," he said firmly. "You must trust me on that as well. No Zondarian could be prouder of his mate than I."

He embraced her then, and she held him tight. And as he held her, he could not help but wonder if he was ever going to see her again.

* * *

The exact location of the convocation had been hotly debated, and had been solved in a rather unique manner. There had been no question that the convocation should be held in a temple, but naturally both the Unglza and the Eenza were at odds over whose it should be. With time ticking down and no immediate consensus apparent, an intriguing idea was suggested and immediately adopted. A special temple would be built that would represent the first co-venture between the two groups. Contractors, architects, builders had all assembled their workforces and thrown the temple together in what was not only record time for Zondar, but possibly for the entire sector of space. It was nothing fancy; more utilitarian than anything else. There wasn't time to do something with a lot of flourishes. It was spherical to represent the entirety of the world of Zondar, and two large hands were intertwined on the front—one presumably Eenza, the other Unglza.

At the appointed time, as the *Excalibur* moved into orbit around Zondar, the assemblage began. Killick was there, as was Ramed, of course. From the eastern territories arrived the Clans of Sulimin the Planner, Arbora the Unseen, and Freenaux the Undesirable (who showed up despite popular demand to the contrary). From the northern plains came the offshoot group of the Unglza known only as the Dissuaders, an arbitrarily negative group who intended to spend much—if not all—of the convocation trying to convince everyone else that they were wasting their time. From the western tropical region came Maro the Questioner, Quinzix the Unforgiving, Tulaman the Misbegotten, and Vonce of the Many Fortunes. All of them converged on the eastern territory where the Savior was to arrive.

The Zondarians were not entirely sure just how the

Savior was actually going to show up. There were rumors that He possessed transmat technology that far outstripped anything existing on Zondar. There were other rumors that He was, quite simply, a being of magic, who could come and go wherever and whenever He pleased. Walls were as nothing to Him, distances merely something to be traversed in an eye blink through force of will alone.

Nonetheless, to play it safe the Zondarians constructed the equivalent of a "landing pad." It was festooned with decorations, flowers, and greetings of welcome sent from all over the world. As Zondarians of all sizes, shapes, and castes converged on the spot, there was a festive atmosphere. Everyone felt that they were present at the beginning of what was to be a new golden age for Zondar.

The *Excalibur* had signaled down to the planet surface to let them know precisely when the Savior would be arriving, and they in turn indicated the precise spot that they desired Him to make His entrance. At the appointed time, Zondarians (some of whom had been waiting from the previous day) packed in the area. They kept a respectful distance from the appointed landing place, but were crushed in so tightly that it was believed a Zondarian could drop dead in the midst of the crowd and still remain standing just by dint of the crush of bodies all around. Unglza were pressed up against Eenza, and although the initial close contact prompted some grumbling, overall it was a fairly well-behaved throng, particularly considering that there had to be close to two thousand Zondarians crushed into an area that would have been better suited for half that number.

There was talking, there was chattering, there was singing, there was all manner of vocal discourse both loud and soft, and then slowly, as the appointed time drew near, it all trailed off into silence. All over Zondar, people began to look to the sky. No one knew quite what to expect. Perhaps the mighty vessel of the Savior might descend from the sky. Perhaps the Savior Himself would appear on a raft made of purest spun clouds. No one knew for certain.

And at precisely the appointed time, the Zondarians who were fortunate enough or highly ranked enough to be on the actual spot of contact heard a humming in the air. They looked up, looked around to see if they could determine the source. It sounded vaguely like their own transmat booths, but the sound was far more focused.

And then there was a collective gasp as Mackenzie Calhoun materialized out of thin air, his body a haze of shimmering sparkles that quickly coalesced into a human body.

There were two others, one on either side of him. One of them was instantly recognizable to many in the crowd as Lord Si Cwan, formerly of the Thallonian Empire. The other was a sight such as none on that world had ever seen. He was as wide across as any three Zondarians, and his skin was dark and leathery. He surveyed the crowd with eyes that were quite small, and yet seemed to take in everything.

And then a collective roar, a cheer, went up from the throat of the entire assemblage. The Savior's arrival had been simultaneously broadcast all through Zondar, and around the world the cheer went up as well.

It was certainly a good day for a rally. There were almost no clouds in the sky, which seemed to sparkle blue with hints of purple slathered across it, as if a painter had designed it and decided to toss in just a dollop of another color. The air was warm, even a little bit dry in his lungs.

At the forefront of the crowd were Killick and Ramed. They strode forward, bowing deeply in the presence of their Savior. They remained that way until Calhoun finally said, "Up. You can get up now."

They rose fully. "Savior," said Killick, forgetting himself long enough to genuflect, however briefly. "You will be interested to know, I think, that the prophecies regarding your coming state, and I quote: 'He will come from air and return to air.' You see? You have already fulfilled that portion of the prophecy."

"I didn't come from air, technically," Calhoun said, sounding reasonable. "I came from my ship. The air was simply an environment—"

"Savior," and Killick smiled beatifically. "You must learn not to question yourself or your destiny. Self-doubt ill suits you. The Savior will be—is—a man of character and determination who will unite the world. There is no place in that destiny for uncertainty."

Calhoun was about to debate the point further, but he saw how Killick, Ramed, and all the others were looking at him, and instead he simply shrugged graciously. "All right," Calhoun said, not wanting to sound unreasonable. "I will certainly accept your view of the events."

"Thank you, Great One." Killick seemed about to touch him on the arm, but then thought better of it, instead gesturing to the others in an encompassing sweep. "Everyone here has waited most eagerly for you."

"Greetings," Calhoun called to them, and a roar of approval went up. Truthfully, Calhoun felt a bit exposed and vulnerable with so many people packed in so tightly. His old warrior's antennae went up as he swept the crowd, trying to see some sign of danger. He knew that Zak Kebron, the mountainous security chief, was doing the exact same thing. It gave him a certain degree of confidence, but he was still duly suspicious and apprehensive of the situation. But it was hard to remain so in the face of such open and unstinting adulation.

Theoretically, this entire business should present no problem to him.

"We have private quarters prepared for you, Great One . . . and for you also, of course, Lord Si Cwan," said Killick. "And for . . ." He turned and looked at Zak Kebron, and tried to smile in amusement. "Well, I certainly hope that we have something large enough for you, sir. It is 'sir,' is it not?"

Kebron didn't bother to nod. He didn't even seem interested in acknowledging that Killick had spoken. But then he said, "I will need to remain in proximity to the captain."

"As you wish," Ramed spoke up.

They proceeded to leave, and the crowd parted before them. Many of them were bowing, or trying to reach up and ever so tentatively touch the trouser leg of Calhoun as he passed by. It was an odd sensation for him . . . and not entirely unpleasant.

"The quarters are quite nice, Commander," Calhoun said, speaking into the monitor as he glanced around. Indeed, "quite nice" understated it. They were rather posh.

From the bridge of the *Excalibur,* Shelby nodded thoughtfully, not caring overmuch what the quarters looked like but wanting to remain politely attentive. "And what is next on the schedule, Captain?" she inquired.

"They're having some sort of welcoming banquet

tonight. They want me to stay here overnight. And tomorrow, the peace talks begin in this temple that they've built."

"Is it necessary for you to stay there?" she asked cautiously. "Is there any reason you can't return to the ship? Security considerations would dictate—"

"I understand what you're saying, Commander, but I think I'll be safe enough here. Kebron's hovering over me, plus Si Cwan is busily paving the way; he's already having discussions with the assorted heads of their religious castes. This may be the simplest peace anyone's ever negotiated."

"I know, I know. That may be what makes me nervous. It seems too easy."

"Very little in this galaxy, Commander, is too easy."

"Watch yourself, Captain," she said cautiously.

"I always do. Calhoun out," he said. His image blinked off the screen to be replaced by the rotating orb of the planet.

She didn't like it. Anytime the captain left the vessel, it was asking for trouble. But obviously in this instance, there was simply no choice. Calhoun the Savior was who they wanted to see. She hadn't even asked Calhoun if he was trying to be circumspect in terms of how he was presenting himself to the crowd. The entire "anointed one" business was still fraught with peril, as far as she was concerned, from a Prime Directive point of view.

She hoped like anything that Calhoun wasn't making a mistake, and worse, that she wasn't just sitting around letting him make it.

Si Cwan was becoming slightly worried.

Certainly the enthusiasm for Calhoun was remaining consistent wherever he went. After being brought to his quarters and informing the Zondarians that the accommodations were more than adequate, Calhoun was paraded around the city. Wherever he went as he was escorted about, people lined up, cheering, shouting, waving. A number sobbed openly, so overwrought were they by his mere presence. It seemed to indicate to Si Cwan that the people were doing everything they could to embrace both the concept and reality of their peace-bringing Savior.

But the leadership, on the other hand, still had Si Cwan nervous.

For the assorted clans were more than just keepers of power. They were also maintainers of petty squabbles that seemed to go back generations. Sulimin was not speaking to Maro, Quinzix seemed totally disinterested in conversing with Vonce, and so on. Si Cwan had asked all parties involved in the discussions—and it was well over a dozen people—for a list of grievances to be discussed. He had been staggered to see that the list went on for page after page. Some of the disputes were centuries old; indeed, Si Cwan was astounded to discover that one of them involved a territorial dispute over land that had been victimized by shifts in tectonic plates and had, in fact, slid into the ocean two hundred years previously. But both the Unglza and the Eenza said that they had title to it, and were standing firm on one side or the other, neither admitting that they were in the wrong.

"Gentlemen, ladies, we must reach some accords here," Si Cwan said finally. He was addressing the group that was seated around a large round table. He noticed that they had split up so that they were sitting along caste lines. He was holding the list, but was doing so with all the enthusiasm of massaging toxic waste. "Rather than obsessing about the individual grievances, of which there are many, perhaps we might wish to get to the core of the disputes between the two groups. We acknowledge and understand that the Unglza and the Eenza have been at war with each

Star Trek New Frontier

other for nearly a millennium. But why? What began it? What set it off? I have studied your philosophies, your religious beliefs—they are fundamentally the same. There do not seem to be vast gulfs between you. Why, in short, are you not able to live in peace with one another?"

They looked at each other, scowling across the table, and then slowly Quinzix rose on somewhat shaky legs, for Quinzix was not as young as he once was. "The Eenza religion," he said slowly, "places the Eenza above all others on this world. It is their belief that, at the time of judgment, it will be the Eenza who are given preferential treatment at the hands of the one who sits in judgment over all. We of the Unglza believe that they are wrong. We believe that the Unglza will be valued most highly. And we consider it an affront to us, and a self-worshiping elevation of the Eenza, for them to think otherwise."

There were nods from around the table, or scowls, depending upon who was nodding. Tulaman now rose, casting an angry glance at Quinzix, who had remained standing. "He oversimplies, Lord Cwan. The truth is that once the Eenza and Unglza were as one. But individual caste and family members desired to take control of the leadership, determined to force out the Eenza leaders. To do whatever was necessary to take over the governing and land that they desired. It all comes down to territory, Lord Cwan, at its heart. That's what this dispute has always been about. Do not let them convince you otherwise."

There was already the grumbling of rising disputes around the table, and Si Cwan put up his hands for silence. "But this is absurd," he said. "Certainly we can come to some sort of arrangement. You're speaking of leadership struggles among people who have been dead for centuries, and philosophical debates about matters that will only be pertinent after those of

159

you at this table, and all of your constituents, pass away. In the here and now, there seems to be no reason—"

"The reason is, they are Unglza!" shouted Tulaman, stabbing a finger at Quinzix. Quinzix for his part trembled with outrage, and seemed prepared to shout back. All around the table, participants were starting to get to their feet, and Si Cwan could feel the rage bubbling through the room.

At that moment, the doors to the chamber opened wide. Calhoun entered, Killick and Ramed on either side of him, Zak Kebron directly behind him.

"Great One," murmured the various people around the table.

Si Cwan said, "Captain, it was my understanding that you would not be joining us here at the temple until tomorrow."

"I know," Calhoun said sounding disturbingly cheerful. "But there's only so much adulation one can take before one feels the need to accomplish a bit more with the day than just shake hands and provide spiritual comfort. So, my friends," Calhoun continued, briskly clapping his hands together and rubbing his palms as if preparing to deal a deck of cards, "what are we discussing?"

The summary did not go particularly well. Si Cwan attempted to outline the disputes in as straightforward and neutral a manner as he could, but it didn't appear to help. He was interrupted no fewer than three times and, by the end of the summation, arguments had erupted throughout the room. There was pointing, there was shouting, there were accusations, there were claims and cross-claims, threats of assault, threats of retribution, threats and more threats . . .

Kebron grabbed the table.

This was not a light table. It was solid metal, having sat in the home of one of the under-bishops of the

Eenza caste and having been donated to the temple specifically for the arrival of the Savior. It was ornately carved and it was massive. It had taken twenty Zondarians half a day, moving it with gravity negators which kept burning out, before they'd managed to transport the monstrosity into the conference room within the temple that had been set aside for it.

With the slightest of grunts, Kebron lifted one end completely clear of the floor. His leverage wasn't properly set for him to raise the entire thing clear, but nonetheless it was an astounding feat. There were gasps of astonishment, and the assembled Zondarians jumped back as Kebron then slammed the table back to the floor.

The clang of the metal on the floor was one of the most earsplitting things that anyone gathered in the room had ever heard. Nor was it confined to the room. The echo resounded throughout the temple and out into the street, where passersby stopped in their tracks at the sound of the massive chime emanating from the temple.

Everyone within the room was clutching their ears, save Calhoun, who simply stood there with a rather satisfied expression on his face. This was not done without effort; Calhoun's head was ringing no less than anyone else's, but he felt it necessary to maintain utter composure.

"Great One—" Killick started to say, but Calhoun silenced him with a glance. Then he looked back at the room full of assorted leaders.

"I've been out among your people," Calhoun said slowly. He circled the room, his hands draped behind his back. "While you were in here, tossing around accusations, defending a status quo built upon a legacy of bloodshed, I walked among the Zondarians, those whom you supposedly represent. And I saw faces filled with such eagerness, such hope. They offered up prayers to me, did you know that? They begged me to help them, just through my mere presence. I spoke to parents who are afraid to send their children to school, for fear that they will end the day burying the bodies of their beloved children. I spoke to people who came out of their homes for the first time in ages without fear, confident for the first time that there may be a hope for peace. There is still a great deal of suspicion out there, my friends." He stopped and put one hand on Quinzix's shoulder and the other on Tulaman's. "There is fear. There is anger. However, it's microscopic compared to the intensity and depth of hostility that I feel when I am in here. Now the people out there have bought into this 'Savior' business. I do not know that I have, especially. But if it will help your people, then you, my friends, will buy into it. You will work with me. You will work together. And if not . . ."

Suddenly the friendly hand on the respective shoulders of Quinzix and Tulaman increased in pressure, and he snapped both of them around so that they were facing one another. "If not, I will knock your heads together, with the aid of Mister Kebron here. Do I make myself clear?"

"Great One, you do not understand the difficulties—" began Quinzix.

At the same time, Tulaman started to say, "We will not simply accept, on their say-so—"

Calhoun knocked their heads together.

It was relatively gentle; he could have done it a great deal harder. But it made a very loud and satisfying thud when their skulls came into contact with one another. Both of them yelped in a most impressive manner, and Tulaman was immediately on his feet, although it was clear that the room was spinning for him somewhat. The others were looking on, aghast. *"Do you know who I am?"* raged Tulaman.

"Yes." In comparison to Tulaman's anger, Calhoun was the soul of calm. "And do you know who *I* am?"

Tulaman looked squarely into Calhoun's purple eyes, and saw the fearsome scar that seemed to be blazing a darker red than it had before. And Tulaman looked down. "Yes," he said reluctantly. "Yes, I do."

"Damn right you do," Calhoun told him. He took in the rest of the room with a glance. "This is not the first world I've brought peace to, gentlemen and ladies. When I last accomplished that, I was half the age I am now. I did it with the strength of my right arm and a refusal to see good people suffer anymore. Now I didn't ask to be your 'Savior.' You came to me. You wanted me to step in, to try and bring you a peace that has long been predicted but never really considered to be a possibility. Well, I'm here, friends, whether you still want me or not. Lord Cwan, Mister Kebron, and I, we are the negotiating team that is going to bring your dreams to fruition. I am the Savior, predicted, believed in, and trusted. Lord Cwan is the experienced negotiator, skilled in dealing with recalcitrant world leaders. And Mister Kebron here . . ."

"Breaks people in half," offered Kebron.

"Well put," said Calhoun. "We are in a life-and-death situation, my friends. We do not end this business until it is concluded to my satisfaction. Anyone who stands in the way of that . . . Well, Mister Kebron here will make certain that any man who blocks the peace process will die a man of parts. Do we understand each other?"

There was a collective numbed nodding of heads from around the table.

"Excellent," said Calhoun with remarkable cheerfulness. "That being the case, my friends, let's get to work."

The official banquet that night was remarkably festive. There was a sense of exhilaration in the air, largely because so much had been accomplished. Whether it was from a genuine desire to help the good people of Zondar, or whether from an equally genuine desire to keep all their limbs intact, the religious and caste leaders of Zondar worked with an amazing amount of effort in negotiating various treaties, agreements, and the like.

After his initial threats of violence, knocking heads, and dismemberment, Calhoun had been surprisingly quiet. It was not necessary, he felt, to be a continued intimidating presence. Rather he came to regard himself as something of a sergeant-at-arms. One who both inspired the peace and then made sure it was enforced. Si Cwan, for his part, handled the actual "dirty work," as it were. His familiarity with the long-standing hostilities of the Zondarians, as well as his own previous experience in creating an enforced peace on Zondar, served him extremely well. By the end of the day when they discontinued talks to allow for the celebratory banquet, everyone in the room felt that they might actually have something genuine to celebrate.

The dining hall was elaborately festooned with decorations. Alcoholic libations were flowing freely, and there was much laughter and polite discourse. Arbora the Unseen was spotted repeatedly as she pirouetted across the dance floor. Maro the Questioner was seen fielding questions from Vonce of the Many Fortunes. The Dissuaders, under the watchful and threatening eye of Zak Kebron, kept more or less to themselves, got quietly drunk, and wound up having to be picked up from under the tables.

Through it all, and above it all, Calhoun watched the festivities.

And felt concerned.

Calhoun had always had something of a sixth sense for danger. It was hardly infallible, to be sure, but there was something there. He'd even been tested for it at Starfleet Academy, and researchers had found nothing in particular. Calhoun's contention was that there was nothing to find because, during the research, no danger was present. Ultimately, whether they found something that they could justify or not was of no consequence to Calhoun at all. He simply knew that he had a sort of "warrior's instinct" for danger. It might have been based upon his being able to look over a situation, instinctively know that something was wrong, and act accordingly. It might have been something on a psionic level. It might have been plain old dumb luck; after all, if one was suspicious all the time (as Calhoun was) and if one faced an assortment of people who wanted to kill one (as Calhoun had) then it was only natural that one would say, "Ah-hah! I had a feeling something was up!"

Whatever the reason, whatever the cause, Calhoun was concerned that danger was present during this festive occasion. He couldn't place exactly what the source was; his instinct wasn't always that specific. But in this instance, he felt a general free-floating apprehension. He wondered if Shelby hadn't been right and perhaps the smart thing to do was return to the ship. But something in him railed against the idea. He had talked tough. He had threatened, he had badgered, he had cajoled, and, above all else, he had acted with supreme confidence. To tuck tail and run now just because he was having an attack of nerves just didn't sit right with him. It stung his pride.

Something Shelby had said to him any number of times rang in his head: "Pride Goeth Before a Fall."

He was aware of someone at his side, and he glanced over to see Si Cwan there. Cwan was regarding him with what seemed to be a mixture of disapproval and amusement. "I am not entirely certain, Captain, whether Commander Shelby would approve of your negotiation style."

"It's hardly my universal approach to situations, Lord Cwan," replied Calhoun. A server brought him a large glass of wine. He sniffed it experimentally, sipped it slightly, and wasn't thrilled with the taste. He put it aside. "In this instance, the people of this world have endowed me with a tremendous amount of power through their perception of me. There's a good deal to accomplish on this world, a lot of walls to deal with. In some cases, I try to get around a wall. Other times I try to burrow under it. In this case—"

"You're simply smashing directly through it."

"Exactly. It's direct, it's simple—"

"And it leaves rubble in your wake."

"These people need help, Cwan."

"No argument there, Captain. But Commander Shelby was right; we must tread carefully. After all, in using your strength as their savior to ramrod through needed changes, you run the risk of their becoming dependent upon you in order to do what needs to be done."

"I certainly hope you're wrong about that, Cwan," replied Calhoun. "It's daunting enough having the crew of the *Excalibur* dependent on me, and that's in my job description."

He looked out upon the celebration once more. "Look at them, Si Cwan. They're happy. They have hope. We're responsible for that. Does it matter how we get them to that point?"

"Yes," Si Cwan said immediately.

"Let me remind you of something, Cwan: Your hands aren't exactly clean in this matter. It was your people who forced a cease-fire down their throats by blowing up part of their geography. The Thallonians set the precedent. If I have to stay consistent with that in order to accomplish what needs to be done, well, I may not be happy about it, but that's what I'll do."

"I don't know about that, Calhoun."

"Don't know about what?"

"About your not being happy about it. I think you're perfectly happy about it." He leaned forward and Calhoun smelled the whiff of alcohol on his breath. Si Cwan was definitely speaking with a looser tongue than he usually had. "Just between us, I think you're a bloody bastard who'd just as soon throw himself into a fight as walk away from one."

Calhoun smiled thinly. "And why do you think that, may I ask? That I'm a bloody bastard?"

"Because," Si Cwan told him, "it takes one to know one." He winked heavily, rose to his feet and walked away with an ever-so-slight swagger.

A moment later, Zak Kebron was looming over Calhoun. "Captain," he said softly—which, for him, was a low rumble—"do you wish to return to the ship?"

From nearby, Killick's voice shouted out, "To the Savior!"

Everyone in the room echoed the sentiment, repeating the word "Savior!" or "Calhoun!" and his name rose in volume, thundering through the room, out into the streets beyond. And in the streets, people took up the chant, shouting, "Calhoun! Calhoun!"

And for a moment, just a moment, he was back on Xenex. Back in his heyday, with the mobs of warriors shouting his name as he would stand there, sword raised triumphantly over his head, declaring that

Xenex's oppressors would be driven from the surface of the planet, even if it took his dying breath.

He had never realized just how happy he had been at that moment. In a bleak fashion, he couldn't help but wonder if perhaps his best days weren't already long behind him. No matter what he accomplished, in many ways it would be nothing more than a mere rehash, a shadow of that which he had achieved so many years ago.

Calhoun drank it in. And for the first time in a long time, he was happy.

Shelby did not sleep well that night.

She tossed and turned, unable to get comfortable, and visions of Calhoun filled her head. Calhoun in pain, Calhoun in danger. When she awoke, she was covered with sweat, her simple white shift clinging to her body. Despite the constant, comfortable temperature of her cabin, she felt as if she were suffocating.

"Damn the man," she whispered. "Damn the man."

She called out in the darkness, cursing herself silently even as she did, "Shelby to Calhoun." At the command of her voice, the computer-operated comm system immediately patched her through to Calhoun's comm link. She knew that he would awaken instantly, as he always did. When they were together, it had always bugged the hell out of her. She couldn't so much as sneak out of the bed to go to the bathroom at night without Calhoun coming to instant, immediate wakefulness.

At this point she was prepared for the reception she knew she'd get. The confused and irritated voice, the demand to know why she had bothered him so early in the morning. He might even take offense that she had so little faith in him that she felt the need to check up on him.

What she was not prepared for was the dead silence on the other end.

Moments before she had felt mild alarm and major embarrassment over endeavoring to get in contact with her captain. Now the "mild" and "major" considerations had switched positions as her alarm swelled and her embarrassment evaporated. "Shelby to Calhoun. Captain, report in," she said more loudly, as if he'd have a better shot at hearing her from the planet's surface if she raised her voice.

Still nothing.

She had fully risen from the bed, and once more she said, "Shelby to Calhoun. Damn it, Mac, report!" She didn't wait more than half a heartbeat before switching and saying, "Shelby to Zak Kebron."

This time there was only a pause of a couple of seconds, and then Kebron's voice responded. "Kebron here. Go ahead, Commander."

"I'm trying to reach the captain. He's not responding."

"On it," was the terse reply. And then she heard what sounded like a crash, and shouting.

And barely a minute or two after that, Kebron reported back—and Shelby felt as if her life were spinning away.

Kebron had been sleeping lightly, as he usually did.

He was fully dressed, as was his custom. Furthermore he had discovered some time back that he rested best when he was on his feet. The Brikar security chief would stabilize his balance, becoming about as moveable as an Easter Island statue, and then he would consciously slow down his body functions to an even slower state than they usually were. Even in his semi–dream state, however, he remained alert and aware.

He had offered to stay within the captain's quarters,

but Calhoun had told Kebron that it wasn't necessary. Kebron couldn't help but observe that the captain certainly carried his warrior's pride close to the surface. He hadn't even wanted Kebron to stand directly outside his door. "I'm supposed to be the most worshiped individual on this planet, powerful and unafraid," Calhoun had told him. "How is it going to look if I have to hide behind my security chief?"

So Kebron had settled for being in the room next door and resting as lightly as he possibly could. Consequently he had come around immediately when Shelby had summoned him.

When he learned that the captain was incommunicado, Kebron did not hesitate. He and Calhoun had had adjoining rooms, but they were not connecting. A second later, however, they were indeed connecting, as Kebron charged forward and slammed one of his massive shoulders into the wall. It bent from the impact, shuddering. Kebron backed up a few steps and then barreled forward once more, and this time succeeded in plowing directly through. Mortar and rubble rained down around him as Zak Kebron stumbled slightly, but righted himself as he entered the captain's quarters.

He wasn't entirely certain what he had expected to see, but the sight that greeted his eyes certainly wasn't it.

Assorted members of the Zondarian ruling and religious castes were grouped around the bed that Calhoun had presumably been lying in. The sheets, however, were in disarray, and there was no sign of the captain anywhere.

The smashing down of the wall was hardly subtle, and the others looked around in shocked confusion as Kebron stood there, quickly brushing off the powder and traces of dust. His eyes had narrowed to a diamond-hard glitter as his gaze focused on Killick. "Where's the captain?" he demanded, and his voice was a terrible thing to hear. The men and women assembled in that room were the cream of Zondarian society, the best and brightest that their people had to offer. The masters of their race who feared nothing and no one. And every single one of them trembled upon hearing that voice. "Where . . . is . . . the captain?" Kebron repeated.

"He . . ." Killick seemed anxious to try and find the words, and was unable to frame them. He looked helplessly to the others.

It was Tulaman who stepped forward, doing everything he could to steel himself for the purpose of facing down Kebron.

"The Savior is dead," said Tulaman.

XII.

KEBRON SLOWLY STARED around the room before his gaze returned to, and focused on, Tulaman.

"What are you talking about?" In direct contrast to his bulk, his voice was at that point so soft that everyone in the room had to strain to hear him.

"We . . ." It was Killick who answered. "We sought the advice of the Great One on a matter of some debate—"

"At this time of morning?"

"The Savior had told us that, had we any questions, we were to ask Him regardless of time. We believed Him, for anything He told us was, naturally, true. We came here, to His room, knocked on His door, and when He did not respond to our summons, we came here and found Him—"

"Found him what? Where is he?"

"He was dead, Kebron," Tulaman said with certainty. "With my own eyes, I saw. His head to one side, eyes wide open, mouth partly open. It is my belief that He suffered some sort of seizure and simply . . . died. Heir to the frailties of the flesh, as much as any other man."

"Indeed." Kebron's voice was so flat, so monotone, that the Zondarians at first thought that he had failed to grasp the severity of the situation. "Where is the body?" he asked.

"He was removed from here, of course," Tulaman said. "None but the highest of the high in our caste— the wisest, the most holy, the most educated—would be worthy of seeing the deceased body of the Savior Himself."

"I want to see the body immediately," Kebron informed them. "Providing it can be produced, which I am beginning to doubt. He will immediately be returned to the *Excalibur* for proper medical treatment."

"Treatment!" Tulaman was beginning to sound annoyed with statements that he considered to be beyond obvious. "What treatment is there for a dead man?"

"If he is dead, then none. If he is not, then I will go through each and every one of you until he is found. Bring me the body of Captain Calhoun, Tulaman."

"Impossible," said Tulaman with conviction.

"Wrong answer," Kebron informed him. And before Tulaman could say another word, Kebron's right hand swung around with what seemed a very slow, relaxed manner. The back of his three-fingered hand struck Tulaman squarely in the side of the head. Kebron had judged the impact quite precisely; if he'd hit Tulaman with any greater force, he'd easily have caved in Tulaman's skull. As it was, the eyes of Tulaman the Misbegotten rolled up into his skull and he fell without another word.

The others stood there in stunned silence, and then Kebron turned to Freenaux and said, "Bring me the body of Captain Calhoun, Freenaux."

"That . . . that isn't possible," Freenaux started to say. He got as far as "That isn't," however, and then his unconscious body joined Tulaman on the floor.

"Wrong answer," Kebron informed the insensate Freenaux, and then he surveyed the remainder of the room's inhabitants. "Sulimin," he said. "Bring me the body of Captain Calhoun."

"Right away, Lieutenant Kebron," was Sulimin's rather panicked reply.

This satisfied Kebron as being the right answer. Then he walked back into his quarters through the rubble of the wall and tapped his commbadge. "Commander," he said as soon as he had Shelby on the line. "This is Kebron."

"Report, Lieutenant," said Shelby, and he could tell that she was keeping her voice steady with effort.

He paused, contemplating the best way to put it, and decided that ultimately there was really only one way to say it. "Commander, Captain Calhoun is missing and presumed dead."

There was total silence on the other end, and for a moment Kebron thought he'd lost contact. "Commander?" he prompted.

"I heard you, Kebron," and there was cold fury in her voice. "What the hell happened?"

He told her in as quick strokes as he could, and when he finished, Shelby said, "Stay on post there. I'm coming down with Doctor Selar immediately. The three of us are going to find out exactly what the hell is going on. Because I'll tell you right now, Kebron, the Mackenzie Calhouns of this universe don't just die quietly in their sleep. They die with their teeth firmly buried in the throats of their adversaries."

"Understood," Kebron said.

And he waited for the advent of Commander Shelby.

* * *

Shelby steadied herself in her cabin, determined not to let the world swirl around her as it was threatening to do.

It couldn't be that Mackenzie Calhoun was gone. It simply couldn't be.

It was some sort of bizarre trick. That had to be it. It was the only thing that made sense. The Zondarians were trying to pull some sort of . . . of spectacular hoax. And she was going to make damn sure that it failed.

"Shelby to Selar!" she shouted, much more loudly than she had intended, even as she yanked her shift off and fumbled for her uniform out of the closet.

"Selar here," came the Vulcan's voice. She sounded sleepy but alert.

"We're going planetside, doctor. The captain is missing, and the Zondarians claim that he's dead. We're going to find him. Meet me in the main transporter room."

"I shall be there immediately," said Selar. There was something to be said, Shelby realized at that moment, for having a Vulcan for a CMO. There were no emotions, no histrionics, no demands to know what had happened. She knew that the moment she arrived in the transporter room, Selar was going to be standing there waiting with her medical equipment and an entirely business-oriented demeanor. She would ask no questions beyond what she needed to know in order to deal with a medical emergency. There was no excess verbiage required by her.

"Shelby to security," she continued, and upon receiving the acknowledgment, said, "I want two security officers, heavily armed, to meet me at the transporter room." She had no intention of screwing around with the Zondarians: When she went in, she was going to go in with a show of force. Shelby finished dressing, charged out of her quarters, and was at the transporter room, as it turned out, in just under three minutes. Selar was standing there waiting for her. Shelby's hair was disheveled, her manner one of barely contained anger, outrage, and confusion. Selar, on the other hand, looked calm and cool. For one moment, Shelby found that she no longer appreciated Selar's unflappable demeanor. Instead she discovered the truth of the age-old adage, namely that misery loves company. The security guards, Hecht and Scannell, were there as well. They had obeyed her instructions to the letter. Hecht had heavy-duty hand phasers strapped to either side of his uniform, looking for all the world like a cowboy. Scannell had a phaser rifle slung under his arm.

"Very impressive, gentlemen," she said with approval.

Ensign Watson had just taken position behind the transporter controls, and she immediately configured the coordinates for the point of transmission from which Zak Kebron communicated mere minutes before. "Energize!" called Shelby as she stepped onto the platform, a slightly sloppy maneuver that could have had a costly effect. If Watson hadn't been paying attention and simply activated the beams on command, the front portion of Shelby's body would have preceded her to the planet's surface. As it was, Watson was cautious enough to wait until Shelby was completely on the platform before beaming her down to Zondar.

Kebron was waiting for her when the four of them arrived seconds later. Kebron glanced in acknowledgment at Hecht and Scannell. Had he so chosen, he could have expressed annoyance that the bringing out of security guards without clearing it through him was a breach of protocol, but he didn't bother.

"Where was his room?" demanded Shelby without preamble.

Instead of answering, Kebron led her to the quarters where assorted Zondarians were still milling around in what appeared to be barely controlled chaos. Shelby spotted Killick, the one Zondarian she recognized, and without even bothering to offer greetings, said, "Where the hell is the captain?"

The question prompted a barrage of responses, not just from Killick but from everyone around. As Shelby tried to sort out who was saying what, she started to hear something else as well. A chorus of voices, but it was not coming from within the temple. Instead it rose from outside, high-pitched and frightening in the depth of its grief. A thousand voices, more, rising as one and giving vent to some sort of deep-seated mourning. "What is that?" she demanded, but even as she asked, she already knew.

"Word of the Savior's passing has spread to the populace," said Killick. "They are bemoaning the passing of—*urkh!*"

The last part of the sentence came as a result of Shelby's hand at his throat.

Killick gasped, unable to get air to his lungs, as Shelby pushed him up against the nearest wall with astounding force. She was unaware that Kebron had already knocked cold two of the Zondarians. It's unlikely that, even had she known, it would have made the slightest difference in how she conducted herself.

Hecht and Scannell looked at each other, and the same thought was clearly on both their faces: They weren't entirely sure what Shelby needed with additional security guards. She was turning into a one-woman army.

Through gritted teeth, she said, "Understand: I am not a morning person. And on mornings where my commanding officer supposedly dies—and vanishes—I am really, truly, not someone that *you want to* groz *with!"* she finished, her voice rising in volume. "Don't you dare stand there and tell me that Captain Calhoun is dead unless you are prepared to produce a steaming corpse. And if you can't do that, then you had damn well better be prepared to bring him here safe and sound. Have I made myself clear?"

A thoroughly intimidated Killick nodded his head. "I . . ." and his throat was so choked that the word was virtually inaudible. Shelby removed her hand and Killick tried to straighten his garments and repair the disarray that he was in. "I found the body myself. Lying in the bed, staring off into the abyss to which we are all destined."

"Some of us," Kebron rumbled, "may be destined sooner than others."

The threat was not lost on Killick or anyone of the others in the room. "We are . . . locating the Great One's body . . . even as we speak," Killick assured them, "so that you may see for yourselves the tragedy of this event."

"Very wise," she told him flatly. "And let me tell you one thing right now: God help you if there is any sign of foul play. Because I swear to you, if one of you brought harm to the captain, then I will bring you to justice or, failing that, I will bring this place down around your ears. Have I made myself sufficiently clear on that point?"

There was mute nodding from all around.

Selar, for her part, was running the medical tricorder over the bed that had been occupied by Calhoun. She checked the readings once more, and then gestured for Shelby to come over and join her. Shelby did so, leaving Killick rubbing his throat. The others gave her a wide berth as she passed. It would have been a tough call to determine at that point who was more intimidating to the Zondarians: the mammoth

Zak Kebron or the smaller but extremely vicious Elizabeth Shelby.

"What have you got?" she asked.

"It is difficult to be certain, but I am reasonably sure that the captain did not die in this bed."

Shelby felt the first bubble of real hope beginning to surface in her heart. "Why do you say that?"

"The humanoid body, when it ceases function, does not generally do so in a neat or tidy manner," Selar said. "The bowels and bladder relax and evacuate any matter left in them, or there is excretion of—"

"I get the idea," Shelby said quickly. "You're saying that there's usually some sort of physical trace left behind."

"However minute it might be, yes," Selar said. "But in this instance, I find nothing. Not so much as a stray bit of spittle on the pillow."

Shelby wasted no time, turning immediately back to Killick and saying, "You're lying to me, Killick."

"I am not! As the Savior is my witness—" He stopped, realizing the inappropriateness of the statement. It was a reflexive comment, one that he had made any number of times throughout the years before there was an actual, flesh-and-blood Savior to which the invocation could be attached. "I swear to you," he amended. "It is as I described it. His body was right there. He was not, to the best of my ability to ascertain, alive."

As he had been speaking, Selar had had her tricorder focused on him. "Commander," she said, "I believe he is telling the truth."

"Are you sure?" asked Shelby.

"To a ninety-eight percent probability," Selar told her, showing her the tricorder readings. Shelby, of course, did not quite understand what she was looking at, but was loath to admit it, so she feigned thoughtful expertise as she regarded the readings.

"Making allowances for the stress of the moment, his pulse and respiration remained relatively close to the Zondarian norm when he was making the statements. Either it is the truth, or at the very least he believes it to be the truth."

"What is going on in here?" came the startled voice of Si Cwan. He was standing in the doorway, having thrown a robe on, looking around in confusion at the assemblage before him. He took it all in in a glance, and then his face darkened as he said, "What happened to the captain?"

Kebron, ever suspicious, said, "How do you know that something happened to the captain?"

"In the name of the gods, Kebron, I'm not completely dim," retorted Si Cwan. "Everyone is standing here looking disconcerted, there's no sign of Calhoun, and Shelby, Selar, and two security goons have shown up. One does not have to be a detective to figure this out."

At that moment, one of the servants to Killick came running in, looking extremely concerned. He motioned for Killick to come over to him, and Killick did so. What followed was a rapid exchange of words, with Killick looking increasingly disturbed, shaking his head in what was clear disbelief. Shelby tried to listen in on what they were saying, but it was hard to hear anything—even her own thoughts—over the wailing and moaning that was coming from just outside. As this happened, Kebron quickly outlined the situation for Si Cwan. The red face of the Thallonian noble became darker and darker by the moment.

Finally, looking for all the world as if he'd rather be anywhere else, Killick turned back to them and cleared his throat apprehensively. "The Savior's body is, uhm . . ."

"If you say 'cremated,' you're next," Shelby told him in no uncertain terms.

"No, but it is . . . it is gone."

"Gone," said Si Cwan in astonishment, beating Shelby and Kebron to the punch by a fraction of a second. "What do you mean, gone?"

"It was brought to a sacred place of preparation, where only the noblest and best of Zondarians are taken for handling," Killick said. "But we have checked there now, and there does not seem to be any sign of him. It has . . . has disappeared. The only thing remaining is . . . is this," and he held up Calhoun's communicator badge.

Before any of the *Excalibur* crew could say anything, Vonce spoke up, and it was in a voice that was filled with joy and reverence. "It is a miracle!" he cried out. "It is as Ontear foresaw! A miracle, I say!"

"What are you talking about?!" demanded Shelby.

" 'He will come from air and return to air!' " Vonce explained eagerly. "Don't you see? The prophecy has been fulfilled! He came from air, via your transportation device. And now, with His passing, He has vanished into the air as well! There is no trace of Him to be found! We are dealing with the miraculous, I say!"

"Don't be a fool!" said Maro the Questioner. "We are dealing with thievery! Thievery of the most vile and depraved sort! That is what faces us! Thievery on the part of the Unglza, who are probably behind all of this!"

This immediately prompted a firestorm of protest from the Unglza representatives, a chorus of agreement among the Eenza present, and a few holdouts who agreed with the miracle theory postulated by Vonce.

Shelby pulled out her phaser and discharged it once

skyward. She only had it set on stun, so the result was simply a very loud noise rather than any damage being done. It was, however, enough to immediately seize their attention.

"We," she said with great control, "are going to look for the captain. We are going to operate on the assumption that he is alive, well, and being held by person or persons unknown. We will find him, make no mistake. And when we do, if we discover that any of you had any involvement in this matter . . ."

She let the threat trail off, reasoning that whatever they might come up with would likely be far more frightening than anything she could possibly say.

"Shall we . . . shall we bring you to the last known location of his body?" asked Killick.

"That should not be necessary," Selar said. "Commander, with your permission . . . ?"

"Whatever you have in mind, Doctor, I'm all ears," Shelby told her.

Selar tapped her comm link and said, "Selar to transporter room."

"Transporter room, Watson here."

"Watson," Selar said, "I require your aid in locating Captain Calhoun."

"Yes, Doctor," came back Watson's voice. "Uhm . . . how are we going to go about that?"

"Elementary, Watson," said Selar, and she was about to continue when she was interrupted by a rather surprising guffaw from Shelby. She looked questioningly at the commander. It hardly seemed the time for any sort of levity, and she was at a loss to determine just what it was that Shelby considered so funny. Shelby waved it off and gestured for Selar to continue.

"Doctor?" came Watson's mildly confused voice.

"We have the captain's DNA records and molecular

patterns in the transporter buffer files," continued Selar after one more puzzled glance at Shelby. "Use the shipboard computer medlink and download that information directly into my medical tricorder."

"Will do, Doctor. Give me a minute to pull up the pertinent data. Keep your tricorder on in order to ensure proper information retrieval."

"Understood."

While they were waiting for the information to be processed, Shelby turned to Si Cwan. "I want you back on the ship," she said.

"What?" demanded Si Cwan. "For what purpose? If I remain here——"

"If you remain here, you could wind up in the same trouble that the captain's in, whatever that may be," Shelby told him. "I'm not going to have any more dealings with these people until we know exactly what's going on around here. Nor am I going to have any non-Starfleet personnel putting themselves at risk."

"I can take care of myself, Commander," Si Cwan informed her.

"Lord Cwan," Shelby said with fading patience, "there is not a single individual in this galaxy whom I would have thought more capable of taking care of himself than Mackenzie Calhoun. He's now missing. So don't for one moment think that your protestations of your own capabilities are going to cut any ice with me. Do we understand each other?"

"Perfectly," said an annoyed Si Cwan, clearly disagreeing but realizing that he wasn't going to make any headway against the immovable object of Commander Shelby. And then he turned to face Zak Kebron. "Bring him back, Kebron. Bring him back safely. If anyone can, you can."

"A compliment?" said Kebron with mild amusement.

"No. A challenge." He tapped the commbadge that he had been issued and said, "Si Cwan to *Excalibur*. One to beam up." And, moments later, he had dematerialized in a sparkle of molecules.

"Well done, Watson," Selar was saying in the meantime.

"Not a problem, Doctor. Anything else you need, just ask."

"Understood. Selar out."

"All right, Doctor," Shelby said, her arms folded and looking barely patient. "What have you got in mind?"

"We can use the tricorder as a localized detection device," Selar said, after making a few adjustments. "Lock on to traces of his DNA or molecular structure in the same way that a tricorder can be utilized to locate any other specific trace elements."

"If we can lock on to where he is, let's just find his coordinates and have him beamed up to the ship."

"The equipment is not quite that localized, Commander. It will indicate direction, but not the final destination."

"Wait a minute." Shelby tapped her commbadge. "Shelby to Bridge."

"Bridge. Lieutenant Soleta here."

"Just the person I wanted to speak to." She quickly outlined what it was that Selar had planned, and then said, "Can we run the same information through the ship's sensors? Do a sensor sweep of the planet using his molecular structure as a guide?"

"Absolutely," Soleta replied. "But via our sensors, it would be more of a selective process. Essentially we'd have to filter through all the biological organisms within the area of the sensor sweep and detect the captain either using his molecular patterns as a guide, or else by process of elimination. That is to say, we eliminate everyone we know is not the captain and, in doing so, eventually find him."

"Sounds like a plan," said Shelby, who then almost bit her tongue since she had inadvertently blurted out Calhoun's favorite expression. The last thing she wanted to admit was that she had been influenced by him in any way. "Do it," she said. "Until I return, you have the conn, Soleta."

"Yes, sir. I'll get right on it."

Shelby turned to Soleta and said briskly, "All right, Doctor. Fire up the tricorder, and let's track down the captain. Between our being on the scent down here, and the *Excalibur* tracking him on their end, we should be able to do this in no time. Gentlemen," and she addressed Kebron, Hecht, and Scannell, "let's go find the captain."

Killick quickly made his way to what he hoped would be a private communication point, deep in his own personal sanctum. Quickly he used it to contact Ramed's home and, to his concern, Talila appeared on the screen. "Killick!" she said, making no effort to hide her surprise. She knew of Killick, certainly, but since he was of the Unglza, she had never actually had any direct communication with him. "This is a surprise."

"Yes, I imagine it would be," he said, trying to remain calm. "Is Ramed there?"

"Here?" The genuine puzzlement on her face was all the answer he needed, but it would have been rude to simply shut off the link. "Why would he be here? He's there, isn't he? He . . . he left for there. He even spoke with me just the other day to tell me that he had arrived."

"Did he say anything to you, Talila?"

Talila was completely confused, to say nothing of

frustrated. She was, after all, speaking with someone whom she regarded as the enemy. She knew, however, that Zondar was endeavoring to enter a new age of tolerance, and what sort of mother and wife would she be if she resisted something as positive as cooperation and brotherhood? So she put aside her immediate temptation to bite off a sharp answer and instead replied, "Did he say anything? What would he have said, Killick? I . . . do not understand."

"I'm not sure," he admitted in annoyance. "But—"

"But what?"

He took a deep breath, and said, "The Savior is dead. Dead and gone. I saw His body myself, and that body has now vanished. And Ramed is gone as well."

"Gone?" She stared at him, and he could almost see the wheels turning in her mind, almost perceive the actual thought process as it was reflected on her face in growing disbelief. "Dead and gone . . . and you . . . you are implying that Ramed had something to do with it?"

"I don't know," Killick said in frustration. "All I know is that he is gone. That makes him a suspect."

"No," Talila shot back at him.

"Talila, listen to me—"

"No!" she said again, even more forcefully. "Ramed's absence does not make him a suspect. Any one of a dozen reasons would suffice to explain that. No, what makes him a suspect is you. You and years, centuries of distrust of him and all those like him. All those like me. I resent your implications, Killick. Resent them most deeply, and you would be well advised not to be in contact with me again."

"Talila," he started to say.

"Never again!" she reiterated more forcefully, and shut off the connection.

Killick leaned back in his chair and let out a slow sigh of dread.

"I dislike the way this matter is developing," he said.

Talila sagged against the wall, shaking her head and murmuring, "No, no, please, no," over and over again. From his room, Rab heard her and emerged, going to her and touching her leg gently.

"Mother?" he inquired. "What's wrong?"

She looked down at him and then, rather than say anything, she took him up in her arms and rocked gently back and forth with him, all the time praying that what she feared could not possibly, under any circumstances, be the truth. She tried to tell herself that Killick had called her up out of some misplaced sense of spite. That the conclusions she was drawing could not possibly be accurate.

She told herself so many things, but the bottom line was that she was terrified. And she had never in her life felt more helpless.

XIII.

THE HIGH PRIEST OF ALPHA CARINAE looked down from the high window in the Central Hall of Worship, and for the first time felt apprehension.

Then he quickly fought to rein in his concerns. It was absurd for him to worry, he realized. His personal safety was simply not a consideration. Everyone, even the relative barbarians of Alpha Carinae, knew his person was sacrosanct. Had they not had that reality drilled into them sufficiently when the Redeemers first arrived upon their world?

The High Priest remembered those first, glorious days. The Redeemers had a fairly standard method of operation. When they targeted a world for redemption, they would sweep in with the full force of their armada behind them. Any initial battle against the Redeemers would very quickly be snuffed out. The current religious leaders of the world were targeted for primary redemption: Either they would accept Xant as their one, true deity or, failing that, they were executed. Usually the Redeemer board of inquiry could determine very quickly whether or not there was going to be cooperation with the redemption. More often than not, there wasn't. In the final analysis, it never really mattered.

Once the world had sworn allegiance to Xant, a High Priest was left in place. One was usually all that was needed, although occasionally two would be left in place on a particularly populous planet. In the case of Alpha Carinae, however, the one had been deemed more than sufficient.

Now the High Priest was beginning to wonder if that confidence had not been misplaced.

Whereas once he had walked the streets with impunity, now he found that the hostility that was greeting him was simply too much. No one had assaulted him; no one would possibly be that foolish. But he could feel the glares, the anger drilling into the base of his skull. Everywhere he went now, he heard the name of Calhoun being bandied about. Calhoun and the *Excalibur*. He was finding leaflets being handed out, some of them being brought to him by his spies, others pasted up on buildings with an audacity he once would not have thought possible.

Part of him wanted to contact the Overlord immediately, to tell him of the further disintegration of the situation on Alpha Carinae. Prime One had certainly been polite and responsive enough when he had sounded the initial warning. But he was concerned that, should he contact them as a follow-up so quickly, it might seem that he was weak and fearful. It was one thing to apprise the Overlord of a situation, as he had already done. It was quite another to run back to him repeatedly as if he, the High Priest, were unable to attend to his own territory.

One of his more trusted servants knocked on the door and waited politely for the High Priest to turn and face him. "There is a delegation here to see you, High One," said the servant.

"A delegation?" The High Priest had been sitting, but he pulled himself to standing while leaning on his cane. "From whom, may I ask?"

"From the . . ." He paused and pulled out a piece of paper, clearly having written it down to make certain that he got it correct. "From the People's Association for Peace."

"A gentle name, certainly," the High Priest acknowledged. "A name designed to put one at ease." He tapped his staff thoughtfully. "One would almost assume that it is deceptively obvious that the name is created so as not to arouse suspicion. Nonetheless, we cannot allow our fears to govern us, can we? Send them in."

The servant nodded once and walked out of the door. Less than a minute later, a group of four male Alphans entered, looking not particularly threatening. One of them, the High Priest immediately noted, was Saulcram. He looked none the worse for wear, considering the severe banging up he had received earlier.

"Gentlemen," the High Priest said slowly, "to what do I owe the pleasure?"

The four men glanced at each other, as if needing to silently affirm one more time what it was that they wished to discuss. Saulcram took an unsteady step forward. Apparently he, the lucky devil, had been selected to serve as the group's spokesman. "We have an . . . an issue that needs to be discussed, High One."

"Indeed. And what might that be?"

Saulcram readied himself for what he felt had potential to be a major problem. As it turned out, he could not even begin to grasp the accuracy of that sentiment. "We wish to worship Calhoun."

Although he was not entirely surprised at the words, the High Priest was still rocked to hear them. He did not let his surprise show, however. He was far too much of a professional for that.

To play it safe, he thumbed a small switch on the inside of his staff. Immediately it triggered a recording device safely hidden within the staff, with a backup copy being made deep within the confines of his private office. "You wish to worship Calhoun instead of Xant. Is that correct?" he said slowly.

There was hesitant nodding of heads from the envoys.

"And you ask my blessing to do so. Is that what this is about?"

"We . . ." and Saulcram drew himself up straighter, prouder. It was as if the fact that he had not simply been struck down by a thunderbolt from on high had given him a measure of new and increased confidence. "We are not seeking your blessing. We will do as we wish."

"My dear friends," the High Priest said expansively. "This Calhoun is not unknown to me, nor is his vessel. He is a mere mortal, dear friends. A brave one, to be sure. A staunch leader, so I am told. But a mortal nonetheless. You cannot seriously expect to forsake a god, to turn your back on one such as Xant, simply for the purpose of attending to the word of a mortal."

"You are mortal," another of Saulcram's colleagues pointed out. "We attend to your word."

"But my word is the word of Xant."

"How do we know?" came the challenging reply.

The High Priest chose not to rise to the belligerence inherent in the tone. "It is enough that I know, my friends—"

"We are not your friends!" Saulcram said sharply, pointing a quivering finger at the High Priest. Slowly he started to approach him. The High Priest's instinct was to back up, but he resisted it. Instead he maintained his ground as Saulcram advanced on him. "You and your kind overthrew us, remember? Overthrew our belief in ourselves. Battered us down, forced your god upon us—"

"We forced nothing! We saved you. You do not fully comprehend that yet, but we—"

"You took away from us our right to choose for ourselves! To think for ourselves! You ask us to trust you when you clearly do not trust us, even for something as simple as making up our own minds about the world in which we live!"

"Stop where you are," the High Priest said fiercely, his veneer of polite patience slipping somewhat. Out of long habit, Saulcram halted in his tracks. "You are tempting a terrible punishment. Terrible beyond your ability to grasp."

"I can 'grasp' just fine, oh High One," Saulcram told him. "And what I grasp is that, for the first time, the Redeemers are wallowing in the stench of fear. You cling to your musty belief in Xant, and in the meantime a true redeemer is here! On Zondar they call Him the Savior!"

"They can call him whatever they wish, but in the end he is no replacement for Xant!" the High Priest declared. His voice had been getting louder and louder, but now he pulled it back to a low and deadly tone. "I have been more than patient with you, Saulcram. With all of you. You have taken it upon yourselves to indulge in some foolish notion of worshiping another, when we both know that the way of Xant is the one, true way. It is my very strong advice that you leave now."

"You don't yet understand, priest," Saulcram told him angrily. "We are not the ones who will be leaving. You will be the one who leaves."

The High Priest tilted his head as if he could not quite believe what had just been said. "I beg your pardon?" he said. This time there was no threat in his voice. If anything, he sounded amused.

"You will leave. Now. This day. You will pack your book, your statues, your teaching scrolls, your tools of consecration. All of it," Saulcram said. Any last vestiges of nervousness had evaporated. "You will take it and you will depart this world, and that is the only way that you will live to see another sunrise. Do we make ourselves clear?" There was silent bobbing of heads from his associates. "We have spoken to thousands of our peers, and they all feel the same way. They want you out, and the advent of Calhoun into this sector is the sign that we have been waiting for."

"A sign." The High Priest scratched his chin thoughtfully. "Let me tell you of signs. The great flaming bird signals the coming of Xant. I do not speak of some uncertain and distant future that you and your descendants may or may not live to see. I am speaking of soon, within your own lifetime. I have spoken to the Overlord himself," which was something of an exaggeration since he had spoken only to Prime One. "It is his proclamation that the return of Xant is near. You would be most ill advised to ignore this very important news. How do you think Xant, and the Overlord, would feel if a previously colonized world had an uprising just in time for Xant's restoration to power and glory? An uprising, the main theme of which was that you did not believe in Xant or his message. What possible purpose could such a happenstance serve you, eh?"

And suddenly, with absolutely no warning at all, Saulcram grabbed the High Priest by the front of his robes. The very act of laying hands upon a High Priest caused gasps of surprise from the others. It took the High Priest no time at all to realize that Saulcram was acting on his own. The others had wanted to draw a hard line, but it was Saulcram who was becoming excessively physical.

"We do not believe you!" Saulcram fairly shouted in his face. "We do not believe you, and we do not believe *in* you! Xant is not coming! Xant is never going to come, and even if he does, then he can trot right back to the great unknown because we have no use for him! You say Calhoun is merely a man. Fine, then, if that is what it takes to survive on our world! I would sooner admire, work with, and worship a living, breathing man that I can see rather than some mysterious unknown deity who will likely never show up in this or any other lifetime!"

"You are wrong," the High Priest shouted back, and he pulled away from Saulcram. "And you are dangerously close to being not only a dead man yourself, but the executioner of your entire race."

"Again come the threats!" said Saulcram angrily. "We are tired of your threats, High Priest! And we are tired of you! You threaten us with the extinction of our entire race if we should so much as lift a hand against you. You have traded upon the reputation of the dreaded Redeemers. But perhaps that reputation is not so deserved! Perhaps we should not be afraid of you!"

"If you are not, then that will be your error. And a most costly error it—"

Saulcram's fist lashed out and slammed the High Priest in the face. The force of the blow took him completely off his feet, knocking the startled High Priest to his back. He lay there, momentarily stunned, reaching up to feel the blood beginning to fountain from his nose. With his free hand he was still clutching his staff. "You . . . idiot!" he yelled. "You have no idea what you've done! No idea at all! Our persons are sacrosanct! They—"

Another of the Alphans stepped forward, eager for a piece of the retribution that was being dealt out, and kicked the High Priest squarely in the stomach. The High Priest moaned, and a gurgle barely recognizable as something made by a living being, rattled around in his throat. With boiling fury, the High Priest lashed out with his staff, trying to trip up his assailants, but they were too nimble. Saulcram leaped over the hooked end of the staff, then slammed down on it with both feet, immobilizing it. The High Priest pulled on it desperately, and he muttered an imprecation as best he could, considering that he could barely form a coherent sentence.

Saulcram yanked the staff away, gripped the shaft firmly, and then swung it up and over his head. The High Priest looked up, saw what was about to happen, and managed to shake his head and mouth the word, "Sacrosanct," just before the hooked end of the staff slammed down on him, splitting his skull. His body trembled, shuddered, and continued to twitch for a moment or two more before ceasing.

His assailants stood there for a moment, barely able to believe what they had done. The first moments of nervousness crossed their faces then, for this was not exactly what they had planned. Threats, yes, they had planned threats. They had even anticipated having to use force in order to get the High Priest to leave.

But the violence . . . the violence had simply seemed to arise from nowhere.

"It was necessary," Saulcram said sharply, as if to bolster the failing confidence of his companions.

"But . . . but the person of the High Priest is sacrosanct . . ."

"Shut up!" Saulcram shouted. "That's their rhetoric you're spouting! The threats they use to keep us in line! Now that the threats have failed, we have to prepare for the inevitable attack, the attempted retribution. We have to muster our forces! We must steel ourselves for battle! We must win back our freedom from the aggressors! We must follow the way of—"

Saulcram suddenly found it very difficult to speak. His tongue felt swollen, his throat suddenly quite dry. He wanted to lick his lips and discovered that his jaw was unable to move. He looked to the others, and his eyes widened in horror as he saw that the man nearest him seemed to be rotting from the inside out. His skin was turning a dark, dusky black and sliding away from his face, his eyes bugging out, the blood vessels within bursting and trickling down his face.

Then Saulcram went blind and he realized with a fading desperation that the exact same thing was happening to him. He clutched at his throat, trying to get air to pass through, fighting desperately for life even when he knew that it was already hopeless, that he was already dead. He fell to the ground, clutching at his mouth, trying to physically pry the jaws open so that he could get some air down his throat. He gave it all the power that his fading strength had, and finally he succeeded in a manner of speaking: His entire jaw snapped off, clattering to the floor and shattering into powdery remains.

The four of them writhed on the floor and died without uttering a single sound except for a few stray gurgles that escaped their lips, or whatever was left of their lips.

So perished the People's Association for Peace, resting in not-so-peaceful a state in the Central Hall of Worship. They were not destined to be alone in their hideous deaths for very long.

The disease that spread from the body of the High Priest, triggered to life by his death, was an airborne virus that made twentieth-century Earth plagues such as the *Ebola* virus look like the chicken pox. It spread through the ventilation ducts of the Hall itself, bringing swift and violent death to all inside within several minutes. None of them had the slightest comprehension of what was happening to them. They had been going about their lives, making preparations for the evening meal, intending to cater to the needs of the High Priest. Ultimately, in a manner of speaking, they accomplished that end, for the High Priest needed them to die in order to prove a point. And so they died, just as rapidly, hideously and uncomprehendingly as the four individuals who had murdered the High Priest minutes before.

Having done its work there, the virus swept out onto the four winds across the surface of Alpha Carinae. No city, no town, no village or hamlet was spared. The virus knew no innocent blood. The very old collapsed into gasping heaps next to the very young. All over Alpha Carinae, from one pole to the other, across the face of the globe, the disease marched, more unstoppable than any army, more merciless, more pitiless. Frantic doctors fought to discover a cure, but there was no cure. The Redeemers had seen to that. They had had, after all, plenty of time to perfect it. Anything that any Alphan doctor might be able to discover or come up with had already been anticipated and attended to.

Within twenty-four hours, half the populace of Alpha Carinae had the disease. It slowed down briefly, then renewed its march across the planet, getting into the water, poisoning the air. There was no escape, no hope, no prayer, even though there were prayers in abundance. The Alphans prayed to the Redeemers for forgiveness, they prayed to Calhoun for salvation, they prayed to whatever gods, goddesses, and holy figures they could think of. And their response was nothing but the crashing silence of entities or deities who were unable or unwilling to help.

The Alphans died abandoned, they died unloved, and ultimately, they just died. Sixty-one hours after the High Priest had fallen to the ground, bleeding and dying, the last of the Alphans hit the floor. The last Alphan was precisely four years old, that very day, and she gurgled out the name of her mother by way of her last words. Her mother, who was lying in a crumbled heap on the floor not ten yards away.

And then the last living being on Alpha Carinae twitched ever so slightly, and stopped moving.

For a long, long while, not a sound was made on the entire planet.

Then a shadow was cast over it. A shadow as if the great spirit of death was hovering over the world, examining it carefully to see precisely what had been wrought.

The shadow came from a great ship, a ship that descended through the atmosphere of Alpha Carinae and did a slow fly-by over selected portions of the planet. The inhabitants of the vessel had been instantly aware of the crisis that had faced the doomed world, but had been forced to allow the disease to do the job for which it had been so thoroughly and mercilessly designed. Having thoroughly obliterated all life on Alpha Carinae, the virus had lingered another twenty-four hours in the air, land, and water, and then, as it had been created to do, the virus simply self-destructed. In no time at all, the surface of Alpha Carinae was perfectly habitable, if one did not mind stepping over all the corpses. Although, on the other hand, there wasn't that much left of them. The virus was extremely thorough in its rotting properties.

The great ship cruised over the surface, inspecting the damage that had been done, the wrath that had been inflicted upon the helpless inhabitants. Finally it hovered over the Central Hall of Worship before landing directly in front of it. In landing, the ship crushed the remains of at least fifty bodies, but this was of no consequence to the inhabitants of the mighty vessel.

A door irised open and the Overlord of the Redeemers emerged. He looked neither left nor right, for the desiccated remains of an unredeemable race were of no interest to him whatsoever. Instead he entered the Central Hall, barely bothering to afford a glance at the fallen bodies except to step over any that happened to be in his way. Very quickly he found the room where the body of the High Priest lay.

The Overlord had not felt particularly close to this particular priest. He had not been one of those whom the Overlord had trained himself. Nonetheless, there were certain obligations upon the Overlord that came not as a result of personal closeness, but from his position and a sense of loyalty to his fellow Redeemers.

He stood over the fallen priest and mourned his passing. The Overlord's personal escort did likewise, their heads bowed and their lips murmuring invocations to Xant that the fallen priest would walk with him in the light.

Then the Overlord picked up the fallen staff and nodded approvingly to see that the recording device within had been functioning. He looked distastefully at the blood on it, and one of his entourage ripped off a piece of clothing from the body of Saulcram and used it to clean off the staff as best he could. Some of the blood was dried on and there was nothing he could do about it, but the Overlord accepted the staff as it was.

He returned to the ship without a word, removed the recording chip, and plugged it into the ship's computer. Immediately the voice of the fallen High Priest filled the control room, and the discussion that had filled his last moments. The Overlord listened dispassionately, no flicker of emotion whatsoever registering on his face throughout the entire recording. When it was done, he played it once more, as if wanting to be sure that no mistake was made.

Then he turned to his fellow Redeemers and said simply, "I want Calhoun and the *Excalibur*."

And the Redeemers immediately set about to put the order into action.

XIV.

Soleta was becoming extremely worried.

She paced across the bridge in an extremely un-Vulcan like fashion and then said, "Time, Mister McHenry?"

"Two minutes later than the last time you asked, sir," McHenry replied, turning in his chair. "I thought you Vulcans had an internal clock or something."

"Perhaps mine needs adjusting," said Soleta. "The away team is overdue to check in."

'Yes, it is," affirmed Lefler. "Fifteen minutes."

"They've got two heavily armed guards with them, and Kebron, who's the equivalent of five more guards," McHenry said confidently. "What can happen to them with him along?"

"I know you intended that as a rhetorical question, Mark, but I'm getting the distinct feeling that I've no desire to learn the answer," replied Soleta. "Lefler, try to raise them."

"Aye, sir," said Lefler, and she immediately set about doing so.

Soleta stared at the planet as it turned below them. It seemed to calm, so peaceful. And yet there was so much wrong down there, so much that had happened. The captain, missing, perhaps dead, and now the away team having lost touch with the *Excalibur*. She did not like how this was shaping up at all.

"Lieutenant," Lefler said, trying to keep the apprehension out of her voice, "I'm not getting a response from them. I can't raise Shelby, Selar, or Kebron."

"Can you get a lock on them at all?"

Lefler quickly checked, sending a locate beam through to their communicator badges. "There's . . ." She shook her head in frustration. "There's some sort of heavy interference. I'm not sure what's causing it. It is the same sort of interference that is impeding our sensor sweep for the captain."

"Atmospheric disturbance?"

"Negative. Seems man-made. Artificial. It's blocking my primary sweep."

"Punch through it, Lefler. I want them out of there."

"Out of there, sir?" Robin looked at her in surprise. "Without a distress call or an order from the Commander?"

"They're overdue," Soleta reminded her. "Weighing the safety of the away team against the chance that Commander Shelby might yell at me, I'll risk the latter. Now get me the away team."

"Working on it, sir," said Lefler. For minutes she adjusted the frequency of the search probe, trying to pull up a contact with the away team, and finally she called out, "Got four of the five, sir! Managed to crack through whatever the local interference is, at least for the moment!"

"Send it through to the transporter room. Bridge to transporter room, four to beam up, now!" called Soleta.

"Starting to lose them!" Lefler called.

"Transporter room, get on it!" Soleta said urgently.

"Beaming them up now, sir!" came Watson's voice. "Having trouble reintegrating the signal, but I think I've got them cl—"

There was a pause, and Soleta fancied that she felt her blood chill ever so slightly. "Transporter room, report!" she ordered. "Who have you got? Are they okay?"

"Bridge, transporter room!" Watson cried out, and there was no mistaking the alarm in her voice. "Medical emergency! Sickbay already summoned! You better get down here! They—oh, God!"

"On my way!" Soleta called out, stopping only long enough to say, "McHenry, you have the conn!" before dashing into the turbolift.

McHenry slowly turned and looked at Lefler with clear concern. "I don't know which is more frightening," he said slowly. "That something's happened to Selar and Shelby . . . or that I have the conn."

"Shut up, Mark," said Robin with no trace of amusement. McHenry, wisely, said nothing.

Soleta barreled through the corridors of the *Excalibur* and arrived just as the team from sickbay was hauling the remains of the away team out of the transporter room. It took all of her carefully learned stoicism not to turn away in horror.

Shelby and Selar looked like hell. Half of Shelby's uniform was torn away, and there were burns all over her, huge patches of charred skin on her upper body. Her head lolled to one side; she barely appeared to be breathing. Selar had not fared much better. She appeared to have been lashed by some sort of tendril, tearing away her clothing and skin in vicious strips. The tip of her right ear had been torn off, and there was blood all over the side of her face.

Hecht was dead. Soleta could tell just from looking at him. His body lay on the rolling cart, twisted at an impossible angle. As for Scannell, physically he appeared untouched. But his mind was gone. His eyes stared blankly, although whether it was into the air or into himself, Soleta could not be sure. His back was arched, and he was babbling inarticulately, shaking his head every so often as if trying to ward off something that only he could see.

Shelby seemed to be barely conscious, and Soleta ran along side the antigrav gurney as it was rushed toward sickbay. "Commander," she said urgently, "can you speak?"

"Lieutenant," Doctor Maxwell began, trying to shoo her away even as he was putting a stasis field in place, while running, in order to stabilize Shelby's condition. "Now is not the time—"

"Commander, what happened?" demanded Soleta, ignoring Maxwell completely. "Did you find the captain? Where is Kebron? What happened down there?"

Shelby's mouth moved, but no words came out. Then, with great effort, she formed a word . . . one word:

"Borg," she managed to say.

Then she lapsed into unconsciousness, leaving a stunned Soleta in the corridor as the gurneys were sent into sickbay.

Burgoyne looked up from hir work in engineering to see the ashen face of Ensign Ronni Beth. "I take it that further analysis of the energy drain—" Burgoyne started to say, but then s/he saw the look on Beth's face. "What's wrong?" s/he demanded.

"Did you hear?"

"About the captain? Yes." Burgoyne shook hir head. "I don't believe it for a moment. I know this captain. It's going to take more than—"

"Not him. He's still missing," Beth said quickly, "but I mean, about the away team. The one that was looking for him."

Slowly Burgoyne got to hir feet. "What happened?" s/he said slowly.

"I cannot say that I am surprised," Killick was saying.

He was speaking via the screen to Soleta, who was seated in the unaccustomed place of the command chair, her fingers steepled. Si Cwan was standing just behind her. "Why, may I ask, are you unsurprised?" inquired Soleta.

"From the coordinates you've given me, it is my estimation that your away team had trespassed into Ontear's Realm."

"Excuse me?" said Soleta, leaning forward in polite confusion. "Ontear's Realm?"

"It is a sacred land," Killick informed her. "It was there that Ontear dwelt. It is believed by many that he dwells there still."

"Ontear," Si Cwan now spoke up. "That would be the philosopher and seer who died five hundred years ago."

"Ontear did not die," Killick said, sounding just slightly defensive. "He was taken away to join the gods, as anyone who has read the books of—"

"Fine, then," Si Cwan saw absolutely no point in disputing it. "Either way, we're agreed that it's not terribly likely he would still be around."

"Do not underestimate the power of Ontear, or the spirit of Ontear"—and Killick's voice dropped to a level that was tinged with menace—"or the vengeance of Ontear."

"Nor should we underestimate your obsession with saying the name 'Ontear,'" commented Soleta. "Are you claiming, Killick, that our away team fell victim to some sort of curse?"

"I would not have put it quite that way, but it is an acceptable summation."

"It is not acceptable to me, sir," replied Soleta. "It is, in fact, illogical. I have an away team with members that are variously injured, dead, and missing. Their intention was to find the commanding officer of this vessel—"

"If their trail led them truly, Lieutenant," Killick informed her, "and your captain is within Ontear's Realm, then you will not be bringing him back. The Realm of Ontear was consecrated after the death of his greatest acolyte, Suti, and forbidden to all Zondarians. Forbidden, in fact, to all who live."

"Even the Savior?" asked Soleta drily.

Slowly, Killick nodded. "Even to one such as He. If He is there, then He is already dead. As for you, Lieutenant, I would consider myself fortunate if I were you."

"And why is that?"

"The fact that you got any of your people back alive. That, in and of itself, is nothing short of miraculous. You should thank the spirit of the Savior for your good fortune."

"I will be certain to keep that in mind," Soleta said with more sarcasm than Si Cwan would have supposed a Vulcan was capable of.

Killick's image blinked out, and all eyes turned to Soleta.

"Now what?" said Si Cwan.

And Soleta—Soleta, who had once resigned from Starfleet when she discovered her Vulcan/Romulan breeding; Soleta, who had until relatively recently been content teaching science courses at Starfleet Academy; Soleta, who, truth to tell, would have been perfectly content never to set foot on a starship again in her life, much less suddenly find herself in a position of command upon one—said the most difficult four words that she had ever uttered in her life.

"I am not sure," she replied.

Burgoyne strode into sickbay like a force of nature. Several medtechs tried to stop hir, but were utterly unsuccessful. Burgoyne pushed them aside, with strength in hir wiry frame that surprised anyone endeavoring to get in hir way. S/he cast a quick, pained glance in the direction of Shelby. S/he had served with Shelby before, thought her a fine officer and a good person, not to mention possessing one seriously fine body from this angle at least. (the latter comment, for reasons of discretion, never having passed through Burgy's lips). But the majority of hir attention was focused on Selar, who lay nearby, eyes closed and breathing shallowly but steadily.

Dr. Maxwell stood near her, checking readings, when Burgoyne walked up. Maxwell glanced up at hir and said, "I would appreciate it if you chose to visit at a later hour."

Burgoyne fixed Maxwell with a dark stare. "Doctor, out of my way."

Maxwell drew himself up, squaring off against Burgoyne. "There is no need, Chief, to be rude."

With a flash of hir canines, Burgoyne said, "That, Doctor, depends entirely upon you."

Maxwell was prepared to say something further, but wisely decided that it would do him little-to-no good, and possibly even some serious harm. With one more quick glance at the readings, Maxwell walked away, allowing Burgoyne some time with Selar.

Burgoyne leaned over her, running hir long, tapered fingers over Selar's battered face. S/he saw a patch of Selar's head where the hair had been burned away. What could possibly have happened to her? What could have done this to her? Slowly Burgoyne felt a deep, burning anger building within hir chest.

"They will pay," Burgoyne whispered to her. "I swear to the gods, whoever did this will pay."

Suddenly Selar's eyes snapped open. She didn't seem focused on anything, her gaze instead darting around as if looking for something.

"Selar!" Burgoyne said in a harsh, amazed whisper, and then s/he called, "She opened her eyes! She—"

Burgoyne's hand was on Selar's temple, and then Selar's eyes snapped into focus on Burgoyne's. Her hand, down at her side, wrapped around Burgoyne's free hand, snapping on to it and grasping it like an infant reflexively holding on to anything thrust in its palm.

Burgoyne gasped as sickbay fell away from hir, and suddenly there was sand and dirt beneath hir feet, hot air burning in hir lungs, and a roar from all around, roaring in hir ears, in hir mind. S/he became aware of the fact that s/he was no longer perceiving things solely through hir own mind, but s/he was having trouble distinguishing hir own state of mind.

And the roaring . . . no, it was howling. Like a massive wind rushing, except the wind was alive somehow. It burned into hir, and s/he felt something angry and ancient flailing at hir, trying to beat hir away.

And Burgoyne would not be intimidated. Instead s/he snarled back, hir canines fully exposed, ready to rend and tear, and s/he howled defiance and swore an oath of bloody vengeance. S/he saw caves and cliffs, and the aged evil bellowed a challenge that Burgoyne eagerly accepted.

And Burgoyne knew at that point, beyond any question that s/he was suddenly in a war. A war that had become very personal.

Then something seemed to insinuate itself into Burgoyne's mind, wrap itself around hir, and hir first instinct was to fight it. But then s/he realized that it was Selar. Selar in a way that s/he had never seen her. Selar, desirous, eager, hungry, wanting and striving and trying to reach out from the depths of her injuries, driven by an instinct for self-preservation and by something else as well. Something that Burgoyne didn't quite understand, but it was a need, a deep, sexual hunger consuming both Burgoyne and Selar as well. Heat seemed to pound through Burgoyne. And just like that, s/he knew Selar, knew her in and out, felt a connection as deep and as full as anything that Burgoyne had ever felt and would ever feel. Burgoyne cried out, and then the creature roared in hir head once more, splitting Burgoyne and Selar from one another. Burgoyne reached out, hearing Selar howling away in the grip of her memories of what she had faced, and then Burgoyne hit the floor.

As opposed to the subjectivity of what s/he had just seen, the floor was all too real. Burgoyne sat there, feeling rather foolish, hir head swirling even as a couple of medtechs helped hir to hir feet. Maxwell, to his credit, had put aside whatever bruised feelings he might have sustained from his high-handed treatment by Burgoyne before, saying, "Chief, are you okay?"

"Fine," Burgoyne said in a voice that was much huskier than s/he was accustomed to. "I'm . . . I'm fine. How long was I out?"

"Only a second. From the moment you said her eyes were open to when you hit the floor, it couldn't have been more than a second." Maxwell glanced over at Selar, checking her readings. "Her eyes are closed again."

"It's okay," Burgoyne said, sounding stunned for a moment. Then hir full concentration returned, with an intensity like a beacon. "It's okay. I . . . know what I need to know." S/he headed for the door.

"Chief," said Maxwell. "Did she make some sort of . . . contact with you? A meld or . . . ?"

"She did something, all right," Burgoyne affirmed.

"What did you see?"

"Enough," Burgoyne said. "More than, in fact." And s/he headed out the door and down the corridor.

Soleta was in the main transporter room, speaking with Watson and endeavoring to refine the search pattern for the captain when Burgoyne entered the transporter room and strode over to the platform. Soleta and Watson both watched hir step onto the platform, whirl to face Watson, and say, "Wherever you brought them up from—beam me down there."

Watson and Soleta exchanged looks, and then with a shrug Watson reached for the controls.

"Belay that order, Ensign," Soleta said quietly.

Burgoyne's dark eyes narrowed and sized up Soleta like a hawk considering a rabbit. "Ensign," s/he said, although s/he never took hir eyes off Soleta, "carry out my order. Energize."

"Watson," Soleta told her, "I believe it's time for your break."

"It is?" asked Polly Watson, and then when she saw Soleta's expression, she quickly said, "You know, you're right. What was I thinking?" and she vacated the transporter room as quickly as she could.

"Would you mind telling me what you think you're doing?" Burgoyne said to Soleta, sounding very dangerous. "In case it's slipped your notice, I outrank you. What you've just done is insubordination."

"That's one interpretation," replied Soleta evenly. "On the other hand, Commander Shelby left me in authority. She trusted me to attend to the welfare of the entire crew complement, and that would include you."

"Soleta, we don't know each other all that well," Burgoyne said with very forced patience. S/he descended from the transporter platform and continued, "When I take it into my head to do something, I do it. This has become a *Gi'jan* to me. A quest. Something of a personal nature."

"Personal considerations have no place in deciding who is and is not to be sent into a hazardous situation," Soleta replied evenly.

"Perhaps not to you," Burgoyne shot back, "but it does to me. Now, Lieutenant"—and s/he moved briskly to the control board—"I am programming my destination. I am setting it to a timer so that I can simply walk over there, step onto the platform, and beam down. And last, I am personally encoding it, on my authority, to my own private password override, so that nothing you can say or do can prevent the beams from functioning. I believe that covers all the bases, Lieutenant, unless you intend, for some reason, to get in my way."

"That," replied Soleta, "would not be logical."

"Very wise," said Burgoyne, completing the last of the adjustments to the controls. S/he nodded in quick approval of hir work, and headed back toward the platform, walking past Soleta as s/he did so.

S/he never even felt the feather-light touch of Soleta's fingers on hir shoulder. All s/he knew was that suddenly the world was going dark and the floor was approaching hir at a depressingly rapid speed.

When s/he came to some minutes later, Soleta was standing over hir, her arms folded. "In case you wish to keep a tally," Soleta informed her, "that could be construed as assaulting a superior officer."

"What did you do?" asked Burgoyne. S/he sat up, hir head spinning ever so slightly.

"The Vulcan nerve pinch. I momentarily stopped the flow of blood to your brain, causing unconsciousness."

"Heh." Burgoyne actually allowed a moment of self-mocking amusement, which was a fairly sporting attitude for hir to take, all things considered. "There are some people around here who would think that kicking me in the buttocks would accomplish that."

"That would be an acceptable fall-back technique." She cocked her head slightly. "You do not seem dismayed that I rendered you insensate."

"You got me fair and square. I can appreciate that. I don't have to be thrilled by it, mind you, but I can appreciate it." S/he rubbed the base of hir neck regretfully. "Where did you grab me? Here and here?" S/he indicated two spots on hir neck.

"Yes," Soleta said. "Although non-Vulcans generally do not master the technique. Some study for years and still fail."

"Well, I can be a fast learner." Then s/he paused and said, "Look, Soleta, when I said it was personal, that . . . that doesn't even begin to cover it. Selar and I, we have some sort of . . . of bond."

"Bond?" Soleta said skeptically.

"I don't know how it happened. She came to in sickbay, and we, we . . . linked somehow. I can't begin to describe it. I knew what she knew, what she experienced. I felt a part of her. I—" S/he hesitated, and then shrugged. "I also feel an overwhelming need to have sex with her. Understand, a high sex drive is certainly nothing new for me, but this . . . this is something I can't even begin to describe."

Burgoyne didn't notice the change in Soleta's expression. Clearly somehow Selar had established a rapport with Burgoyne, had zeroed in on hir as a mate. She might very well not have been in her right mind when she did it, lying on a med table in sickbay and reaching out for the first sympathetic mind that was in proximity. Or there might be something deeper there; Soleta had no way to be sure. Either way, Burgoyne's personal stake in the matter had definitely increased.

"I want to go down there, Soleta," Burgoyne said. "I need to. It's a *Gi'jan,* as I told you. I need to find the captain, and find whoever it was that hurt Selar. They must pay. There must be justice for the crime." S/he shrugged. "If nothing else, think of it as a means of utilizing all the energy I've got running through me right now. Soleta, I'm going to get down there. With or without your help, I'm going to do it. We both know it, unless you intend to try and stick the chief engineer in the brig."

"I'd rather not," Soleta admitted.

"So it would be simpler for all concerned if you would just cooperate."

"A valid point. However, Burgoyne, you must admit that it is a daunting task you are setting up for yourself. An entire, experienced away team is damaged, dead, or missing."

"So you see what happens when you send a large number of people in. Send in one person who can take care of hirself, however—a smaller target, as it were—and we might stand a better chance. Besides, I have an advantage," s/he said. "I have a link, a sense of what they faced. I'll be ready for it."

"Was it the Borg?" asked Soleta.

Burgoyne shook hir head. "Not that I saw. Although from what I glimpsed—and I can't even begin to describe it—it may very well have been worse."

"This is not encouraging my cooperation."

"Soleta . . ." Burgoyne tried to find the words, and then simply said, "I've got to do this. Do you understand? I have got to do this. Give me twenty-four hours—"

"Twelve," Soleta counter-offered. "And you will have to bring someone with you. I will not have you down there alone."

"Let me guess: You."

Burgoyne was quite surprised when Soleta shook her head. "I am needed here," she replied, "to endeavor to coordinate the sensor search for Captain Calhoun. Besides, what you need is someone from the security force."

"I'm going to be moving pretty quickly," said Burgoyne. "You have to understand, Soleta, there are various aspects to me that you never see in day-to-day life here on the *Excalibur*."

"That may very well be, but as my ability to render you unconscious indicates, you are in need of someone to watch your back. Furthermore, I am quite aware of your more . . . feral attributes," Soleta informed hir. "I have someone in mind who I believe would be capable of accompanying you on this quixotic quest of yours. Someone who will be able to 'keep up with you.' "

"Who?" And then Burgoyne realized even before Soleta said it. "You can't mean—"

"Ensign Janos."

"Soleta, be reasonable," Burgoyne started to say.

"I am being most reasonable. Janos is ideally suited."

"Janos makes me nervous," protested Burgoyne. "He makes everybody nervous!"

"So do you," shot back Soleta.

"That's not exactly fair," Burgoyne said, although s/he did allow a small smile. "Janos works the graveyard shift by popular demand. He prefers it that way and so does most of the crew."

"Granted," agreed Soleta. "But the bottom line is that he's a formidable security guard, incredibly strong, remarkably intelligent. If you want someone to be watching out for you, Janos is your—"

"I hope you weren't going to say 'man.'"

"You, of all people, Chief Engineer, should not find amusement when a crewmember eludes easy categorization."

"All right, all right, point taken."

"Good. Then we have an agreement. Twelve hours, with Ensign Janos as your back-up."

"You drive a hard bargain, Lieutenant," Burgoyne told her.

Soleta tapped her commbadge. "Transporter room to Ensign Janos." They waited, and when no response was forthcoming, Soleta tried again. Still no answer. "I was afraid of this," Soleta admitted. "He's off shift, so he's likely asleep. He is sometimes difficult to awaken."

"All right. I'll do it." S/he shook hir head as s/he walked out of the transporter room.

The door slid shut behind hir, and Soleta said calmly, "I'll be certain to change my door lock code."

* * *

Burgoyne stood outside Ensign Janos' quarters and rang the chime once more. There was no reply from within. Not wanting to waste any more time, Burgoyne tapped in the security override code that was known only to hirself and a handful of other ranking officers. The door beeped in acknowledgment and slid open.

Burgoyne stepped into darkness, hir eyes adjusting with preternatural speed. She was able to pick out a bulky body hanging upside down in a corner of the room. "Janos," s/he hissed. "Ensign Janos . . ."

Suddenly the bulk was gone. S/he tried to refocus and then, right in hir face, something large and bulky roared at hir with deafening volume. The breath was not especially pleasant either. Even with hir excellent night vision, s/he sensed rather than saw the behemoth raging in front of her.

"Ensign, it's Chief Engineer Burgoyne! Burgoyne one-seventy-two!" s/he said loudly. "You weren't answering the comm! You're needed for a special assignment!"

The mass in front of hir paused, and s/he heard the deep rasping slowly fade, to be replaced by normal, if heavy, breathing. "Special assignment?" came the thick-voiced reply.

"That's right. The captain's disappeared, the away team was slaughtered, Lieutenant Kebron is missing, and you and I are going down alone."

"Why?"

"Why? To show everyone else how it's done, that's why."

There was a pause. "Lights to half," said Ensign Janos. The lights in the cabin obediently came to half illumination.

Burgoyne immediately saw that Janos was unclothed, which was not particularly unusual for him.

He preferred a state of undress, considering it more natural, although of course he did follow Starfleet constraints and wear a uniform when he was on-duty. Even so, no one would have found it particularly disconcerting since Ensign Janos was covered, head to toe, with thick white fur.

Janos, as did others of his species, also had a general ape-like appearance, and was likely the only other individual on the ship, aside from Burgoyne, to sport fangs. However, that was where his resemblance to others of his kind ended, something that became immediately clear the moment he opened his mouth.

"Sounds brilliant," Janos said. "A real rip-snorter of an escapade. I appreciate your thinking of me for it."

Wasn't my idea, thought Burgoyne, but rather than admit that, s/he said, "Not a problem."

"Hope I didn't startle you overmuch. I have that sort of killer-instinct thing on when I'm slumbering. Anyone who startles me, well, you get the idea."

"Oh, definitely. How long will it take you to get ready?"

"Half a mo'. Just need to pull on a clean pair of woollies and then we're off to the races!" Ensign Janos, the mugato security guard, didn't grin. His face wasn't built in a manner that allowed him to. But he did seem exceedingly chipper about it. "You can wait here if you wish, Chief. Not as if I have anything to hide, and besides, I hear you're somewhat the frisky one when it comes to matters of sexual orientation, eh? Watching a fellow like me get dressed shouldn't be too much of a shocker for you, I'd surmise."

Burgoyne considered it for a moment, and then said, "I think I'll wait outside, if it's all the same to you."

"As you wish. Pass up the thrill of a lifetime, if that's your pleasure."

Burgoyne stepped into the hallway, waited until the door shut behind hir, and then muttered, "Soleta, I'll get you for this. I'm not certain how or where, but I will get you for this. And Captain, if you're alive, I certainly hope you appreciate this."

XV.

ACROSS THE BELEAGUERED WORLD of Zondar, arguments spilled over into feuds. Skirmishes became outright battles. Accusations ricocheted, counteraccusations flew. Mourning took hold of the entire populace as they came to feel that a golden age of growth, a time of peace and prosperity, had been snatched away from them. It seemed to many that night and day became filled with nothing but ululations of grief, cries that could be heard from one side of Zondar to the other.

Mackenzie Calhoun was deaf to all of them.

He lay inside the cave, unable to move, barely even able to think. Slowly he felt his strength starting to return, but when he tried to move his arms and legs, nothing seemed interested in functioning. It took a massive amount of effort just to be able to open his eyes, and when he did, the entirety of his reward was darkness. Slowly he started to be able to make out things, except all he was making out was cave walls. There was no chill in the cave, however; instead he felt a distant warmth, leading him to believe that he was in a fairly arrid area.

He tried to call out, but his mouth was dry and raspy, his throat not much better. He cleared his throat, took another stab at it, and this time managed to get out, "Hello?"

He didn't get an immediate response, and he wasn't entirely certain if that was a good thing or not. He felt the bonds at his wrists and ankles, tested his strength against them, and found that they were more than capable of standing up to his best efforts. That didn't stop him from trying to pull his wrists clear, but after several minutes that only resulted in severe abrasions, he stopped to reconsider the matter.

He tried to remember how he had arrived at his present situation, but his memory was hazy at best. He recalled the banquet, and the vague sense of danger. He remembered retiring to his room. Beyond that—nothing. He looked down at his chest and noticed that his communicator was gone. Well, whoever had made off with him was thorough, he would certainly give him that.

Slowly he surveyed his surroundings. Definitely a simple cave, fairly unremarkable. Now if he could just figure out what in hell he was doing there. Who could possibly have done this to him, and for what possible reason?

Then something flickered over near the wall. He looked up at it, squinting, trying to make it out.

It was some sort of light emission, that much he could see. And it appeared to be taking some sort of form, coalescing into . . .

A Zondarian.

But it was not one that Calhoun had seen before. He was hairless, with the same glistening leathery skin that the rest of the people shared, but he seemed older somehow.

Calhoun sat up, propping himself up on one elbow, and said to the image, "Who are you?"

He wasn't entirely certain if he expected an answer, but was rather startled to receive one, although it wasn't much of one: "I know who you are," replied the image. It had only partly materialized; Calhoun could still clearly see the cave wall behind him.

"Oh?" was all Calhoun replied. It wasn't the most useful of responses; after all, Calhoun knew perfectly well who he himself was.

"I watched you," said the new arrival. "I watched you arrive. I watched you hailed as the Savior. That is what I do, much of the time. I watch. Watch and record."

"Would you be kind enough to tell someone where I am?"

"They will know," replied the image cryptically. "I have already seen that. That is what I do, you see. I notice certain moments, and then track them to see how they develop. I have already seen what will happen to you. Now, for curiosity's sake, I am studying to see how you got to that point."

"I'm flattered I'm of such interest to you." He felt his arm becoming numb and shifted his position. "Since you seem to be so cognizant of what's to come, would you mind telling me if I get out of here?"

"You will be saved by neither man nor woman," replied the image, and then slowly it began to fade out.

"I appreciate the encouraging words!" Calhoun called out. "Get back here!"

But the image was gone.

Insanely, Calhoun sensed that the floor was warm directly beneath where the image had been, as if it had been generating body heat. But that was impossible. It had been nothing more than a hologram . . .

For, for all Calhoun knew, it had been a complete delusion. Perhaps he was simply losing his mind. Now there was a cheery thought. The image had vanished and he'd been left with more questions than answers.

And then it appeared that his questions were going to be answered in very short order, because he heard a soft footfall approaching him. Rather than immediately tip off the fact that he was conscious, Calhoun laid his head down and narrowed his eyes to slits so that he could still see. He slowed his breathing down as best he could to try and simulate an unconscious state.

He saw someone approaching him, and this, in contrast to his previous visitor, was very much a flesh-and-blood Zondarian. His captor stopped several feet away from him and said, "Feigning unconsciousness is rather pointless. I heard you talking to yourself before, so I know you are awake."

Slowly Calhoun lifted his head. "Ramed, if I'm not mistaken."

"I am honored that you remember me, oh Great One," Ramed said with a slight inclination of his head. "You have, after all, met a great many of us. It is flattering to know you can keep track of who is who."

Ramed's comment about "talking to himself" had immediately struck Calhoun as odd. Ramed had apparently been oblivious to Calhoun's visitor from moments before. Calhoun decided to keep that information to himself. He wasn't sure if that was going to be of any use, but when one is in a hostile situation, any knowledge one possesses that is not shared by one's opponent is inherently some sort of advantage, even if the details of that advantage are not readily apparent. "So, what did you do to me?" asked Calhoun. "To get me here. To knock me out?"

"A simple drug in your food."

"But I ate and drank the same as everyone else. You couldn't have singled mine out."

"I did not have to. I put it into everyone's drink. However, a drug that can reduce your bodily functions to simulate death can also be completely harm-less to Zondarians."

So much for my vaunted sixth sense, Calhoun mused. He rationalized to himself that perhaps he hadn't realized specifically where the danger was coming from because, to so many people in the room, it presented no danger at all. Or, more likely, he just wasn't perfect. That was something he definitely hated to admit.

"And then I simply brought you here after your body was taken to the sacred place of preparation. I am somewhat stronger than I may appear to you, oh Great One. I admit, you did become a bit heavy the last mile or so, but it was nothing I could not handle. I have, after all, the strength of my convictions."

"Would you mind telling me what the hell we're doing here? I take it that this isn't something being sanctioned by your peers."

Ramed shook his head. "No. No, not at all. At the moment, in fact, there is great consternation among my people. You made quite the impression upon them in a fairly short time. Although admittedly, you did have help. We told the people of your coming, we told them that you were the fulfillment of prophecy. Naturally they could not help but love you. See you as a symbol of something truly great."

"And you, for some reason, feel the need to undo all that?"

Slowly, Ramed sank down to the ground near him, as if he were commiserating somehow. "I have no choice," he said simply. "My part in these matters is as predestined as your arrival was. As your death is."

"You are so certain, then, that I am going to die."

From the folds of his clothes, Ramed pulled out a wooden handle. He pushed on it and a long and sharpened point snapped out. "Neither man nor woman will save you," Ramed said.

The words immediately struck a cord within Calhoun. It had been the exact words of his ghostly visitor from earlier. But Ramed had made quite clear that he had not heard the exchange; unless, for some reason, Ramed was endeavoring to completely confuse him. But that didn't seem likely. Ramed might be deluded, even demented, and certainly bent on Calhoun's destruction, but remarkably subtle he most definitely was not.

They stared at each other for a time. Then Ramed said, "Are you not going to beg for your life?"

"Am I supposed to?" Calhoun asked sarcastically. "You seem to be rather cognizant of what's to come. You tell me."

"I do not claim to know *every* detail," Ramed replied.

"Ah. Well, thank you for clearing that up." Calhoun's eyes narrowed. He struggled to bring himself up to a fully sitting position and managed by dint of pulling his back up against the wall. "Why do you think I'm going to beg for my life?"

"Well, that is a natural action for one who is destined to die."

"We're all destined to die, Ramed. Beg for my life? I've been prepared to die since age fifteen. I never expected to live to see twenty. Every day beyond that, I've considered to be something of a gift. So if you're expecting to see me grovel and crawl now, if that's what this is about—"

"No, that's not what this is about. This is about saving my world."

"I thought that's what my presence here was doing."

"You have no say in the matter either, oh Great One. You are as caught up in all this as I am."

"Caught up in all *what?*" Calhoun said slowly, as if addressing a child. "You have yet to tell me what the hell this is all about."

"You truly desire to know?"

"No, Ramed, it's always been my goal to die in ignorance. Yes, of course I want to know."

Ramed rose, walking away from him and disappearing into the inner recesses of the cave. This, to Calhoun, did not seem the most straightforward manner of answering a question. Moments later, however, Ramed returned with a scroll. It was carefully preserved within a tube, and Ramed removed it from the cylinder with extreme delicacy. He began to read from it, and Calhoun could tell from the way that Ramed wasn't even truly looking at it that either he was making it up as he went, or else he had read it so many times that he more or less had it memorized.

"'Look to the stars, for from there will come the Messiah,'" Ramed said. "'The bird of flame will signal his coming. He will bear a scar, and he will be a great leader. He will come from air and return to air. And he will be slain by the appointed one. The appointed one, who will be privy to great knowledge. The appointed one, a great spiritual and religious leader, one to whom many will look for guidance, who will hear these words and know, within his heart, that he is the one who is chosen to slay the Savior. He and no other. There will be a great festival to celebrate the Savior, from which the Savior will disappear. And he will then live for three days and three hours exactly after that disappearance. There will come a great confrontation within the place that was once my home. The Savior will be saved by neither man nor woman, and he will die, impaled on the great spear passed down by my descendants. And in that slaying, the Messiah's death will unite our planet. And . . .'" Ramed's voice trailed off.

"Oh, don't stop now," Calhoun said drily. "This was just getting interesting."

"'And if he does not die in the appointed way, then the final war will destroy all? All. All!'" he added for emphasis.

"That was truly riveting," Calhoun told him. "And what am I supposed to learn from that?"

"You are supposed to understand," Ramed said in genuine confusion. He waved the spear around for emphasis. "This is prophecy. These are the words of Ontear himself. Most of it has not been made known to the good people of Zondar. Only that the Savior would one day come. That is all they know. But it was the wish of Ontear—a wish carried out by his greatest acolyte, Suti—that only the innermost circle know of the true, full details of what was to happen. After all, who would willingly wish to become known as the Savior of the Zondarian people if he knew that his destiny was to die in order to obtain that unity?"

"I can see where that would be a problem."

"Suti kept the sacred knowledge within his own family, and that knowledge was handed down, from one generation to the next. The secret scroll, passed down, the information waiting for the time that was to come."

"And you're certain that I am the Savior," Calhoun said. "You're so certain of that. And that you are the appointed one who is supposed to kill me."

"Of course," Ramed said in clear confusion. "How can you possibly dispute it? The prophecy is clear—"

"Is it? How do you know?"

"It could not be more clear!"

"*T'han*chips. I think you're looking for an excuse," Calhoun told him. "I think you're just a deluded, would-be murdering bastard who's looking for any excuse—"

Ramed was literally trembling with rage. "How can you say that? You know nothing of me! *You know nothing!*" He drew closer to Calhoun. "I have a wife! A son! I am a good man, a decent man, who has never harmed a soul in my entire life! Do you think I wanted this task? Do you? I lived in dread of being the appointed one! As did my father, and his father before him! You have no idea what it was like, Calhoun! No idea of the burden my family has carried! Every day, for generations, Zondarians have hoped and prayed that the Savior would come! And every day, for generations, my clan has dreaded that moment, for we knew that the knowledge we possessed ensured our damnation! If I lived my entire life and never set eye on the Savior, I would have died in peace—no! I lie, for I would have had to pass the knowledge on to my son, thereby condemning him to a life of apprehension! I have spared him that, at least. For that, I suppose, I should be grateful. I must do this thing, Calhoun. I have no choice, no free will. My people, the fate of my very world, depends on my next actions! I must do that which I find personally repugnant in order to ensure that my planet is united! For if I do not, if my will is weak, if I fail in the endeavor, then there will come a great war which will destroy everything! How can I condemn my people, my world, to that?"

"Your destiny is no more and no less than what you make of it," Calhoun said. "Letting your every move be dictated by vague prophecy . . ."

"There is nothing vague about it!"

"There sure as hell is."

"It speaks of your coming from the stars, with the flame bird as your avatar!"

"The flame bird merely speaks of the timing of it. Even if you judge that this is the time, that doesn't mean I'm necessarily the one you're expecting. All our worlds orbit stars, or suns. We owe our lives, our existence to them. We all come from the stars, Ramed. All of us. Singling me out simply because I come from a starship is folly."

"'He will come from air and return to air!' You materialized out of the air itself!"

"You're a spiritual individual, Ramed. Don't you

believe in the ephemeral nature of the spirit? We are plucked from nothingness, and to nothingness we return."

Ramed shook his head and pointed accusingly at Calhoun, coming to within a foot of him. "This is absurd," he said. "In most cultures, prophecies are vague, and those with something to gain try to find the specifics that will serve them. Here the prophecies could not be more specific, and you seek to dilute them."

"I'm simply pointing out that maybe they're not as precise as you thought. You could just as easily be the savior as me. You're a great leader, after all."

"Oh really?" Ramed smiled patronizingly. "'He will bear a scar.' What of that? I have no scar."

That was when Calhoun lunged forward.

He'd slowly been positioning himself, maintaining what seemed a casual sitting position. The moment that Ramed was close enough, however, Calhoun made his move.

His intention was to slam into Ramed with such force that he would knock him cold. He would then grab the sharpened pike and use it to cut through the ropes that were binding him. For a spur of the moment plan, it wasn't bad.

Unfortunately the ground betrayed him.

There was a thin layer of gravel. Had his feet been free so that he could properly maneuver, he would have easily been able to vault it or maneuver around it. But with his feet tied up, it was impossible for him to move with his usual agility.

Consequently his bound feet went out from under him, and he collided with Ramed in a totally off-balance fashion. Ramed staggered back, spinning away, and his face smashed into the cave wall. He slid to the ground, momentarily dropping his spear, and Calhoun tried to angle around to get it. But Ramed was too quick, snatching it up and holding it between them, point directly aimed at Calhoun's chest. Calhoun lay on the ground, his purple eyes focused pitilessly on Ramed.

"What did you think you were doing?" Ramed gasped out. Blood was pouring down the side of his face from where he'd slammed it against the wall.

"Trying to make my own destiny, you pathetic idiot," Calhoun snapped at him. "Just as I've been doing all my life. You—you're a slave to yours. But I'll shape my own. By the way, congratulations. That's going to leave a rather impressive scar."

Ramed was trying to staunch the bleeding. He tore off a portion of his sleeve and used it to put pressure on the wound. "Very amusing, Great One," he said, with as heavy sarcasm as he could muster. "Very, very amusing. You're trying to confuse matters. To confuse me. But it's not going to work, do you understand?"

"I understand perfectly. You're obviously the one who doesn't understa—"

He didn't have the opportunity to complete the sentence, because a chime began to sound from within the cave. Calhoun looked around. "What's that?" he asked. "An alarm clock to tell you that now's when you're supposed to butcher me?"

"No. It's a proximity alarm," Ramed told him. He pulled the cloth away and saw that it was soaked with blood, but also could see that the flow had slowed down appreciably.

"An alarm? We're in a cave in the middle of nowhere. What kind of alarms and technology do you have in a place like this?"

Ramed stared at him. "You'd be amazed," he said.

"If someone's coming," Calhoun told him, "particularly if it's my people, I assure you, they'll get past whatever it is you've got prepared."

"Your confidence in your crew is most heartening,

even though it indicates an unwillingness to accept the hopelessness of your situation. This area has been prepared, you see. Prepared for centuries by my ancestors, who have known that this would be the place where the Savior would be taken to meet His destiny. There is technology here that is undreamt of, even by your standards. It's one of our other great secrets. Anything that your people might have prepared has already been considered and guarded against."

"I was unaware that you were that technologically advanced a race."

"We're not," Ramed smiled ruefully. "That is both our blessing and our curse. Your people have already made a foray to find you. They were rebuffed."

"Rebuffed?" This caught Calhoun's attention. He started to sit up, but Ramed held the spear out in a vaguely threatening fashion and Calhoun stopped moving. "What do you mean, rebuffed? What did you do to my people?"

"I? I did nothing. They did it to themselves, just as these newcomers will. And once they are disposed of, well, the third hour of the third day beckons, oh Great One. That which will be your last hour."

"Or yours," Calhoun replied.

Ramed looked at him sadly. "Poor, sad Savior. Still hoping to be rescued. Still refusing to believe that neither man nor woman will save you."

And Calhoun smiled. "Believe me, Ramed, with my crew, that isn't necessarily as much of an obstacle as you might think."

XVI.

IT WAS LATE AT NIGHT on Zondar as Burgoyne stood on the rocky outcropping, hir nostrils flaring, feeling more alive than s/he had in ages. The moons of Zondar were full, providing a healthy dose of light. Nearby Ensign Janos—looking cramped, as always, in his Starfleet uniform—cracked his knuckles with a sound that seemed like a cannon shot.

The area around them did not seem particularly inviting. It was fairly mountainous, with a myriad of caves. Burgoyne realized that there was any number of hiding places where the captain and his captor could be. S/he held up a medical tricorder, packing the same information that Selar's had held, as a means of tracking down the captain. But a quick readout of the immediate area revealed a problem. "We're getting some sort of interference," Burgoyne said. S/he tried adjusting the tricorder but had no success with it."

"Which would lead us to assume," Ensign Janos

231

observed, "that someone is actively trying to discourage us from locating the captain."

"Obviously. This must be one of the things that caused the other away team to run into problems. So," and Burgoyne snapped the tricorder closed, "we're just going to have to go about this the old-fashioned away. How's your sense of smell, Janos?"

"My olfactory abilities are exceptional, as befits my race, if not necessarily my breeding."

"All right, then. Start sniffing around. You take east, I'll take west."

No words were exchanged for some minutes after that. Burgoyne prowled the area, paying little attention to Janos at that point. All of hir senses were extended, trying to pick up some physical trace of the captain. S/he sniffed the air, s/he scented around rock and rocky trails, trying to detect some sort of lead, some vague hint as to where the captain might have gone to.

"Chief!" called Janos. Janos was approximately a hundred yards away, but Burgoyne crossed the distance quickly and efficiently, moving with a grace and ease that would have startled any onlooker with the possible exception of McHenry. Janos was down on the ground, sniffing around one particular section, and he grunted, "I think I've got something."

"The captain?"

"No. I think it's Kebron."

Burgoyne quickly dropped to the ground next to Janos. It would have been a strange sight, had anyone been around: two Starfleet officers, crawling about on the ground, sniffing. Fortunately enough for decorum and the image of the fleet, no one was around at that particular moment.

"I think you're right," Burgoyne said after a moment. "Let's go."

They stayed low to the ground, on the scent. Burgoyne quickly took the lead, moving on all fours across the rough terrain, hir arms and legs bending at joints usually covered by hir uniform. S/he hit an incline at one point, and hir hardened nails dug into the rocky ground with efficiency. There was no unnecessary chatter between the two of them; they were moving entirely on instinct, and Burgoyne came to the reluctant realization that Soleta had known what she was about when she insisted on pairing Burgoyne with Janos.

And as s/he moved across the terrain, as all of hir tracking senses came to the fore, subtle changes came over Burgoyne. Hir lips drew back to reveal hir canines, but it was not in the teasing or slightly threatening manner in which s/he usually displayed them. Rather, it was as if s/he was prepared to use them—indeed, couldn't wait to do so. Hir normally dark eyes had clouded over completely as s/he tapped deeply into hirself, into an essence that was hir natural state but one that s/he normally did everything s/he could to keep hidden away. Hir claws—for that was, indeed, the best way to describe them, since "nails" somehow didn't do them justice—clicked against the rocky surface as s/he made hir way across it. S/he sensed rather than saw that Janos was directly behind hir, smelled his thick fur and distinctive scent.

There was a deep crevice just ahead of them, and Burgoyne—disdaining to scamper the rest of the way—coiled and then leaped, clearing the distance of fifteen feet in one vault. Cautious of a possible booby trap, Burgoyne tentatively stuck hir head over the edge and peered down.

Wedged in, far below, was a familiar dark-skinned form.

"Kebron!" called Burgoyne. "Kebron, it's me! Burgoyne one-seventy-two! Kebron!" A moment later, Janos appeared at Burgoyne's side. "Kebron, can you hear me?"

There seemed to be a slight appearance of movement on Kebron's part. He tried to angle his head upward, but since his neck was virtually nonexistent, this was somewhat problematic for him. He had to try and tilt his entire torso back as best he could, and was only partly successful. His voice strained with the effort. "I . . . hear you," he said slowly.

The crevice had to be at least twenty feet down. "Kebron, we'll get you out of there!" called Burgoyne.

"Can't," he told them, and he'd never sounded so tired. "Grav generator . . . out . . . can barely . . . move. . . ."

Immediately Burgoyne knew what had happened. Zak Kebron was so massive, that the only way he was able to move in a non-Brikar gravity field was with a small portable gravity generator that he wore in his belt. It was virtually impossible to break the generator through conventional means. Something had managed to short it out, however, and Kebron was clearly finding it impossible to do anything.

Burgoyne tapped hir commbadge in an endeavor to raise the *Excalibur*. Hir reasoning was simple: Beam Kebron up out of the crevice. This intention, however, was quickly thwarted when all s/he could get over hir commbadge was static. And the idea of Burgoyne and Janos going down and trying to pull Kebron out was simply an impossibility. Even between the two of them, and the considerable strength that Janos possessed, there was just no way that they could possibly haul Kebron out from the crevice.

"Kebron!" Burgoyne called down to him. "You'll have to wait there until we find some way to get you out!"

"Wait . . . fine . . . not planning on . . . going anywhere . . ."

"What happened, Lieutenant?" Janos called down. "What did this to you? How many of them are there?"

Kebron didn't seem to hear at first. He appeared stunned, and Burgoyne realized that it was a condition beyond anything that the simple deprivation of the field generator could have caused. Kebron was in shock.

"Hundreds of them . . ." Kebron said. "Thousands . . . couldn't stop them . . ."

Burgoyne and Janos looked at each other. "That sounds pleasant," Janos observed.

"Kebron, be strong," Burgoyne urged him, although s/he wasn't sure just exactly how much good that was going to do. "We'll be back for you as soon as we can."

No reply came back.

Quickly the two officers vaulted the crevice, sniffing the air, the dirt, anything they could. And this time it was Burgoyne who picked up the scent. S/he had been crouched on the ground, running the crumbling dirt under hir fingers, and s/he detected something that became stronger as s/he moved off to hir right. "Got it!" Burgoyne called. "Got the captain!"

"Brilliant!" crowed Janos.

"It seems as if—" S/he prowled the area, trying to confirm what s/he already suspected. "Yes. Whoever took the captain was likely carrying him, and then became tired and started dragging him. This way."

"I'm with you, Chief."

Quickly they set off across the terrain, moving with amazing speed. The scent grew stronger the farther along that Burgoyne went, and within moments s/he was no longer running in anything that vaguely approximated humanoid manner. S/he was sprinting on all fours, a satisfied growl low in hir throat, and there was no concern whatsoever about what s/he might run into. S/he was completely focused on the hunt.

And it wasn't just about finding the captain, either. S/he was eager to track down the person or persons who had abused Selar. S/he wanted to wrap hir fingers around their throats, s/he wanted to sink hir teeth deep into their flesh, to rend and tear . . .

There was a faint buzzing in hir head that began to grow louder and louder, but s/he wasn't fully aware of it. Instead s/he was completely wrapped up in the thoughts of what s/he was going to do to Selar's assailants when s/he got hir hands on them. S/he could almost taste the sweetness of their blood pumping into hir, could savor the screams for mercy that they would utter. But there would be no mercy. There would only be slaughter, and blood, and Burgoyne's laughter combined with a triumphant roar . . .

S/he took another step, then another, and the buzzing was becoming louder still, and finally s/he became aware of it in a distant manner, wondering what it was . . .

And suddenly s/he was on the *Excalibur.*

S/he looked around in confusion, not entirely sure how the devil s/he'd gotten back there. The corridors were empty. S/he began to run, calling out names of various crewmembers, trying to find someone. S/he didn't even think to hit the commbadge on hir chest. S/he just yelled, becoming angrier as hir cries were ignored.

S/he ran into engineering, and everyone was there. Everyone. Everyone s/he'd ever known, everyone s/he'd ever encountered. Hir parents were there, and others from Hermat—not friends, certainly, for s/he'd had no real friends on Hermat—and the engineering crew, and the command crew. There was Calhoun standing there, arms folded, shaking his head in clear disdain, and Shelby's face twisted in contempt, and the others were all pointing, shouting at hir.

"Freak!" they called out. Over and over came the

word, "Freak, freak!" spoken with derision, cried out in a hundred different voices that combined as one.

A freak to hir own people, for the outgoing and sexually joyful Burgoyne had never truly fit in with other Hermats, who tended to prefer their own kind. Freak to the people of the *Excalibur,* who had never known a Hermat before and didn't at all know what to make of hir. All the suspicious glances, the scornful looks, all aimed at hir. S/he tried to back out of engineering, but the door had closed behind hir and refused to open.

"Get away from me!" shouted Burgoyne. "Get away!"

Instead, they advanced, and there was McHenry in the forefront, shaking his head and saying, "You were just an experiment! An exercise in weirdness! I never found you attractive, never!" and there was Selar, as burned and battered as when s/he'd last seen her, and Selar was sneering, "Even on my deathbed I'd never want you! You vile, bizarre thing! You sickening, perverted monster!"

Burgoyne roared in fury. The hackles on the back of hir neck rose, hir eyes went completely dark, and hir claws were fully extended. All of the playfulness, all of the confidence, everything that made hir what s/he was, had vanished. All s/he knew were those who feared hir, hated hir, despised hir either behind her back or to hir face.

"I'll kill you!" s/he howled, and with uncontrolled frenzy s/he leaped forward . . .

And crashed squarely into Ensign Janos.

Janos, who was surrounded by mugatos, his own kind with whom he had as much in common as he had with an amoeba. Mugatos jumping around, snarling at him, picking at him and poking at him in the midst of the jungle on Tyree's World to which mugatos were native. Janos had never set foot, paw, or anything else upon Tyree's World, but he had known it just the same. They prodded at him with their horns, they tore at him with their poisonous fangs, which were not toxic to him, but could rip him up and injure him just the same. He cried out as they came at him from all directions, and then the carefully cultivated personality that he'd worked so long to develop evaporated, and Janos bellowed, a truly frightening sound of a mugato in full rage. A mugato seeking an enemy to rend limb from limb.

It was in this state of mind that Burgoyne and Janos slammed into each other.

And nearby, something formed of coalescing energy took shape and started to advance upon them.

XVII.

THE LONG RANGE SENSORS gave the *Excalibur* her first warning that there was danger imminent.

Boyajian, the tactical officer filling in for Kebron due to the security chief's absence, called out to Soleta, who was in the command chair. "We have an incoming vessel, Lieutenant. And it's big."

"Put it on screen," Soleta said calmly.

"Not yet possible, sir. Hasn't emerged from warp space yet." He paused and then said, "Orders, sir?"

Soleta considered the situation a moment. Unknown territory, an unknown vessel coming toward them, intentions unknown. She didn't like to take an immediate defensive posture with a new encounter, since it could make them look as if they were combative or spoiling for a fight. Nonetheless, not doing anything would be tempting fate, particularly if the other vessel dropped out of warp space with all weapons blazing.

Lefler and McHenry were both looking at her expectantly, as were the other members of the bridge crew. Soleta began to feel, once again, the gnawing doubt of someone who believed that she was in way over her head. But there was absolutely no way that she was going to share that sentiment or concern with the rest of the crew.

"Yellow alert," Soleta said after a moment. "Raise shields. Bring weapons and targeting systems on line, but do not energize weapons."

"Do not—" repeated Boyajian.

"No. The chances are that their scans won't be able to detect that we've got them targeted, but would be able to determine that we're running weapons hot."

"So we're hedging our bets," commented Lefler.

"Precisely, Lieutenant. Our bets are significantly hedged. Continue sensor sweeps for the captain."

"Lieutenant," and McHenry leaned back in his chair to address Soleta. There was a trace of worry in his voice. "We haven't heard from Burgoyne or Janos."

"I didn't expect to, Mister McHenry," replied Soleta. "The area that they are exploring is in the heart of the interference zone. That's the territory that we're having difficulty scanning or getting any communications from. The likelihood that they would be able to keep us apprised of their progress is fairly slim. It is my assumption that if we do hear from them before the end of the twelve-hour period I've given them—of which eight hours, fourteen minutes remains—it will be because they have accomplished their task and emerged from the zone." She hesitated and then added, in as close to an understanding voice as she could muster, "I'm sure Burgoyne is fine, Lieutenant. S/he is a rather resourceful individual."

"Believe me, I know," McHenry said.

Boyajian suddenly looked up from tactical. "Lieutenant, she's coming out of warp."

"All departments report confirmation of yellow alert status," Lefler confirmed.

"Ship coming in at nine-hundred-thousand kilometers, bearing two-eleven mark three."

"Bring us about, Mister McHenry. Let's keep some distance between us," Soleta said.

"Aye, sir."

"Bridge to Ambassador Si Cwan," she added after a moment's consideration.

"Si Cwan here," came the brisk reply.

"Ambassador, your presence on the bridge would be most appreciated. We seem to have visitors."

"On my way."

The *Excalibur* angled out of orbit and came around to face the newcomer. The vessel's warp drive bubble evaporated as the ship entered normal space and came to a halt approximately 850,000 kilometers from the starship. The ship was pyramidal, powerful-looking, and half again as large as the *Excalibur*.

"Hail on all frequencies, Mister Boyajian," Soleta said, drumming her fingers gently on the armrest. "Let them know we're not out to start a fight."

"I am hailing them, sir, but they're not responding."

"That could be unfortunate." She leaned forward, studying the ship's configuration. Soleta was not entirely unfamiliar with Sector 221-G; she had spent some time exploring the once-Thallonian Empire at a time when outsiders were not only unwelcome, but more often than not, put to death. She had acquired some knowledge in her travels, and she had the suspicion that she recognized the ship's configuration. If she was correct, then the situation with which they were faced was a fairly incendiary one.

The turbolift doors hissed open and Si Cwan strode onto the bridge. Immediately his gaze went to the front screen, and he slowed to a halt. Then he spat out a word that Soleta immediately recognized as a rather extreme Thallonian profanity. "I take your reaction," she said slowly, "to be an indicator that our new arrivals are, in fact, who I think they are."

"The Redeemers," Si Cwan nodded. "Just what we needed."

"I take it that's not good," Lefler surmised.

"Not in the least. Boyajian, sensor scan?"

"They are heavily armed, Lieutenant. They have not as of yet activated their weapons array. Their shields are likewise in place."

"In other words, we're both suspicious, but neither of us wants to provoke the other."

"An accurate assessment, Lieutenant."

"Lieutenant, these are Redeemers we're talking about," Si Cwan told her. "They are missionary zealots, and if you do not accept their particular deity—Xant—then they will have no use for you."

"Meaning they'll leave us alone?" McHenry suggested optimistically.

"Meaning they will endeavor to blow us out of space," replied Soleta.

"Oh. Well, that's not quite as good."

"Let me try to talk to them. We've dealt with them before. The royal family has always managed to avoid Holy Wars with the Redeemers; perhaps I can continue our run of good luck."

"Be my guest, Ambassador," said Soleta.

"Put me on a hailing frequency," Si Cwan said to Boyajian, and when the latter nodded confirmation that he was on, Si Cwan said, "Attention, Redeemer vessel. This is the *Starship Excalibur*. This is Ambassador Si Cwan speaking. Perhaps you remember me; you've had dealings with both myself, and my ancestors, for many years. We have always managed to have mutual respect for each other's concerns, and I see no reason that that has to change now. Please inform us of your concerns, and we will endeavor to answer them." He stopped and turned back to Boyajian. "Did they get that? Did they hear me?"

"I broadcast it, Ambassador," said Boyajian. "Whether they actually listened, I couldn't tell y—" Then he paused, checking the readings on his board. "Lieutenant, we're getting an incoming hail."

"It would seem they indeed heard you, Ambassador," Soleta said. "Well done."

"Let us save the congratulations until we see whether they are saying anything we wish to hear."

"A valid point. Put them on, Mister Boyajian."

The screen rippled and, a moment later, the ebony face of a Redeemer appeared on the screen. He gazed at them with eyes that seemed to glow a deep and frightening red.

Lefler immediately felt a chill at the base of her spine. Her impulse was to look away, but she didn't want to appear weak or faint of heart. She glanced over at McHenry and took a small measure of comfort in seeing that he appeared to have the same reaction. It appeared as if McHenry would rather be looking anywhere else than directly at the viewscreen. But he couldn't take his eyes away from it: Not just out of a sense of duty, as was the case with Lefler, but also out of a deep fascination. He found the Redeemer just too compelling, in a negative away, to look away from him.

Soleta, for her part, remained impassive. As for Si Cwan, he had seen enough Redeemers in his life not to be put off or intimidated by their frankly frightening air.

"I am Prime One," said the Redeemer. His voice was an odd combination of deep but brittle. "I am

second only to the Overlord in the Redeemer hierarchy."

"Greetings, Prime One," said Si Cwan. He made a
small hand gesture that Soleta surmised to be some
sort of ritual greeting. "We have not met, but I know
of you. I am Si Cwan."

"I know of you, Thallonian. I have heard many
positive things about you. Also"—and his eyes
seemed to glow more brightly—"some rather negative things."

"That is the way of all things, is it not, Prime One?
Even in the light of Xant, there must be darkness."

Prime One inclined his head slightly to indicate
that Si Cwan had a point. He glanced around the
bridge from his vantage point. "We desire to speak to
the captain."

"The captain is not available," Soleta said, rising
from her chair. "I am Lieutenant Soleta. You may
address me in any matters pertaining to this vessel."

"Where is your captain? Where is the one called
Calhoun? Is he on your vessel?"

"The captain," Soleta repeated guardedly, "is not
available. If you have business, it can be discussed
with me."

"Our business is not with you," Prime One said. "It
is with Calhoun. The one whom those on the world
below call 'Savior.' The one whose name and reputation spreads from one world to the next, like a
plague."

"I'm not quite following," admitted Soleta.

Prime One let out an irritated sigh, as if he felt he
was speaking to someone who wasn't worth the effort.
"We have been preparing the worlds under our sphere
of influence, plus other worlds that may be worth our
while, to prepare for the return of Xant. Xant, the one
true god. Xant, the one true Savior of all worlds."

"I see," said Soleta. "And why would this be pertinent to us?"

"Do not be coy with me, Vulcan. It ill befits you or your eminently logical kind. We both know that various planets—including, most conspicuously, the one directly below us—are espousing the opinion that Calhoun's arrival is tantamount to, and even more important than, the return of Xant. Calhoun is working to supplant Xant's rightful place in the galaxy."

"Captain Calhoun is doing no such thing," replied Soleta.

"We have information to the contrary," began Prime One.

But Si Cwan stepped in quickly before Prime One could continue. "Your information, I must tell you, is faulty," he assured Prime One. "I will grant you, the people of Zondar seem to have elevated Captain Calhoun to some sort of god-like status. But that was the decision of their world, and one that was not supported by Captain Calhoun himself."

"From our understanding, he presented himself as the Savior of Zondar."

"He was endeavoring to save a race from destroying itself," Si Cwan pointed out. "Further, he presented himself as nothing. They believed him to be their Savior. What matters what a race believes when one is trying to save it? You know of the civil war that grips the Zondarians."

"Yes, we were aware," said Prime One. "It was, and is, a tragic situation that brother should slay brother."

"You see, we are in agreement then."

"About the situation, yes. But we had every intention of attending to Zondar in our own way."

That comment, and the implied threat, were unmistakable. "Are you saying that you intended to . . . redeem Zondar?"

"It was a planet ripe for redemption. And with the demise of the Thallonian Empire, all agreements between ourselves and your family are, obviously, in abeyance."

"Even so," Si Cwan said, "you cannot feel that Mackenzie Calhoun has undercut the divine Xant simply because he was doing his job. He is here to help. To aid a belligerent people in setting aside their differences. What matter the method?"

"It matters to us," Prime One told him flatly. "What Calhoun has done is nothing less than pose a threat to the entire structure of the Redeemers. At least you Thallonians did not trespass into the realm of the theological. Yours was a straightforward environment of warfare and business. You conquered and controlled, not out of a sense of divine right, but out of a belief in your own intrinsic strength. We believed it to be shortsighted and limited, but it was a mind-set with which we could co-exist. Calhoun, on the other hand, is being perceived as some sort of Savior."

"Mackenzie Calhoun cannot control how he is perceived by others."

"Granted," said Prime One. "We, however, can."

McHenry turned to Lefler and in a very low voice, said, "I do *not* like the sound of that."

Nor did Si Cwan. "May I ask," he said slowly, "how you would propose to exercise that control?"

"By destroying both Calhoun and his vessel," said Prime One matter-of-factly.

And now Lefler murmured to McHenry, in an equally low voice, "Yup. That would do it."

Soleta now took a step forward before Si Cwan could reply. "I must warn you, sir, if you fire upon this vessel, we will take retaliatory action. Furthermore, bear in mind that this is a Federation starship. To fire unprovoked upon us is to risk direct confrontation with the Federation itself."

"Unprovoked?" Prime One retorted. "We have endeavored to save the souls of the races in this sector before your Federation had even assembled its meager membership. You come in here, on your supposed mission of mercy, when in fact the Redeemers consider it nothing less than trespass. And then to foist one of your own off as a major religious figure . . ."

"We have been over that, Prime One," Si Cwan said. "The primary mandate of this vessel is to save lives, and Captain Calhoun—"

"And our primary mandate is to save souls!" shot back Prime One. "And how is that to be accomplished if Xant is to return, only to discover that he has been forsaken in the name of some upstart Starfleet captain?! A world already lies in ruins because of him."

"What do you mean?"

"Alpha Carinae, Lord Cwan. The people there came to believe in the influence of Mackenzie Calhoun. In so doing, they attacked and killed the High Priest of that world. You know the consequences of such an act."

For a moment, Si Cwan felt the strength draining from his legs. He reached back and gripped the upper rail behind him. Soleta looked to him questioningly, standing with her back to the screen so that they had a fraction of privacy despite the height difference between them.

"High Priests are equipped with a sort of fail-safe device," Si Cwan said, after he'd taken a moment to steady himself. "A particularly virulent strain of virus. It's contained within their bodies, in a device that is keyed to the heartbeat of the priest. If the priest is critically injured or killed—in short, if they die of anything save natural causes—the virus is released. Within seventy-two hours, no one is left alive on the world."

Soleta's eyes went wide.

Si Cwan then looked to the screen, his face hardening. "And you would blame this . . . this tragedy on Calhoun?"

"On whom else, Lord Cwan?" demanded the Prime One.

"On whom else? And on whom did you place the blame when there was revolt on Oxon Three, eh? And your little plague-retaliation lay waste to that race? Or what about the brutal beating of a High Priest on Lesikor, eh? That time, you intervened quickly enough so that merely half the population of the planet was destroyed. And where was Calhoun then, eh? No, no, Prime One. Look elsewhere for your precious blame. Look to yourselves. Your converts balk against your restrictions and your oppression. They rebel against you. You try to redeem them when the only thing they need saving from is you yourselves! So if the people of Alpha Carinae latched onto the legend building around Calhoun, what of it? Sooner or later they would have seized upon someone or something else. They were not turning toward another. They were turning away from you, and that's the truth of it! Rather than seek out Calhoun to punish him for your own shortcomings and oppression, look on this as an object lesson in the danger of domination!"

Very quietly, Prime One replied, "I hardly think that you, of all people, are qualified to spout lessons on the danger of domination, oh fallen Lord Cwan."

Si Cwan's face darkened slightly, and he said, "Actually, I beg to differ. I think I am eminently qualified. After all, who knows better of the hazards of dictatorship than a fallen dictator?"

Through the distance of space, the two of them stared at each other for a long moment.

"Calhoun is no threat to you," Si Cwan said at last.

"Perhaps you are right," Prime One said.

Several members of the bridge crew let out sighs of relief.

"But then again, perhaps you are wrong," continued Prime One. "We cannot take that chance."

Boyajian looked up from his sensors. "Lieutenant, they're going weapons hot!"

"Red alert, sound battle stations," Soleta said, icy calm descending upon her. She was now faced with a worst-case scenario, and she had absolutely no choice but to try and see it through. In a way, it was almost a relief. Now she knew what she had to face. "Prime One," she said as she took one more try at the screen, "I must warn you once more: We will defend ourselves if fired upon."

"I would hope so," replied Prime One.

"Calhoun is not aboard this ship!" Si Cwan called above the klaxon of the red alert. "You're accomplishing nothing!"

"The ship is doomed anyway, for we would hardly want the vessel of a martyred captain cruising the spaceways, spreading word of his great deeds," reasoned Prime One. "If you are lying and the captain is on the vessel, then we have accomplished our mission. If not, and he is on the planet surface, then we will either redeem the planet or—if it is irredeemable—obliterate the populace as well. The infection of Calhoun worship will end, here and now. May Xant light your way to the next life." And the screen blinked out.

"At least he gave us his blessing," McHenry commented.

"Incoming!" called Boyajian. "High energy concentration plasma torpedoes! Locked on and tracking us!"

"Evasive maneuvers!" called Soleta.

And McHenry promptly slammed the *Excalibur* into reverse.

At high speed, increasing with every moment, the *Excalibur* hurtled backward on full reverse thrust, the torpedoes in hot pursuit.

"Thirty thousand kilometers and closing!" called McHenry.

"Locking on counters!" Boyajian said. "Keep us steady, McHenry! Just need another few seconds!"

"Maintaining course and speed!"

"Counter torpedoes locked on! Firing!"

Photon torpedoes leaped out from underneath the ship, hitting the plasma torpedoes squarely. The explosion rippled outward, but the *Excalibur* gracefully sailed around it.

"Redeemer vessel in pursuit," called Boyajian. "Orders, Lieutenant?"

Soleta hesitated, unsure of exactly how to proceed.

And at that moment, she heard the hissing of the turbolift door and a strong, if struggling voice, say, "I'll take this one, Lieutenant."

Everyone on the bridge turned and reacted with similar astonishment, except for Soleta, who was well-trained enough to mask not only her surprise, but a vague sense of relief.

Shelby was standing in the doorway. She was still clearly injured, and she was laboring to keep herself standing. Skin grafts had been attached to replace the areas where her face and body had been lacerated, but the healing process had only just begun. Nonetheless, Shelby forced her legs to carry her forward.

"Commander?" gasped out Lefler.

"I heard a red alert. We're in trouble. If you think I'm going to lie around in sickbay, you can forget it." She staggered, gripped the command chair, and eased herself in.

"Commander, are you sure—" asked Soleta.

"No," Shelby told her. "No, I'm not sure. But I'm here, much to the chagrin of Doctor Maxwell, who's still on the verge of apoplexy that I walked out. So . . . status report."

"We are under assault by a warship belonging to a race known as the Redeemers. They are heavily armed and shielded, and have a stated intention of destroying us and, after that, Captain Calhoun. Orders, sir?"

Shelby leaned forward. "Prepare to kick 'em to hell, Lieutenant."

And Soleta came as close to smiling as she ever did. "All prepared, Commander."

XVIII.

WITH A SNARL, Burgoyne ripped a chunk out of Ensign Janos.

Janos roared in fury as his thick white fur quickly became blood-stained around his ribs. Burgoyne sank hir canines squarely into Janos's upper shoulder and, bracing hir feet against his upper chest, did everything s/he could to rip Janos's arm out of its socket.

Furious, Janos grabbed Burgoyne by the back of hir uniform and pulled hir off him, losing some more fur in the process. He hurled Burgoyne across the rocky terrain, and Burgoyne slammed into an outcropping, momentarily stunned. Without hesitation, Janos lowered his head and charged, driving his horn straight at Burgoyne's chest. Burgoyne had been momentarily stunned, and hir vision cleared just in time to see the horn bearing down straight at hir. Just before Janos made contact, Burgoyne took a quick step forward and leaped high, somersaulting through the air and over Janos's head. Janos, unable to halt his charge in time, crashed into the rocky wall, chipping off some of the rock and some fur off his head as well.

Janos spun, baring his fangs and howling his fury at Burgoyne. He charged after hir, the ground shaking under him. Burgoyne, had s/he been in hir right mind, would have run. Instead s/he maintained her ground to meet the charge. It was nothing short of suicidal, for the fangs of the enraged ensign were poisoned, and the slightest scratch from those frightening weapons would kill anyone: even a Hermat chief engineer.

Janos lunged, sweeping his right claw through the air. Burgoyne ducked under it, not even moving hir feet. S/he snarled derisively, and the move further enraged Janos. He swung a left, another right, just trying to get a grip on Burgoyne, but the Hermat was too quick. S/he maneuvered as if Janos were moving in slow motion. Quickly becoming fed up, Janos charged forward with his entire body. Burgoyne darted between his legs, taking a moment to sweep with hir talons across the upper portion of Janos's thigh. The ensign went down, howling, clutching at his leg. He didn't know how lucky he was. Burgoyne had been moving quickly, and if s/he hadn't had to hurry hir thrust and had, in fact, hit where s/he was aiming, Janos's scream would have been considerably higher-pitched.

Burgoyne started to scramble to hir feet, and suddenly Janos hurled himself backward. He did so blindly, but he had a general sense of where Burgoyne was, and the move caught hir by surprise. All four hundred and fifty pounds of ensign landed squarely on top of hir, knocking the wind out of hir and pinning hir.

Janos tried to reach around, find a part of hir that he could grab, get to his mouth, and chomp down on. The moment he accomplished that, the battle would effectively be over.

Moving quickly, fired by desperation, Burgoyne swung hir talons around and raked the side of Janos's face. Janos let out a yelp and Burgoyne quickly squirmed out from under the massive fury body, pulling hir legs clear and rolling frantically away.

They faced each other, both crouched, their respective teeth bared, and they circled warily. Burgoyne's talons were poised, ready to strike again, and Janos was maneuvering around to try and find a suitable terrain so that he could charge again with his horn.

And then something sounded within Burgoyne's mind. A voice . . . of someone who wasn't there.

In sickbay, Selar's eyes snapped open. She moaned, trying to sit up.

Maxwell saw it out of the corner of his eye and immediately summoned medtechs over. Selar was babbling incoherently, and Maxwell tried to make out what she was saying. Something about Burgoyne, something about monsters, and she spoke as if someone were standing right there next to her whom only she could see.

"Sedate her!" called Maxwell.

"No!" Selar said with what sounded startlingly like a growl. "*No! Leave me alone! S/he needs me!*"

Burgoyne felt her. Felt her in hir mind, in hir heart. Felt her connection to hir.

For just a moment, Burgoyne's mind cleared. The *Excalibur* evaporated, the assailants vanished, the laughing stopped . . .

And there was Ensign Janos, charging toward hir with an undiluted roar of fury.

"Oh, hell!" Burgoyne cried out, and s/he backpedaled rapidly as Janos came at hir. Realizing that Janos was going to catch up if s/he continued to run backward, Burgoyne whirled and dashed at break-neck speed, arms pumping furiously.

Dead ahead of hir was a solid wall of rock.

Right behind hir was the infuriated mugato.

Burgoyne picked up speed, ran as fast as s/he possibly could. Janos was right behind hir, propelling himself forward even faster with the aid of his knuckles.

And the second that Burgoyne reached the rock wall, s/he ran right up the wall, hurling hirself up and over. As s/he cleared the top of Janos's head, s/he grabbed the horn. The mugato reached around, trying to get at hir, as Burgoyne landed, allowed hir momentum to carry her, and twisted forward and down with all hir strength. Janos was hauled back and over in a flip, slammed down to the ground.

For just a moment, Janos was immobilized. With the blood lust upon hir, Burgoyne would have taken the opportunity to try and tear out Janos's jugular vein. But hir head was clear, and Burgoyne's hand stretched out, clamping onto the mugato's shoulder. Hir long fingers moved in perfect imitation of the way that Soleta had dropped hir with the nerve pinch.

Janos let out a startled yelp. His body trembled for a moment, and then pitched forward. Burgoyne stepped back, still cautious, in case Janos was pulling some sort of trick. But s/he quickly realized that that wasn't the case; Janos wasn't budging.

S/he felt heat beginning to build beneath hir feet, as if some sort of massive machinery was functioning beneath the ground. For a moment s/he considered picking up Janos and trying to lug him along, but quickly dismissed the notion as unworkable.

"Good thing you were here to watch my back," s/he said, before allowing him to slump to the ground.

Then s/he felt it again: that same sensation that

caused the hair on the back of hir neck to stand up. S/he spun . . .

And saw it coming toward her.

It was massive, hundreds of feet tall, and all s/he could make out was its outline. It seemed to shimmer and coalesce in the darkness, and it appeared to fill not only the air all around, but the area within Burgoyne as well. It seemed to have some sort of massive mouth, and a hundred eyes, every one boring its way into hir soul. S/he began to feel the same fears, trepidations . . .

"Get that way from me!" shouted Selar, all thought of Vulcan control tossed aside. She was sitting up in bed, struggling to shove aside the stasis field.

Maxwell came at her with a sedative, but he never had the opportunity to inject it into her. Her hand whipped around and she smacked the hypodermic out of his grasp, sending it clattering to the floor.

"Burgoyne!" she cried out, reaching into thin air. "Come back to me! Come back!"

And then s/he shook it off. The creature raged above hir, and at first Burgoyne backed up, intimidated, afraid. But s/he felt something else within hir mind, something that was helping hir to brace hirself against the beast . . .

And s/he realized what it was doing.

"I am not alone," whispered Burgoyne. "I am not alone, and you have no power over me."

Selar did not understand what was going through her mind. She was operating purely on instinct. She shoved aside the stasis field, and stumbled off the medtable, hitting the ground heavily. She wasn't remotely aware of her surroundings. All she knew was the instinct that was pounding through her, the need for her mate. The need to feel completion. The need to share herself.

She could feel hir. She had no clear idea of how s/he had gotten into her mind, but she was beyond caring. Medtechs approached her, tried to haul her back to the medtable. They made the mistake of doing so by hauling her arms up onto their shoulders. Her instinct in overdrive, she knocked the two of them cold with deftly placed nerve pinches. They slid to the floor and she went down with them, her legs skewed, her eyes staring into nothing and something all at the same time.

"Burgoyne," she whispered.

Burgoyne started forward with slow, measured tread, tapping into the ferocity that rampaged through hir. Ferocity that was born not only of hir own inner nature, but of carefully channeled sexual energy . . . energy that s/he wanted to expend with Selar, but instead focused with the intention of avenging the calamities that had been visited upon the Vulcan doctor.

The creature loomed over hir, and s/he was reminded of the truism that any science, sufficiently advanced, would appear as magic to races that didn't understand it. S/he didn't pretend to comprehend the nature of the being that faced hir. Whether it was biological, whether it was the creation of unseen machines, whatever—s/he didn't care. All s/he knew was that s/he was in another place, another mental realm where nothing was going to stop hir, least of all some static-filled, snarling mass of electrons.

"Take your best shot!" shouted Burgoyne. S/he made no effort to dodge, didn't try to run or maneuver around the energy creature. Instead s/he plunged straight into it, bellowing hir defiance. "I know what you're doing! I know what your design is! We are born alone, and we die alone, all of us! And we spend a lifetime running from that fact! Taking solace in relationships, making children to follow in our footsteps, all to avoid any contemplation of the fact that we are always alone! Always separated by our very natures! But I'm not alone, creature! I'm not!"

S/he shoved hir way squarely into the beast, and was immediately buffeted by high energy emissions that threatened to flay the skin from hir body. But there was more than physical punishment. One had to be battered down mentally in order to succumb to the beast, that much s/he had already figured out. It was the classic divide-and-conquer strategy. Separate the intended victim from all that he or she holds dear: from friends, from loved ones, from self-esteem, from the belief that good ultimately triumphs, and that life has any purpose. Leave all that behind and discover that all you have remaining to you is emptiness and hopelessness, and no point whatsoever in trying to continue one's existence. Flood the mind with that which is most frightening. Or overwhelming, like the Borg imagery for Shelby.

But that wasn't working with Burgoyne, for Burgoyne had drawn into hirself the essence of Selar. S/he held it close to hir, nursed it, drew warmth and confidence from it. The creature roared in fury all around hir, and s/he felt it descending upon hir. It was like trying to walk step by slow step through a tornado, feeling it flailing at you and trying to rend you limb from limb. Burgoyne, however, would not be stopped, would not be slowed.

Shelby, Selar, Hecht, and Scannell, even the mighty Zak Kebron . . . they had all endeavored to enter this realm, and all had failed. All had somehow been battered into submission, had been made to feel small and alone in a hostile galaxy. Not Burgoyne. Burgoyne felt the closeness of the link with Selar, and not only that, but s/he felt the eternal company of hir own nature. Male and female, yin and yang, the two eternal parts kept close with one another. Not only was Burgoyne joined with Selar, but furthermore, Burgoyne was at one with hirself. And as such, s/he would not be stopped.

"Get out of my way!" s/he howled once more, as loudly as s/he could, and then s/he pushed completely through the creature and suddenly felt relief swelling through hir. Relief and a sense of dizzy light-headedness. S/he spun and saw that the beast was raging behind hir, infuriated at hir ability to get past, and then it started to reach for hir.

With a snarl, Burgoyne kept going, no longer moving in anything vaguely resembling something humanoid. In hir four-legged, miles-consuming stride, s/he came across as something akin to one of the great cats of Earth. S/he charged up an incline, gravel rolling away beneath hir, hir nostrils flaring as the scent became stronger and stronger with every passing moment.

And so did hir killer instinct as well. S/he sensed that s/he was drawing close to the individual who was to be held accountable for the injuries to Selar. S/he knew now, beyond a doubt, that it was the energy creature that had been personally responsible for the state of Selar and the others, but something in turn was behind the creature, either having activated it or brought it to full life. Either way, Burgoyne was there to dispatch justice, no matter what it took.

And then, toward the top of the ridge, s/he saw him.

He was standing there with some sort of short spear, about a yard long. He was tapping the pointed end gently into the palm of his hand, as if he were tapping out a tune that only he could hear. He was shaking his head in apparent amazement of Burgoyne's arrival.

"You," he called down, "are going to have to die."

Burgoyne said nothing, but instead scrambled up the side of the hill. Just beyond the man waiting for hir was a cave, and she was positive that the captain was held within, presuming that the captain was still alive.

"I am Ramed," he told her. "You arrive at a propitious moment. It is the third hour of the third day. It is time for the Savior to pass on. Have you come to bear witness?"

Some feet away, Burgoyne had come to a cautious halt. S/he had hir talons extended, and there was a dark and fearsome look in hir eyes. When s/he spoke it was in a low and guttural voice that was barely recognizable as hir own. "Did you . . . do it?' s/he asked.

"Do what?" Ramed seemed only mildly interested.

"Did you hurt Selar?"

"Who is Selar?"

"The Vulcan. The Vulcan doctor." Burgoyne was having trouble focusing on the words; all s/he really wanted to do was leap forward and tear his throat out. But s/he had to be sure.

"Ah, yes. The Vulcan. Not directly, you understand. It was not my hand that inflicted the injuries upon her. However, I did bring into existence the rather devastating creature that attempted to stop you earlier, and that laid waste to your previous rescue attempts. How did you get around that? I must know. Because your friends were so utterly unable to—"

Burgoyne had heard enough. S/he crouched and let out a bellow akin to the roar that a lion used when endeavoring to freeze prey in place in preparation for a charge. It shook Ramed to his core. To his credit, he tried not to let it show. "Most impressive," he said. "A pity that you will not be saving the captain, however. That is impossible."

"Why?" Burgoyne managed to get out.

"Because it is written that the captain will be saved by neither man nor woman. And what does that leave?" Ramed said reasonably.

Burgoyne took another step forward, hir fangs bared. "I am a Hermat. I am both man and woman. No individual, as your prediction might indicate, but rather a merging of both. So it would seem to me that I'm not covered by whatever it is that's written."

It took a moment for this to sink in for Ramed, and when it did, a slow burn of uncertainty began to spread through him. Again, however, he tried to cover it up as best he could. "That is mere semantics," he replied. "Trickery. Word games."

"Perhaps. But nonetheless, it's true. Give me the captain."

"No." Ramed gripped his spear more forcefully.

"Give me the captain and perhaps I'll let you live," Burgoyne said. S/he had dropped to all fours once more. S/he padded toward him. It was a most disconcerting thing to see: S/he spoke with the barely controlled voice of a humanoid, but hir every move and gesture was evocative of a great cat.

"Don't you understand? It's not up to me! This isn't even about me! What I'm doing, I'm doing on behalf of my world! He has to die! You wouldn't understand, because you don't believe! It is from where I draw my strength—the strength that enables me to stand up to you, and do what must be done!"

"I have my own beliefs," Burgoyne told him. "My own religion, which means as much to me as yours does to you. It's where I draw *my* strength from." S/he had stopped hir approach and was starting to circle, trying to find the best angle from which to charge. "I believe in the sacred merging of male and female. Creatures such as yourself go through life as half one or half the other. You always remain separate. Always.

I am complete. I am the embodiment of the sexual union. All strength, all power derives from that union."

"That's ridiculous."

"Is it? No single act is more powerful. A merging of body, and of spirit. A sharing of all aspects of what you are. A uniting of purpose. The creation of new life, and the reaffirmation of one's own. A letting down of shields and barriers in the pursuit of that one, pure, undiluted moment of ecstasy. The most powerful symbol in nature, and my people are a living embodiment of that symbol. Great power is drawn from that. A strength that you, with your enslavement to the scribblings of others, cannot possibly stand up to. Ultimately your faith will fail you."

"My faith is complete unto itself," Ramed said, his anger building. He swept the spear back and forth in an arc, and it whistled through the air. Burgoyne approached cautiously, aware that Ramed seemed rather adept with the weapon. Clearly, he'd been practicing with it. "Don't think to challenge me on the strength of faith, because you will surely lose."

"You've already lost," retorted Burgoyne. "I have faith that I will win. Faith drawn from my unity and holy purpose, my quest that I know I will fulfill. You . . . you have no faith at all. I can tell. I can smell it on you. I can smell the fear radiating off you, oozing through every pore. The fear, the uncertainty. You don't believe in what you're doing. You act out of some misbegotten sense of obligation. But you don't have the stomach to kill. To do what must be done."

"You know nothing! I am a good man! A decent man! And I can kill if I have to!"

And Burgoyne laughed. It was not a pleasant sound. S/he tossed back hir head and a contemptuous snicker erupted from hir throat. "You idiot," s/he told him. "You're not fooling anyone, least of all me."

"I can kill him! I can do what needs to be done!"

"Oh, can you?"

And slowly Burgoyne stood. It took effort, for hir instinct was still to pounce. S/he stood there for a moment, and then gestured. "Come on. Do it. You have that pointed stick of yours. Test yourself out on me. Kill me."

Ramed stood there, the spear wavering uncertainly. "This is—what do you think you're—"

"One of us here isn't afraid, and I guarantee you that it's not you. Take a shot. Go ahead. I won't stop you. Stab me. Stab me to the heart. Here. I'll make it easy for you." Burgoyne tapped the area directly between hir small breasts. "Right here. That's all you have to do. Strike right here. I'll offer no defense." S/he closed hir eyes, hir arms comfortably at hir sides. "Go ahead. Practice on me. Am I not an easy enough target for you?"

"Why . . . why are you doing this?" demanded Ramed.

"Because I have faith that I will win. That my gods will help me. That you do not have what it takes to be a stone cold murderer. That you lack the conviction of your beliefs. Well? Make your move, Ramed. I haven't got all night. Do what you need to do . . . presuming you can do it."

S/he said nothing more, merely stood there, hir eyes serenely closed, hir entire body posture relaxed. Clearly s/he did not believe for a moment that he would try to kill hir.

He gripped the spear with both hands, holding it as tightly as he could. This was his whole life, he realized. His entire existence, boiling down to this moment. He had to do something about hir. If he simply tried to turn and run back into the cave, s/he would surely pounce on him and bring him down. His only chance was to fight. And why shouldn't he? Was he such a coward that he could only kill a helpless victim, tied up?

What had he become? In the final analysis, what had he become? A coward? A murderer, but one unable to commit a simple murder?

In his mind's eye, he saw his wife and child. He saw the faces of Zondarians everywhere, depending upon him to do what had to be done, and he felt his faith beginning to waver. Here, at the final hour, at the moment for which he had prepared his entire life—a moment that his ancestors had prepared for—his nerve was starting to fail him. All thanks to this . . . this creature who stood before him, so contemptuous, so convinced that he did not have the necessary inner strength to do what had to be done.

He would show them. He would show them all.

In the name of eternal peace on Zondar, in the name of the Savior, who had to become a martyr if there was going to be an end to warfare, Ramed would find the inner strength. He would cling to the rightness of his actions. He would do the job that needed doing.

And gripping the spear—the spear of justice—he charged forward, driving the point straight toward Burgoyne's breast.

XIX.

THE *Excalibur* barreled toward the Redeemer vessel, shields on maximum, all weapons fully targeting the ship.

Si Cwan had just finished, in as expeditious a manner as he could, describing for Shelby exactly who the Redeemers were and what their problem was with the *Excalibur*. Shelby nodded repeatedly, seeming to take it all in, and then she ordered, "Lay down a phaser barrage. Let's see what their shields have."

The phasers of the *Excalibur* lashed out, pounding the Redeemer ship. The opposing vessel twisted away, backing off as the starship drove toward it, firing relentlessly.

Shelby pounded the arm of her chair. "Yes! Yes!" she crowed, drawing looks from everyone on the bridge. "Damage report! Did we hurt them?"

"Not to any measurable degree," reported Boya-jian. "Their shields seem unimpaired. Commander, they're firing."

The Redeemers' phaser weapons blasted at the

Excalibur, targeting the engineering and saucer sections. The ship trembled under the pounding as, throughout the vessel, crewmen who weren't belted in to their stations tumbled to the floor.

"Shields at seventy percent and holding!" said Boyajian. "Whatever they've got, it packs more wallop than our phasers do! They're not as maneuverable as we are, but with that kind of shielding and weaponry, they don't have to be."

"Damage reports coming in from all over the ship," Lefler informed her. "Life support Systems out on Deck fourteen. Rerouting power now to restore systems."

"Fire photon torpedo spread and phaser barrage. Double-barrel," Shelby said grimly.

The Redeemer ship didn't budge, didn't even engage in any sort of evasive action, as the starship fired upon them. Their shields sparked under the assault, but otherwise held firm.

"We're not getting through their shields, Commander," Boyajian said. "Still no appreciable damage."

"They're firing again!"

"Evasive maneuvers!"

McHenry tried his best, but the *Excalibur* was slowed by the damage she'd sustained. He avoided two blasts, but a third struck at the upper right nacelle.

"Shields at forty percent and falling!" Boyajian warned. "We cannot sustain another direct hit!"

"Mister McHenry, bring us around at one-four-two mark three. Concentrate all remaining shield power to the rear deflectors. Get us out of here. Full impulse."

"We're running, sir?" McHenry asked.

"Simply changing strategy." She rose and said, "Engineering. I want a full-power magnetic burst channeled through the deflector array, on my order. Then prepare to give me warp power, and we're going to need it fast."

"Acknowledged," came Torelli's voice from engineering, although clearly he didn't understand the reason for the order.

Nor did McHenry. However, he was aware of another situation, which he felt was necessary to bring to Shelby's immediate attention. "Commander," he said. "The course you've ordered . . . it has us on a collision course with the Zondarian sun in just under two minutes."

"I'm fully aware of that."

This pronouncement brought concerned looks from everyone on the bridge, and someone would have said something to Shelby had they not received an incoming hail from the Redeemer ship. "Federation vessel," came the voice of Prime One. "Stand down and surrender. Throwing your vessel into a star will accomplish nothing."

. "We'll be just fine, thanks," Shelby shot back, her voice rising, "because the great god Calhoun will protect us! And Calhoun can wipe up the floor with your god any day of the week! Catch us if you can, you posturing fool! *Excalibur* out!"

A stunned Boyajian cut off the signal as Soleta and Si Cwan stepped forward. "Commander," Soleta said slowly, "is it possible that you released yourself from sickbay too early?"

"This is erratic behavior, at best—" began Si Cwan.

"I didn't ask for your opinion, Ambassador. If you've nothing to contribute of substance, then get the hell off my bridge. Lieutenant, are you challenging my authority?"

Soleta looked long and hard into Shelby's eyes. She felt as if the entire crew were looking to her, waiting on her judgment. She tried to see some indication of whether Shelby was operating in some sort of diminished capacity, or whether she truly had a plan.

She saw craft and cunning and even a sort of demented anticipation in Shelby's eyes. And there seemed to be nothing of unsteadiness about her.

"No, sir," said Soleta.

"One minute, thirty seconds to Zondarian sun, commander," McHenry said. He was trying to put his worries aside as he saw the star dead ahead, apparently waiting for them.

The ship trembled once more under a blast from the Redeemer ship, but it was a glancing blow, and with all power to their rear shields, they were able to sustain it with minimum problems. The *Excalibur* did not slow down as it tore through space, heading straight on what appeared to be a suicidal course.

"One minute to sun," McHenry told her. The ship, shields down in the front, was beginning to feel the heat. "The Redeemer vessel is still in pursuit."

"Of course they are. It's a matter of pride now. They have to show that their god will protect them as well as ours will. When dealing with fanatics, count on their fanaticism," Shelby said.

"Fifty seconds to sun . . . forty, Commander." McHenry, to his credit, didn't sound nervous. He seemed resigned, even interested in what it would feel like to plunge into a star.

"Give me a countdown, McHenry. Bridge to engineering, ready on deflector dish."

Sweat was pouring down the faces of everyone on the bridge, except for Soleta, who handled the heat better than most. The sun was now completely filling the screen, which had automatically dimmed to spare viewers the intensity of the light.

"Thirty . . . twenty-nine . . . twenty-eight . . . twenty-seven . . ."

Shelby seemed to be counting down with him, making rapid-fire calculations in her head, her lips moving soundlessly as if she were talking to herself. The bridge crew gripped their seats, bracing themselves, wondering what in the world they were about to die for.

"Redeemer ship?"

"Two hundred thousand kilometers and closing."

"Maybe they want to be able to kiss us good-bye," Lefler guessed.

"Twenty-one . . . twenty . . . nineteen . . . eighteen . . ."

The star was everywhere. The heat was overwhelming.

And as if shot from a cannon, Shelby leaped to her feet and shouted, "Engineering! Full magnetic burst, on my mark, five seconds' duration! McHenry, same mark minus five, forty five degree down angle, full reverse thrust! *Mark—now!*"

The deflector dish flared to life, driving a full bore magnetic burst straight into the corona of the Zondarian sun. It struck the corona, disrupting the magnetic lines of the star's turbulent surface. Like a vast giant being stung by a hornet, the star slapped back at the irritation . . .

In the form of a gigantic solar flare.

The *Excalibur* screamed into reverse, the ship's structure howling in protest over the abrupt change in direction, pulling against the gravity of the sun that was already starting to take hold of them. For a moment that stretched into infinity, it looked as if they would not be able to break free, and then the starship tore loose of the star's magnetic field and slammed backward and down, away from the sun.

The Redeemer ship was not quite as fortunate.

Unable to turn or handle as deftly as the *Excalibur,* the Redeemers couldn't get out of the way in time.

The last thing they saw was the solar flare belching up at them from the sun's surface, and then the spectacularly erupting discharge, leaping five hundred thousand kilometers from the star and pumping heat approximately twice as hot as the surface of the sun, enveloped the Redeemer vessel. Even the formidable shielding of the Redeemer vessel was unable to stand up to an all-encompassing flare in excess of twenty thousand degrees Fahrenheit. The Redeemer ship was immediately obliterated as the *Excalibur* frantically put as much distance between herself and the momentarily angered star as it could. The flare continued, as if pursuing them, as the starship hurtled backward, but the flare topped out at sixty hundred and fifty thousand kilometers. It continued to erupt for another fifteen minutes, but by that point the starship was safely out of range.

Shelby was on her feet, her fists above her head in triumph. "Hah!" she crowed. "Spectacular! Engineering, great job! You too, McHenry! Excellent all around! Oh! Look!" She pointed to midair.

"Look at what, sir?"

"The colors!" Shelby called out excitedly—and then she pitched forward, Si Cwan just barely catching her before she hit the floor.

XX.

BURGOYNE STOOD THERE, chest bared, eyes closed, a look of serene peace on hir face, as Ramed lunged forward with his spear at hir unprotected breast.

The point slammed toward hir—and stopped two inches from impact.

It did not do so at Ramed's behest. He'd been ready to plunge it through hir. It was because Burgoyne had caught the point, hir hand moving so quickly that Ramed had never even seen it coming. Ramed's full strength from both arms was pitted against Burgoyne's single hand, and still he couldn't make any headway.

"You . . . said you wouldn't defend . . . against me," grunted Ramed.

"What do you think, I'm stupid?" snorted Burgoyne.

Ramed redoubled his efforts, and Burgoyne grabbed the spear with both hands, putting hir full weight against his. They shoved against each other, Burgoyne snarling deep in hir throat. To hir surprise,

Ramed displayed greater strength than s/he'd given him credit for.

And then something caught Burgoyne's eye.

It was a Zondarian, an older one, and he was materializing like a ghost. He was looking at hir with unfeigned surprise.

It startled Burgoyne. Not much. Just enough, however, for Ramed to shove hir back. S/he stumbled and suddenly realized that s/he was treading air.

Ramed's momentary look of triumph quickly faded, however, as Burgoyne's legs scissored around his middle. The two of them plummeted down the side of the incline, hitting the side once or twice. Burgoyne, nude from the waist up, was the more vulnerable, as hir torso was lacerated by the dirt and rocks as they rolled down, down, tumbling one over the other.

They hit the ground at the bottom, separated from one another, and miraculously Ramed had still managed to hold on to the spear. He leaped, trying to drive the point straight through hir, but Burgoyne was too quick, hir rage too towering. S/he dodged to one side, brought hir foot up and smashed him squarely in the stomach. He tried to get to his feet and then s/he swung hir talons, slicing through his upper arm, drawing blood. S/he tried to get closer, to go for his throat, but he warded hir off with the spear point, catching hir just under the ribs and drawing a thin line of blood.

They parried, thrusted, bobbed, and weaved, each jockeying for position, and Ramed fell back, back . . .

Burgoyne covered the distance between them in one jump, twisting in midair and avoiding the point of the spear. S/he gripped the spear firmly, and there was murder in hir eyes, and this time Ramed knew that s/he wasn't going to let go until one of them was dead. He steeled himself.

Suddenly they both felt the energy enveloping them.

The creature, the being of energy, the being of magic, of science—whatever it was—they had drawn within range of it, and now it enveloped them.

Burgoyne was ready for it. S/he still had the peace, the joining of Selar deep within hir. The creature insinuated itself through them, seeking weakness, trying to determine whom it could hurt.

It cascaded through Ramed, enveloping him, searching out all his weaknesses, and Ramed cried out in fear, for it was everywhere, the creature was everywhere, giving him no peace, giving him nowhere to hide.

And he knew his life for the sham that it was. Knew that he was supposed to be someone in a position of power, someone who was wise and knowledgeable and a leader. But everyone had found out, everyone had discovered the truth, that he was just one scared little man who had no true feelings of his own save what he'd been told, no real belief in himself, no confidence. He was alone, all alone, and there was Talila coming toward him, and Rab, and all of the Eenza were crying out that he had betrayed them, and all of the Unglza knew that he was a fool and that they would eventually triumph.

The knowledge tore at him, emotionally eviscerated him, and the creature flailed at him, feasting on his weakness.

And Burgoyne sensed it, sensed all of it, and suddenly, despite hir ferocity, despite hir anger, despite hir eagerness to complete hir blood quest, all s/he felt was pity for this poor, pathetic lost soul who was clutching the spear as if his life were wrapped up in it.

"Let go!" shouted Burgoyne over the howling of the energy being.

Cuts, slices began to appear on Ramed, his clothing becoming torn. He began to sob wildly, calling out names like "Talila" and "Rab," names that meant nothing to Burgoyne. "Let's get out of here!" Burgoyne shouted, and began to drag Ramed, not releasing hir hold on the spear but instead using it as a means of hauling Ramed away from the creature's influence. S/he felt it trying to get in at hir as well, but s/he steeled hirself with hir own security, and with the image of Selar that s/he held dear to hir, and s/he resisted its power.

"I can't!" Ramed howled. And suddenly Ramed began to wrestle with the spear with renewed effort.

Burgoyne braced hirself. "Let go! Let it go! It doesn't mean anything!"

It's everything I am! It's the only thing I am!" Ramed cried out, and with all his weight, all his desperation, all his loneliness, all his hatred of himself and what he had become, he yanked on the spear. He did so with such force and fury that he actually tore it from Burgoyne's grasp.

He was unprepared for the sudden shift in weight. He stumbled forward, and the spear punched through his chest and out his back.

Ramed looked up at Burgoyne with what appeared to be confusion. He reached out a hand to Burgoyne, his fingers flexing on nothing, and then he slid to his knees, running down the length of the spear and coming to a halt as the handle bumped up against his chest.

"Failed . . . failed . . . all my fault . . ." he sobbed, but Burgoyne could not hear his last words over the howling of the creature.

And then, slowly, Burgoyne became aware that the noise was abating. All around them, the creature seemed to be dissipating. S/he couldn't tell whether it was from the creature's own volition, or if some outside force was acting upon it. All s/he knew was that, within moments, it had stopped. The creature was gone as if it had never been there.

Burgoyne crouched over the fallen form of Ramed.

Ramed looked up at hir, the life light flickering out of his eyes. His body spasmed, and he gripped Burgoyne's arm with the last of his strength. "Save . . . my world . . . ask the Savior . . . somehow . . . save my . . ."

"This . . . this didn't have to be," Burgoyne said, unable to contain hir frustration. "What a foolish, foolish waste."

And Ramed smiled.

"Better . . . this way . . ." he whispered. "Better to be . . . a mere fool . . . than a damned fool."

And as the phantom shade called Ontear looked on from a point hundreds of years in the past, Ramed passed into a history that was yet to be.

XXI.

"AND THAT IS HOW I know that I am not your Savior."

Mackenzie Calhoun was circling the large table, as the most holy men of Zondar looked in astonishment at the parchment that he had given them. The parchment, unmistakably in the hand of the holy Suti, that detailed all that had happened. "Ramed," he continued, "was your promised Savior."

Near Calhoun stood Zak Kebron, his arms folded, his gaze baleful, and Ensign Janos, who was eyeing the assemblage with no less suspicion than Kebron. And to the side stood Si Cwan, watching the proceedings.

As voices of protest began to rise, Calhoun raised his voice to silence them. "Read it for yourself!" he said. "Everything that is in those scrolls fits Ramed as well as it does me. And the final proof: Ramed is dead. Slain by the ancient and sacred spear that he and his clan, in their sacred duty, had maintained for just that purpose. In his name, for his sake, in the name of the sacrifices that he made, now is the time to set aside the differences that have wracked this planet with strife for centuries."

"Your people want it, and you want it," said Si Cwan. "When the golden age of peace beckoned you, you could taste it, couldn't you? All of you could. Like honey on your lips, like the sweetest wine filled with the promise of intoxicating peace. It was yours to take. Ramed sacrificed himself to show you the way. You must follow his sacrifice."

"You're suggesting we kill ourselves?" asked Killick in disbelief.

"You've been killing each other long enough, it's almost appropriate," Maro commented drily.

"True enough, but no, that's not what is being suggested," said Calhoun. "It is our recommendation that the Unglza immediately surrender to the Eenza."

This, as Calhoun anticipated, brought a chorus of protest from the Unglza side of the table. "Why should we?" demanded Quinzix.

"Because the Eenza will then promptly surrender to you," replied Si Cwan.

This brought another broadside of objections, but Calhoun steamrolled over them. "You don't understand!" he said angrily. "This is not a request! This is not a plea! I'm telling you that this is what's going to happen! I'm telling you that Ramed lay down his life to show you the way, and you will follow that way! He died for your sins! He died for his people! He martyred himself because he believed that self-sacrifice was the only way that there would ever be peace on this planet, and so help me God, you will follow that lead or you will spiral into the pit and I will make sure that I'm there to give you the swift kick that helps you along!"

There was shaking of heads, there was disbelief, there were loud arguments and objections, there was fury, there was hostility, there were threats and more threats, there was a fistfight, there were sobs, there were pleadings, there was blustering and anger and vituperation . . .

. . . and ultimately . . .

. . . there was acceptance.

The crowds were massed outside the burial site, but for the moment, Talila was the only one allowed in. She stood at the gravesite of her husband, staring at the dirt, as if she could somehow will him back to life.

She became aware of a presence next to her, and she looked around to see a rather odd-looking individual in a Starfleet uniform.

"Who are you?" she asked.

"I am Burgoyne one-seventy-two. Chief engineer. I . . . knew your husband," s/he said. "I was there when he died."

"Did you kill him?" she asked, her voice surprisingly even.

"It was as much at my hand as his," Burgoyne admitted. "He was trying to kill me and I defended myself. But ultimately I don't think his heart was in it. I think he was searching for a way out—and found it."

"Found it in the comfort of the grave," she said hollowly. She shook her head. "Pointless. Pointless and foolish."

"That is what I thought, at first. He . . . he spoke your name at the end. Yours and, I believe, your son's."

"How kind of him," she said icily, "to think of us at the end. To think of those he was leaving behind. The wife with no one to love her, the child with no father to raise him."

"He was trying to save your world," Burgoyne told her.

And her hand snapped around, as s/he knew it would, and caught Burgoyne across the cheek. Burgoyne took the slap and didn't even reach up to rub the redness.

"Then the world can burn," said Talila. "And so can you." And she walked away, leaving Burgoyne at the gravesite of the martyr of Zondar.

"Si Cwan?"

Once again, Lefler felt as if she were talking to thin air as Si Cwan stared out his window. This time, however, rather than looking into space, he was gazing upon the planet Zondar, turning below them.

She was about to start lecturing him again on how the time she was spending as his liaison was somewhat limited. Then again, part of her didn't mind just sitting and staring at him, admiring the rippling muscles, sleek build and remarkably strong chin. But as she wrestled with her priorities, he broke the silence. "I don't know if they're going to make it," he said.

"The Zondarians?"

He nodded. "There are many who want peace, who are so hungry for it that they readily accept Calhoun's interpretation of events. But there are others who are calling Ramed the false Savior. There are others still who, having read Ontear's unexpurgated predictions, not only believe that Calhoun should have died but, in failing to do so, has doomed the entire world. At a time when they should be uniting, we're seeing factions. I just do not know if we're going to be able to pull this off."

"If anyone can, you can," said Lefler.

He turned and smiled at her. "You truly believe that?"

And Lefler, who had just been mentally kicking herself and demanding of herself, *My God, did you* *just **say** that? You sound like a love-struck nitwit,* immediately swtiched gears and said, "Absolutely."

"Thank you. I appreciate your vote of confidence."

Then his computer beeped at him and he glanced at it. "Another incoming message," he said. He looked at it more closely. "Well, now *this* is interesting."

"Who's it from?"

"The Momidiums, over in the Gamma Hydrinae system. They have someone they wish to turn over to us."

"Turn over?"

"Yes," he said slowly. "A human being, apparently. Female. She was on some sort of exploratory mission there. The Momidiums felt she was a spy, but they're very reverential of life, so they didn't execute her. Nor did they turn her over to us because they felt that we would execute her."

"Would you have?" asked Lefler.

He looked at her evenly. "Do you truly wish to know the answer to that, Robin?" When she didn't reply, he took that as her response. "In any event, they simply locked her away. They've kept her there for approximately four years now. However, they wish to embark on solid relations with the Federation since the *Excalibur* is now in the area, so they're interested in turning her over to us in exchange for certain guarantees."

"What sort of guarantees?"

"Look for yourself." He turned the computer screen around so that she could read it. The various conditions were spelled out on the screen, lined up next to a photograph of the human woman.

Si Cwan frowned. "Robin, are you all right?"

Lefler had gone dead white. Her jaw was hanging down to somewhere around the floor.

"Robin?" he asked again.

And she looked up at him and whispered, "That's . . . that's my mother."

"What?" He swung the screen around, as if he would actually recognize a total stranger. The woman had long black hair, a long face, and eyes that seemed to blaze with quiet intelligence. "Are you sure?" he asked.

Lefler nodded wordlessly.

"This is . . . this is incredibly fortunate for you, then!" said Si Cwan. "The Momidiums claim this is a recent photo of her, so apparently she is in in good health."

"Remarkably good health," said Lefler, her voice sounding very distant. "Considering that she died ten years ago."

Burgoyne returned to hir quarters, feeling heavy-hearted and despairing. S/he sank into hir overstuffed couch. The computer was beeping at hir, indicating a message was being held for hir.

"Computer. Message."

The screen came on and Calhoun's face appeared on it. "Chief," he said, "we've received permission from the Zondarians to explore the caves and machinery on their world, in Ontear's Sacred Realm or whatever it's called. There seems to be tremendous potential there for discovery. And hopefully it will provide some answers to some outstanding questions we have. When you get in, coordinate with Lieutenant Soleta."

Burgoyne nodded, as if Calhoun could see hir.

"And Burgoyne, thanks again for saving my ass. I owe you one, Burgy," added Calhoun.

The screen blinked out.

Burgoyne sighed. It was clear that s/he wasn't going to get a break. There was still that bizarre energy situation in the engine room that s/he had to explore. And now there was this mysterious alien machinery, which did hold some fascination, but still . . . Burgoyne felt tired. Wrung out.

"A quick rest," s/he said to hirself. "Five minutes won't kill anyone."

S/he rose and entered hir bedroom.

Selar was waiting for hir.

Burgoyne blinked in surprise to see the doctor standing there. She looked fairly recovered, although there were still bruises on her. Reconstructive surgery had repaired the damage to her ear. Her gaze was steady, her manner calm and collected.

No. No, it wasn't. Her body started trembling the moment that Burgoyne walked in.

"Doctor? What are you doing here? Are you all right?"

Selar tried to speak, but couldn't get words out. Instead she took two steps forward, grabbed Burgoyne, and kissed hir forcefully, swept up in *Pon Farr,* caught up in her need, and knowing, finally, for once, exactly what she wanted.

No words were required.

And Burgoyne never did get that five minutes' rest.

STAR TREK®
VULCAN'S FORGE
by
Josepha Sherman and Susan Shwartz

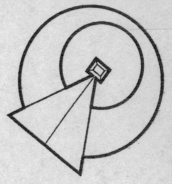

Please turn the page for an excerpt from
Vulcan's Forge . . .

Vulcan, Mount Seleya
Day 6, Seventh Week of Tasmeen,
Year 2247

Dawn hovered over Mount Seleya. A huge *shavokh* glided down on a thermal from the peak, balanced on a wingtip, then soared out toward the desert. Spock heard its hunting call.

Where it stoops, one may find ground water or a soak not too deeply buried, Spock recalled from his survival training. He had no need of such information now. Nevertheless, his gaze followed the creature's effortless flight.

The stairs that swept upward to the narrow bridge still lay in shadow. Faint mist rose about the mountain, perhaps from the snow that capped it, alone of Vulcan's peaks, or perhaps from the lava that bubbled sullenly a thousand meters below. Soon, 40 Eridani A would rise, and the ritual honoring Spock and his agemates would begin.

It was illogical, Spock told himself, for him to assume that all eyes were upon him as he followed his parents.

Instead, he concentrated on his parents' progress. Sustained only by the light touch of Sarek's fingers upon hers, veiled against the coming sunrise, Amanda crossed the narrow span as if she had not conquered her fear of the unrailed bridge only after long meditation.

Few of the many participants from the outworld scientific, diplomatic, and military enclaves on Vulcan could equal her grace. Some had actually arranged to be flown to the amphitheater just to allow them to bypass the bridge that had served as a final defense for the warband that had ruled here in ancient days. Others of the guests crossed unsteadily or too quickly for dignity.

Vertigo might be a reasonable assumption, Spock thought, for beings acclimating themselves to Vulcan's thin air or the altitude of the bridge.

"The air is the air," one of his agemates remarked in the tone of one quoting his elders. "I have heard these *humans* take drugs to help them breathe."

All of the boys eyed the representatives from the Federation as if they were xenobiological specimens in a laboratory. Especially, they surveyed the officials' sons and daughters, who might, one day, be people with whom they would study and work.

"They look sickly," the same boy spoke. His name, Spock recalled, was Stonn. Not only was he a distant kinsman to Sered, he was one of the youths who also eyed Spock as if he expected Spock's human blood to make him fall wheezing to his knees, preferably just when he was supposed to lead his agemates up to the platform where T'Lar and T'Pau would present them with the hereditary—and now symbolic—weapons of their Great Houses. By slipping out early into the desert to undergo his *kahs-wan* ordeal before the others, Spock had made himself forever Eldest among the boys of his year. It was not logical that some, like Stonn, would not forgive him for his presumption, or his survival; but it was so.

A deferential three paces behind his parents and two to the side of Sarek, Spock strode past a series of deeply incised pits—the result of laser cannon fire two millennia back—and up to the entrance of the amphitheater. Two masked guards bearing ceremonial *lirpas* presented arms before his father, then saluted Spock for the first time as an adult. For all his attempts at total control, he felt a little shiver race through him as he returned the salutes as an adult for the first time. The clublike weights that formed the *lirpa* bases shone, a luster of dark metal. The dawn light flashed red on the blades that the guards carried over their shoulders. At the guards' hips, they wore stone-hilted daggers, but no energy weapons—*phasers*—such as a Starfleet officer might wear on duty. Of course, no such weapons might be brought here.

Lady Amanda removed her fingers from her husband's and smiled faintly. "I shall join the other ladies of our House now, my husband, while you bring our son before the Elders. Spock, I shall be watching for you. And I am indeed *very* proud."

As, her gaze told him, *is your father.*

She glided away, a grace note among the taller Vulcans.

Spock fell into step with his father, head high, as if his blood bore no human admixture. *As it was in the beginning* . . . Silently, he reviewed the beginning of the Chant of Generations as he glided down the stairs.

Everyone in the amphitheater rose. T'Lar, adept and First Student, walked onto the platform. Then, two guards, their *lirpa* set aside for the purpose, entered with a curtained carrying chair. From it, robed in black, but with all the crimsons of the dawn in her brocaded overrobe, stepped T'Pau. She leaned on an intricately carved stick.

Spock's father stepped forward as if to help her.

"Thee is kind, Sarek," said the Elder of their House, "but thee is premature. When I can no longer preside unassisted over this rite, it will be time to release my *katra.*"

Sarek bowed. "I ask pardon for my presumption."

"Courtesy"—T'Pau held up a thin, imperious hand—"is never presumptuous." Her long eyes moved over the people in the amphitheater as if delivering some lesson of her own—but to whom? Carefully, she approached the altar and bowed to T'Lar. "Eldest of All, I beg leave to assist thee."

"You honor me," replied T'Lar.

"I live to serve," said T'Pau, an observation that would have left Spock gasping had he not been getting sufficient oxygen.

Both women bowed, this time to the youths who stood waiting their presentation.

Again, the adept struck the gong.

T'Lar raised both arms, the white and silver of her sleeves falling like great wings. *As it was in the beginning, so shall it always be. These sons of our House have shown their worthiness . . .*

"I protest!" came a shout from the amphitheater.

"I protest," Sered declared, "the profanation of these rites. I protest the way they have been stripped of their meaning, contaminated as one might pollute a well in the desert. I protest the way our deepest mysteries have been revealed to *outsiders.*"

T'Pau's eyebrows rose at that last word, which was in the seldom-used invective mode.

"Has thee finished?" asked T'Lar. Adept of *Kolinahr,* she would remain serene if Mount Seleya split along its many fissures and this entire amphitheater crumbled into the pit below.

"No!" Sered cried, his voice sharp as the cry of a *shavokh.* "Above all, I protest the inclusion of an outsider in our rites—yes, as leader of the men to be honored today—when other and worthier men, our exiled cousins, go unhonored and unrecognized."

Sarek drew deep, measured breaths. *He prepares for combat,* Spock realized, and was astonished to feel his own body tensing, alert, aware as he had only been during his *kahs-wan,* when he had faced a full-grown *le-matya* in the deep desert and knew, logically, he could not survive such an encounter. *Fight or flight,* his mother had once called it. That too was a constant across species. *But not here. There must not be combat here.*

"Thee speaks of those who exiled themselves, Sered." Not the slightest trace of emotion tinged T'Pau's voice. "Return lies in their power, not in ours."

"So it does!" Sered shouted. "And so they do!"

He tore off his austere robe. Gasps of astonishment and hisses of outrage sounded as he stood forth in the garb of a Captain of the Hosts from the ancient days. Sunlight picked out the metal of his harness in violent red and exploded into rainbow fire where it touched the gem forming the grip of the ancient energy weapon Sered held—a weapon he had brought, against all law, into Mount Seleya's amphitheater.

"Welcome our lost kindred!" he commanded, and gestured as if leading a charge.

A rainbow shimmer rose about the stage. *Transporter effect,* Spock thought even as it died, leaving behind six tall figures in black and silver. At first glance they were as much like Sered as brothers in their mother's womb. But where Sered wore his rage like a cloak of ceremony, these seemed accustomed to emotion and casual violence.

For an instant no one moved, the Vulcans too stunned by this garish breach of custom, the Federation guests not sure what they were permitted to do. Then, as the intruders raised their weapons, the amphitheater erupted into shouts and motion. From all sides, the guards advanced, holding their *lirpas* at a deadly angle. But *lirpas* were futile against laser rifles.

As the ceremonial guard was cut down, Sarek whispered quick, urgent words to other Vulcans. They nodded. Spock sensed power summoned and joined:

"Now!" whispered the ambassador.

In a phalanx, the Vulcans rushed the dais. They swept across it, bearing T'Pau and T'Lar with them. They, at least, were safe. Only one remained behind. Green blood puddled from his ruined skull, seeping into the dark stone where no blood had flowed for countless generations.

"You dare rise up against me?" Sered shrilled. "One sacrifice is not enough to show the lesser worlds!" He waved his weapon at the boys, at the gorgeously dressed Federation guests. "Take them! We shall make these folk of lesser spirit *crawl.*"

Spock darted forward, not sure what he could do, knowing only that it was not logical to wait meekly for death. And these intruders were not mindless *le-matyas!* They were kindred, of Vulcan stock; surely they could be reasoned with—

As Sered could not. Spock faltered at the sight of the drawn features, the too-bright eyes staring beyond this chaos to a vision only Sered could see. Few Vulcans ever went insane, but here was true madness. Surely his followers, though, clearly Vulcan's long-lost cousins, would not ally themselves with such insanity!

Desperately calm, Spock raised his hand in formal greeting. Surak had been slain trying to bring peace: if Spock fell thus, at least his father would have final proof that he was worthy to be the ambassador's son.

They suddenly seemed to be in a tense little circle of calm. One of the "cousins" pointed at him, while a second nodded, then gestured out into the chaos around them. The language had greatly changed in the sundered years, but Spock understood:

"This one."

"Him."

It may work. They may listen to me. They—

"Get back, son!" a Starfleet officer shouted, racing forward, phaser in outstretched hand, straight at Sered. "Drop that weapon!"

Sered threw back his head. He actually laughed. Then, firing at point-blank range, reflexes swifter than human, he shot the man. The human flared up into flame so fierce that the heat scorched Spock's face and the veils slipped across his eyes, blurring his sight. He blinked, blinked again to clear it, and saw the conflagration that had been a man flash out of existence.

Dead. He's dead. A moment ago alive, and now— Spock stared at Sered across the small space that had held a man, his mind refusing to process what he'd just seen. "Half-blood," muttered Sered. "Weakling shoot of Surak's house. But you will serve—"

"Got him!" came a shout. David Rabin hurled himself into Sered, bringing them both down. The weapon flew from Sered's hand, and Captain Rabin and Sered both scrambled for it. The woman touched it, Sered knocked her hand aside—

And the weapon slid right to Spock. He snatched it up, heart racing faster than a proper Vulcan should permit, and pointed it at Sered.

"Can you kill a brother Vulcan?" Sered hissed, unafraid, from where he lay. "Can you?"

Could he? For an endless moment, Spock froze, seeing Sered's fearless stare, feeling the weapon in his hand. Dimly he was aware of the struggle all around him as the invaders grabbed hostages, but all he could think was that all he need do was one tiny move, only the smallest tightening of a finger—

Can you kill a brother Vulcan?

He'd hesitated too long. What felt like half of Mount Seleya fell on him. Spock thought he heard his father saying, *Exaggeration. Remember your control.*

Then the fierce dawn went black.

Look for STAR TREK Fiction from Pocket Books

Star Trek: The Next Generation®

Star Trek: Deep Space Nine®

Star Trek®: Voyager™

Flashback • Diane Carey
Mosaic • Jeri Taylor

Star Trek®: New Frontier

Star Trek®: Day of Honor